THE GIRL WHO CAME BACK

KERRY WILKINSON

Bookouture

Published by Bookouture
An imprint of StoryFire Ltd.
Carmelite House
50 Victoria Embankment
London EC4Y 0DZ
www.bookouture.com

ISBN: 978-0-34913-247-1
eBook ISBN: 978-1-78681-265-0

Printed and bound in Great Britain by Clays Ltd, Elcograf S.p.A.

Papers used are from well-managed forests
and other responsible sources.

ONE

TUESDAY

My mother doesn't recognise me.

She's on the other side of the café, almost hidden behind her MacBook. She sips her cappuccino, then puts it down and frowns at the screen as if whatever she's looking at is in a foreign language. Her eyes narrow and her nose twitches, then she sucks in her right cheek but not the left. I wonder if I do that when I'm concentrating. It's a long, long time since we saw one another and there's that whole nature-nurture thing.

How much of her is me?

I'm trying to think of the best thing I could say to her when she looks up from the computer, catching my eye before I can turn away. She smiles in the way people do when they realise they're being watched. Lips together, only the merest of upturn and then she focuses back on her laptop. She'll give it a couple of seconds and then check on me once more, making sure I'm not some maniac stalker.

There's no recognition there.

The waitress chooses that moment to drift by, picking up my empty teacup and saucer. She's somewhere around my age – late-teens or early twenties, slim with long red hair, freckles and an apron tied tightly around her.

'Would you like anything else?' she asks.

She sounds perfectly polite but has that passive-aggressive 'paying customers' vibe about her. It's not as if the café is busy. There's only my mother, me and a gossipy part mothers' meeting, part crèche at the back by the door to the toilets.

I ask her about the teas they have and then settle on an Earl Grey. She's about to turn back to the counter when I point towards my mother.

'Can you tell me who that is?' I ask.

The server turns between us. 'That's Sarah.'

'She's the boss…?'

'Right. If you're after a job or something, I can get you a form…?'

'No, I was curious. That's all.'

She gives me a glance as if to say 'weirdo' without actually saying it, then she disappears back behind the counter with my empty cup. I quite like the level of disdain she manages to conceal under a mask of politeness. Takes a blagger to know a blagger, I reckon.

I wonder what my mother is working on. Perhaps the accounts for this place, or a new version of the menu? I watch her in a not watching her kind of way. She never leaves my peripheral vision as I look through the large window at the front of the café towards the street. There are a couple of empty tables out there and someone walking their dog.

The espresso machine is made from shiny aluminium, which makes it a pretty good mirror as I manage to keep an eye on her while facing the opposite direction.

It's hard to work out whether she looks like me. Her hair is a brighter blonde than mine but it has that almost white shade of bleach. Our noses are similar, slim and narrow, rather than squashed. I'm not sure beyond that. Her taste in clothes is brighter than mine. I went black and have never gone back; she's in a floaty, summery sunflower yellow dress that would look awful with my pale skin. She either has a fake tan or has been on holiday recently.

There's a burbling of liquid from behind the counter and then the waitress reappears with my drink and a smile. The napkins have been printed especially, with a logo that reads 'Via's' in the corner. I fumble through my purse for some pound coins and apologise my way through paying, then go back to watching my mother.

She's a two-finger typist, one of each hand, like one of those drinking bird toys that bob back and forth on a pendulum. Not technology-illiterate, more technology-befuddled.

There's not much between us – a few metres, a couple of tables – but it feels like an ocean. She doesn't recognise me now, so what if she never does? Her blank gaze flits across me dismissively and that's it. I'm a nobody.

I should leave. Push my way through the door and follow the High Street back to my car. It was wrong to come here. *I* was wrong to come here.

When she glances up again, I'm too slow in turning away and there's a moment in which it feels like we're locked together. Something *squeezes* my stomach and there's a second where I can't breathe.

She looks at me and I look at her.

There is a strange electricity that we both feel, magnets being dragged together.

She pushes her glasses up from her nose so that they're resting on top of her head. 'Are you okay?' she asks.

I stand and move around the tables, leaving my untouched tea until I'm standing in front of her. I've forgotten how to talk. Like those people in comas who wake up and suddenly know a foreign language but not their own. Even my thoughts are a crumpled, muddied mess, as if they're in another language, too.

'Are you Sarah Adams?' I ask. I've surprised myself at being able to talk.

She squints and then lines are engraved into her forehead as she frowns slightly, trying to place me. I'm someone she met at a conference once, a daughter of someone she knows, some customer with whom she's exchanged words before.

'It's Sarah Pitman now,' she replies. 'Do I know you?'

I want to say the name but the words are stuck – and then I don't have to.

My mother's eyes widen and she takes a huge gulp of breath. 'Oh my God,' she says, 'It's you. It's really you.'

She blinks and there's a moment where it feels as if everything has stopped. The infants at the back are no longer babbling, the waitress isn't clinking cups into the dishwasher, the man walking past the café has frozen in the moment.

The space-time continuum itself has glitched.

Then she says it: 'Olivia.'

SEARCH FOR MISSING GIRL CONTINUES

24 May 2004

The hunt for a missing six-year-old Stoneridge girl has entered a third day as police focus on a stretch of woods on the outskirts of the village.

Olivia Adams was playing in the back garden of her family home when she disappeared a little after four o'clock on Saturday afternoon. The girl, who has long blonde hair, was wearing green shorts with a cream T-shirt featuring a cartoon of a fairy on the front. She was also sporting a red hairband.

Reports say the girl's father, Daniel Adams, was watching the FA Cup Final inside the family home when his daughter disappeared.

Police are looking into reports of a suspicious car left outside the Adams home. A spokesman added that a 27-year-old man was helping them with their inquiries, although he insisted that there had been no breakthrough. The identity of the man is yet to be released.

Mother Sarah said: 'We just want our daughter back. If anyone's seen anything, however insignificant it may seem, please come forward. She's a friendly child and is used to being around adults. She's never run off and is often in the garden. We always keep the gate locked.'

The search for Olivia continued through the night on Saturday and all day Sunday, finishing at sunset. It was due to begin again this morning. The police have been aided by *a large group of Stoneridge residents, who have helped comb through the Canvey Estate as well as fields that back onto the busy A622. The search has now moved further out of the village to centre on the western edge of Stoneridge Woods.*

The disappearance of Olivia, a pupil at Stoneridge Primary School, has left the village in shock.

Georgina Hooper, a teaching assistant who has a daughter the same age as Olivia, said: 'It's devastating. This sort of thing doesn't happen here. Everybody knows everyone else and it's a proper little community. None of us can believe it. Olivia's a lovely little girl and I hope she's found soon.'

Despite the search party continuing largely uninterrupted for more than twenty-four hours, sources close to the investigation have admitted that authorities are baffled by a lack of clues.

'It's like she vanished into thin air,' one observer noted.

Police have distributed maps of the immediate area and are focusing on a lane that runs along the back of the Adams home. More than a hundred officers have been brought in from neighbouring forces, with a helicopter deployed on Saturday evening to help with the search.

On the ground, however, morale appeared to be dimming. A woman who did not wish to be named said: 'Everyone's acting as if it's already too late. One of the officers said the first three hours were critical but we've gone way beyond that.'

Ashley Pitman, who owns Pitmans Garage in the village, has been helping out with the search since the beginning and remains hopeful. 'We'll find her,' he said. 'We'll keep searching for as long as it takes. Someone, somewhere must know something.'

A candlelit vigil and service to pray for her safe return is due to take place at Ridge Park at sunset this evening.

Police are asking for anyone with information to come forward.

TWO

Mum pushes up out of her seat. She's a little shorter than me but only by an inch or so. She shuffles around the table, her gaze not leaving me for a moment, then she tugs at the longer parts of my fringe. It's as if she's making sure I'm real, not a ghost or a figment of her imagination.

'I can't believe it,' she whispers.

She lets go of my hair but then cups my cheek with her hand. It's warm and her touch is soft. When she realises what she's doing, she apologises and hugs her arms across her front, like she's trying to comfort herself.

'You have the same eyes,' she says, tears in her own. 'All these years on and they haven't changed.'

Of all the things I thought might happen, it wasn't this. I had a speech planned about being back – and yet none of it has been necessary. She said the name and then she recognised my eyes. Now I'm here, and away from the, *I'll say this and she'll say that, so I'll reply with this*, it's obvious how silly all that was. I doubt I could've got even half a sentence out, let alone an entire speech.

'I never stopped hoping,' she says. Her voice is croaky, like that of a lifelong smoker.

I realise everyone's watching and the silence I imagined is real. The waitress is holding a dirty cup in mid-air and the mothers have stopped gossiping among themselves. I don't think they can hear anything that's been said but the spark from across the room is too obvious to miss.

'Where've you been?' she asks. The number one question, of course. I have a speech for that, too.

'Shall we go somewhere else?' I reply. They're the first words I've spoken since I asked her name.

It only takes a glance towards the back of the café for Mum to get the message. She stares at me for a moment more, blinks, and then launches into action. She snaps her MacBook lid shut and then fumbles with a bag that was underneath her seat. The laptop and papers are crammed inside and then she flusters her way back around the table.

'I have to head out, Nattie,' she says. The waitress still has the empty cup in her hand and it takes a moment for her to realise she's being spoken to.

She jumps a little: 'Oh, um…'

'I'm on the mobile if you need anything.'

Nattie glances towards me and I wonder if she could hear us after all. She looks towards my table, where the tea sits untouched. She's far too sensible to say anything even if she did overhear, so she smiles her waitress smile and says it's not a problem.

The bell above the door jangles as we head out into what feels like a new world.

I have a mother and she has me.

It's warm, the sun high and the sky blue. Stoneridge has a small High Street of a few dozen shops. There are hardly any chains; no McDonald's or Starbucks, no tacky yellow arches or weird green and white mermaid thing. It's all very Britain in Bloom; hanging baskets suspended from shop awnings and perfectly manicured strips of lawn dividing each side of the road. A summer of bunting and street fairs; bell-ringing on Sundays, with a packed house for the carol service every Christmas Eve.

We walk alongside each other and it's as if we're both too scared to say anything. Mum is a little shorter than I thought – she's wearing low heels that clip-clop across the paving slabs. I'm in flats.

We pass an Italian restaurant that's already open, with metal chairs and tables cluttering up the pavement. There's one bank, then another; a hairdresser, at least three charity shops, a bakery and a WHSmith. There's a pointy stone obelisk seemingly plonked at random at the end of the strip of grass, separating one side of the road from the other. It's all very cosy and comfortable.

'I don't know where to begin,' Mum says eventually. 'I suppose… how did you know I was in the café?'

It's not the question I expected.

I've almost forgotten. It was only this morning and yet everything's a muddled mess in my head. 'I went to the old house and—'

'You went there?'

'I didn't know it was the old house. I thought you might still live there.'

Mum slows her pace by half a step. 'Oh… of course. After your father and I divorced, we—' She stops herself. 'Sorry, there must've been a better way of telling you. Did you know we were separated?'

'No.'

'Oh…' She stumbles over her words, starting to explain a couple of times but interrupting herself until she goes quiet again. 'I have a new husband,' she says. 'His name's Max. We moved to a new place on the other side of the village a couple of years after you, um…'

I wonder what word she's thinking of. After I *left*? *Disappeared*?

'Do you remember the old house?' she asks.

She stops and glances sideways towards me and there's the sense that she wants me to say yes but I can't do that. Her eyes narrow and then open wider. She's not sure what to make of me.

'No,' I reply. 'I saw the name of the road online and it was easy enough to find. A woman opened the door and I asked for you. She said you'd moved out years ago. I thought that you'd moved away completely, another town or city, something like that – but

she said you owned a café on the High Street and that you were
sometimes there during the afternoons.'

'That's Janet,' Mum says, starting to walk again. 'She's lived in
the village all her life. She bought the house for the asking price
when we put it up for sale. Did she recognise you?'

'I don't think so. That was this morning. I poked my head into
the café then but you weren't around, so I tried again at lunch, then
again now. The waitress probably thought I was casing the joint.'

Mum laughs. 'Nattie's your age,' she says. 'You were in the same
class at primary school. Used to play together during the holidays.'

'Oh.'

We continue walking for a few steps. We're past the obelisk
and the end of the High Street. There's a postbox on the corner
and Mum goes in the opposite direction, heading towards a
stone church with a towering steeple. The road has narrowed to
barely a lane in either direction. There are small pebble-dashed
houses on either side, but no pavement. Like a scene from a
postcard.

'Does the café name mean anything?' I ask.

Mum stops again and so do I. She turns to face me, then places
a hand on my shoulder. She squeezes. I'm flesh, blood and bone.
Real.

'Of course it does,' she replies. 'Via's is named after you. I
always hoped this day would come.' She gasps. 'I never forgot.'

There are tears in her eyes which she blinks away before squeezing the top of her nose.

'Do you want to go to the house?' she asks. 'The new one. We
can talk there, perhaps? If that's what you want…?'

'That sounds good.'

She turns back towards the church at the end of the road. 'The
car's parked over there.'

'I can drive myself.'

'Oh.' She snorts in part-surprise, part-amusement. 'Of course. You're…' she starts counting on her fingers.

'Eighteen.'

'Right. Eighteen and a half. You can drive, you can vote, get married. You can do anything now…' She tails off and then adds: 'Where are you parked?'

I point in the direction she indicated. 'That way, near the post office.'

We start walking again and there's a surreal moment as she makes small talk about how the council introduced free parking because the locals made a fuss about the old charge. Small-time politics and letters to the local paper. It all feels very normal, the type of thing that's enormously important to a tiny number of people.

When she finishes the story, she laughs and then I join in. What else is there to do? This is village life. All that time away, all the unanswered questions, and we're talking about free car parking.

We round the row of houses and follow a low drystone wall that rings the church until we're in the car park at the back of the post office. There's a big sign about how it's closed on Thursdays and a sandwich board advertising discounted travel money.

Mum points to a black 4x4-cum-tank. Mine is the battered silver Fiat a few spaces along. She stops at the back of her vehicle and faces me once more. I'm a new puppy that needs to be smoothed and petted, to be hugged and loved. Everything's there in her face. She offers a hand and then withdraws it, wary of letting me out of her sight in case I disappear once more.

'I'll follow you,' I say, digging into my bag for the car keys.

She presses her weight from one leg to the other, still not ready for a goodbye, no matter how temporary. Like if she looks away, even for a moment, I might be gone again. She touches my arm, the gentlest of brushes with the back of her hand but it says more than her words.

'Do you want to come with me instead?' she asks, although it's not really a question. It feels like a 'no' would devastate her. 'It's not far,' she adds. 'I can drop you back later if you want…?'

From nowhere, I'm a little girl again, strapped into the front seat of the car being chauffeured around. 'That sounds good,' I say.

THREE

It's all stone walls, large detached houses, overgrown hedges and vast expanses of green as Mum drives out of the village. The road narrows, widens and then narrows again as she heads through the country lanes. She's at least ten miles per hour under the speed limit, slowing steadily for all the corners, even though she must know when they're coming.

After a few minutes of green, we reach another row of houses and I realise we've looped around the outskirts of the village. There's a newish out-of-place estate of red bricks and cluttered on-road parking, then more hedges as the houses become further spaced apart.

Mum's place has a large pebbled driveway that crunches under the wheels. There's a large lawn at the front and the house itself is twice the size of the old one. It must have at least four bedrooms as well as the attached garage.

We've not spoken the entire trip but I've felt her looking sideways to me, perhaps wondering if anything about the village or journey has been familiar. Maybe it's that she wants to check I haven't gone anywhere, or that she hasn't woken up from the dream.

She parks in front of the house, not bothering with the garage.

'This is home,' she says.

I follow her to the door and she fumbles with her bag, muttering about never being able to find her keys. 'They're in here somewhere,' she insists, her fingers rifling through the various pockets before she eventually holds them aloft. 'Damn things,' she adds. Her hand is trembling as she unlocks the door.

Inside and we're straight into an echoing hallway. There's a view all the way through to the back garden, a tunnel of light beaming through the house, and I find myself drifting along the hall, into the kitchen until I'm staring out to the lawn beyond the window. It's a little ragged, the grass creeping into the flower beds along the side, unmown for a week or three. There's a tree at the furthest end, casting a thick shadow towards the house, and everything is enclosed by high hedges. There's no gate, no way out other than through the back door.

Mum is at my side and she rests a hand on my lower back. She doesn't say anything but she doesn't have to. Her daughter and back gardens don't mix.

'This way,' she says softly.

I follow her into another hall, along the wooden panelled floor and then into a conservatory. It's a few degrees warmer than the rest of the house, offering another view of the back garden. There's a bookshelf full of CDs and books, the spines faded by the sun. A skylight is open, allowing the vague thrum of chirping birds to creep inside. Mum sits on the washed-out sofa but I'm drawn to the bookcase, picking up the framed photograph from the top shelf.

Like everything else, it's been bleached by the sun. The once green grass is a tea-stained brown, the blue sky is grey and murky – but the little girl in the centre is still clear enough. Her blonde pigtails are now a grainy sand colour, the green frog on her T-shirt a swampy brown. She's smiling, holding up what looks like a plastic spade.

'That was taken a month or two before everything happened,' Mum says. She's blinking rapidly, keeping any tears at bay. Trying to be strong. 'Every time it was sunny, you'd want to be out in the garden.'

She sighs and takes a deep breath.

I have an urge to find a mirror, to compare the girl from the photo to the woman I am. The blonde hair must be similar but I wonder what else we have in common. I can't believe my cheeks are as rounded as the girl with the frog T-shirt, but then a five- or six-year-old looks nothing like someone who's eighteen.

After placing the picture back on the bookshelf, I turn and realise Mum is standing right next to me. She tugs the longer bits at the side of my fringe again and I let her. She has a faraway, vacant stare and it's only when she blinks that it feels like she's back in the room.

'Sorry,' she says, taking a step backwards. 'I can't believe it's you… that you're back. I know I said I kept on hoping but I'm not sure that's true. Sometimes I hoped you'd be back but other times… I don't know. People said I had to move on, to stop looking backwards, but it's not as if you can turn it off.'

She bites her lip.

'It's all so… strange,' Mum adds. She tails off and glances upwards momentarily. She gulps and then licks her lips. Her eyes are wet.

She isn't wrong. I was close to chickening out in the café and there's still a part of me that wishes I had. It would have been easier. I could've gone back to my other life.

In my mind, my mother was almost mythical or dream-like. A mother. A mum.

Here, now she's in front of me, she's real. An actual person with emotions and expressions. The things I'd planned to say, the things I *have* to say, feel inadequate.

It isn't only her. It's me. I thought it would be easy, that I'd be strong, almost emotionless. But seeing this real person in front of me has changed that.

She sucks in her right cheek once more but not the left. This is what she does when she's thinking.

She isn't *a* mother any longer, she's *my* mother.

'If you don't want to talk about things, that's fine,' Mum says. 'We can sit here if you want…?'

'We can talk.'

Her chest deflates as she lets out a long breath of relief.

'Can we have something to drink first?' I ask.

'Of course.'

We move back through to the kitchen and then it's more small talk about whether I want 'normal' tea or something else. After that it's talk of milk and sugar and which mug would I like. Anything and everything to avoid the inevitable. She hurries around the kitchen in a blur but keeps drifting back towards me as if to make sure I've not disappeared into thin air. Minutes later and we're back in the conservatory, taking up opposite ends of the sofa. It might be faded and raggedy but it's certainly comfortable.

She sips her tea and waits. There are thirteen years of questions but I suppose there's only one way to begin.

'I don't remember everything too well,' I say. 'There was a man who came to the back gate. I think he had sweets or something like that. I went over to see what he was offering and then… it's a blur.'

'Did he grab you?'

'I guess…'

She's looking directly at me, *staring* at me but I can't return the look. I've twisted to face the garden instead.

'I remember this fuzzy feeling, like I'm running except I don't think it was me.'

'Like he grabbed you and ran off…?'

I shrug and the disappointment is clear as Mum lets out a long breath. When I turn back to her, she is looking towards the photograph on the bookshelf and I wonder what she's thinking. It's probably frustration that, after all these years, I still can't give her the precise answers she wants.

This is the thing I didn't expect, that her disappointment hurts. It actually hurts. It's like catching an elbow on the corner of a table, right on the funny bone where there's that instant stab of pain and the moment of surprise is momentarily worse than the agony.

I thought things would be fine. I'd shrug to myself and move on. She could deal with it – but it's not like that at all. From not knowing her, I now want her acceptance more than anything.

'I remember being in a caravan,' I say. 'There was this U-shaped sofa with a table in the middle and then a sink and microwave along the wall. It was really small and there was the man and another woman. They told me my name was Karen. When I said it was Olivia, they said I couldn't say that any longer. The man took off his belt and said I'd feel it if I ever said that name again.'

Mum has a hand over her mouth and her eyes have widened.

'The woman cut my hair and then she took me into this bathroom. It was really small – there was a toilet, a sink and a shower. No bathtub. She made me stand in the shower and then she squeezed dye into my hair. I didn't know what it was then but it was really thick and smelly. I remember the black streaks running over my arms and down my legs. She rubbed my head really hard, before washing everything down the plughole.'

It looks as if Mum wants to say something. Her mouth is open but no words come out, so I carry on.

'They made me dye my hair until I was about thirteen or fourteen. It was always black and then, one day, they said I didn't have to dye it any longer.'

She's quiet for a moment and then stumbles over some words, before eventually managing: 'Did you stay with them this whole time?'

Her hand is trembling so much that the tea sloshes over the mug onto her hand. She winces and puts the cup down before rubbing at the skin.

'They told me to call them Mum and Dad,' I reply. 'We moved around a lot—'

'So they were gypsies?' She stops herself and then speaks really quickly: 'Or, um… travellers? I don't know the correct term.' She swirls a hand and says something about political correctness. I give her a moment as she seems, unsurprisingly, befuddled.

Another shrug. 'I wasn't allowed out for a while,' I say. 'I don't remember it all properly but the door was locked a lot. There was always food but they'd tell me off for crying. There was a PlayStation and a telly. I didn't want to play at first but that was all there was to do.'

'How long did that go on for?'

'I don't know.' I rub my head, messing up my hair. 'Sometimes it feels like a dream or a TV show. It's grey round the edges, like watching someone else do something. I think it was a few weeks. Maybe a month, or longer. I was allowed out to play, but only in front of the caravan. There were other kids.'

She sighs long and hard, before rubbing her eyes. There's more blinking and then she stares directly at me. It's so intense that it's as if she's trying to will the information from me. 'Didn't anyone say anything about you not being there and then, well… being there?'

'I don't remember…' I tail off, scratch my head and then look up. 'It's hard to explain. They made me call them Mum and Dad and then, I guess, they sort of *became* my mum and dad. That was normal. I forgot about things. It was typical to be on the road, or parked in a field. The other kids knew my name and I knew theirs. I suppose I became Karen…'

She stares at me, biting her lip as if she doesn't trust herself to actually speak. It looks like she's in pain and it's the absolute worst thing. I don't know why I thought this would be easy, that I could walk into someone's life, look them in the eye and change it.

I've had my life changed in the past. One sentence and – BANG – everything's different. I was on the other side then but now I know what it's like to deliver the sledgehammer blow.

What it's shown me is that I'm not the person I thought I was.

I'm not as *strong* as I thought I was.

I thought I could say the words and feel nothing – but I can't. I want to be liked. I want my mother's approval.

'I didn't know where I was,' I add. 'We'd be on a patch of land in the middle of nowhere, or on the outskirts of some village. I was only allowed to talk to the other kids who travelled in the other caravans. I didn't understand England or the UK then, let alone Europe. I had no idea where we were, or who anybody else was. If I ever said anything out of turn, I'd be locked in the caravan again.'

Mum nods but I have no idea what she's thinking. Her eyes are huge, eyebrows high like she's one of those Botox junkies who are permanently surprised.

'Did you go to school?' she asks.

'No. There were books – and I read a lot – but that was all.'

'How did you escape?'

'They wanted me to get married when I was seventeen. It's what everyone does.'

'You were with them for ten years…?'

Mum sounds like she can't believe it but I don't know what else to say. She's so stunned that she starts to cough. She stretches for a box of tissues and conceals her mouth while turning away.

When she's settled once more, I add: 'I didn't want to marry him. It was like one of those old royal weddings where the prince from one country marries a princess from another and it's supposed to bring everyone together. My family wanted to be connected to another.'

It's already out before I realise what I've said.

Mum's eyes widen and it's too late. '*Your* family,' she says.

'I didn't mean it like that. I, um—'

I have no idea what I'm going to add to that, but she cuts me off anyway, speaking so quickly that the words run into one another: 'But you didn't go through with it…?'

She's looking at my hands, searching for a ring that isn't there.

I shake my head. 'I ran away one night. It was really different then. We lived in the same caravan but I had my own key and was allowed out. I waited until everyone was asleep, stole a bit of money from the drawer in the kitchen and then left. I didn't tell anyone. We were in this place outside Sunderland and I got on a train. Hid in the toilets when the ticket inspector came past, so I didn't have to pay. I stayed on it all the way to King's Cross.'

'In London…?' Mum asks as if there's another King's Cross, but I think it's more shock than anything else.

I nod.

'This happened a year ago?' she asks

'A year and a bit,' I reply. 'It was a couple of weeks before I turned seventeen.'

'What did you do then?'

'Walked around. Everything was so big. I was used to caravan parks and fields and wasteland. Sometimes we'd get takeaway but we'd never eat out. I'd never been to a cinema, or the theatre. I was used to seeing the same people every day – or sometimes I wouldn't see anyone. Then, suddenly, there are people everywhere. Lights everywhere. Shops and restaurants; pubs and hotels and noise. It was really disorientating.'

Mum nods along. She touches my arm once more. Only a second or two but she's making sure I'm still there. Still real.

'I'm still like that when I go to a big city,' she says.

'I didn't know anyone. All I had was the money I'd taken – a couple of hundred quid – plus a bag with a few clothes. I didn't have a change of shoes. I didn't know where anything was and I'd never used a mobile phone. I was walking into the shops, pubs and restaurants asking if there was work. Eventually I ended up in this café – like yours but grubbier. The guy behind the counter said there was nothing but then he followed me outside and beckoned me into this alley. He said there was cash-in-hand shifts going if

I could keep quiet. I know now that it was all a bit shady but, at the time, it felt like he was being nice.'

'Was he… *kind* to you?'

She sounds like she'd be heartbroken to hear anything else and I nod.

'Sort of. He wasn't horrible. There was a room above the café that he let me stay in,' I add. 'There was no proper bed and no shower. It was a storeroom and I had to go into the toilet to wash in the sink. He charged me rent, which meant I ended up working for next to nothing. I didn't understand minimum wage at the time and the other people who worked there didn't speak English very well. When my shift finished, I'd go out walking for miles. I'd go around all the touristy areas and then head out further. Then I started to remember…'

Mum has pressed forward to the edge of her seat. 'Remember what?'

'Olivia… Stoneridge. I got a phone and figured out the Internet, so I searched online for the name. Things started to come back but I didn't know what to do. One of the girls from the café taught me to drive and she knew someone who sold cheap cars. I'd drive out this way but was too scared to come all the way into Stoneridge. It took me eight months to get this far.'

She stares at me and her nostrils flare wide. 'You should've… you could've… Do you remember me?'

It feels as if I'm locked to her and I have to force myself to look away. My tea has been going cold on the side and I take a few seconds to sip it before twisting back. 'Bits,' I say. 'It all melds together. I'm sorry but I can't remember what was you and what was my other mum and dad.'

It takes a while but she nods. I think she wants to move on. Dwelling too much will mean tears, and who knows where we go then.

'Do I call you Olivia… or Karen?'

There's no question what she'd prefer. The name 'Karen' escapes through clenched teeth. It would break her heart if I said anything other than what I do.

'Olivia.'

She sighs with relief.

'I remember a flowery dress you used to wear,' I add. 'It was white but there were pink and green bits.'

This brings tears to the corner of her eyes. She blinks and wipes them away. 'I did,' she says. 'What was I thinking?!'

She laughs through the tears and then takes a tissue from the box on the table to blow her nose.

'I remember the beach,' I say. 'I think we played cricket or rounders. Something with a bat…?'

Mum's face brightens. 'That's right – your father, me and you.'

'I think there was a birthday party, too. I remember a cake and candles at a bowling alley. It must've been with you because we'd have never gone from the caravan.'

Another nod. 'That was Nattie's birthday – the girl from the café. You would've been five, I think. I can't believe you remember that. I barely do.'

'It's only flashes, like when you wake up from a dream and you can remember the last bit. Everything's really patchy.'

'Perhaps being around the village will help you remember more…?'

Mum wipes her eyes once more but doesn't push on to ask if I'm staying around. She's about to say something else when there's a loud scratch from the front of the house. She stands automatically, momentarily forgetting I'm there as she wipes her sleeve across her face and then tugs her hair back into a neater ponytail. She's still on her feet as a man ambles into the room. He's short and thickset with hairy arms and a mop of dark unruly hair, plus brown-black eyes to match. He frowns towards me as Mum lets out an 'Oh' of surprise as if she's not expecting whoever this is.

Moments later, there are more footsteps and then a little boy patters into the room. He's unsteady on his feet, wobbling from side to side. Mum scoops him up from the floor and cradles him onto her shoulder as he pokes at her ear. She glances over his head towards me, looking for a reaction.

The final person into the room is a man who looks like the first one to enter. He's equally short with a thick mat of hair across his arms. He's tanned with the sort of leathery brownness that comes from spending too long outside. His hair is shorter than the first man, but it's still a mess of straggly black. He looks from me to Mum and back again, eyes shrinking to slits.

'What's going on?' he asks.

Mum turns to me, balancing the child on her arm. She points to the second man, then the first. 'This is my husband, Max, and his brother, Ashley.' She then twists so that the little boy is looking at me. His eyes seem too big for his skull in the way toddlers do. There's a thin covering of sandy straw hair but he has the same green eyes as my mother.

'Say hello, Harry,' she says. 'This is your older sister, Olivia.'

FOUR

I reach out to take Harry's hand and his tiny twiglet fingers grip mine tightly. It's been a long time since I thought about having brothers or sisters. I'd never particularly wanted siblings before but, now he's in front of me, Harry is the most wondrous thing.

He babbles something about 'bricks' and then lets me go. Mum places him on the floor and he toddles off to a box in the corner. He upends it, scattering a pile of Duplo bricks across the hard floor before plopping himself down among the plastic mess. I watch him but I can sense everyone else looking at me.

'How old is he?' I ask before anyone else can speak.

'Twenty-eight months,' my mum replies quickly.

It takes me a few seconds to figure it out – two years and four months. When do people stop having their ages announced in months?

'He has your eyes,' I say.

'Yours, too,' Mum replies. We glance to each other for a moment but it's she who turns away almost instantly. She seems closer than ever to tears.

Harry is oblivious to it all, clipping a red brick into a blue one and then sucking his fingers. He's jabbering to himself and I'm not sure if it's actual words. I want to pick him up and hold him.

'Olivia.'

The first of the men to enter says the name like a question and I turn to face him. This is Ashley, my mother's brother-in-law; my step-uncle, I guess. If that's a thing. The two brothers look similar but there are differences. Ashley is taller, with thicker arms. There's a blemish that zigzags across his eye and another straight line of scar tissue on his top lip, under his nose. He's unshaven, with dark stubble; but Max, my stepfather, is clean.

'Hi,' I reply.

Neither of the brothers speak. They stare at me as one, eyes narrow with suspicion.

'You're Olivia…?'

It's hard to tell whether Ashley is asking a question. I hold my arms out, palms up as if to say, *here I am*.

'What do you want me to say?'

'You're actually her?'

I don't get a chance to reply because there's a plasticky bang and then Harry starts to cry. He's somehow trapped his finger between two bricks and is staring at it accusingly, not quite understanding what's happened. Mum scoops him up, cooing about boo-boos and rocking him back and forth. Harry stops crying almost immediately and starts playing with her necklace instead. I get the sense this sort of thing happens a lot because she's utterly unfazed as he drags on the silver chain.

Mum says she's going to get a bottle and then carries Harry out of the room, checking on me over her shoulder before leaving. I continue to stand, smiling awkwardly as the two men goggle at me. The room suddenly feels cold. Ashley is eyeing me like I've been caught breaking into his car, while Max is full of bewilderment, watching on as if I'm a new creature he's never seen before.

Thankfully, it's not long before Mum returns. She plonks Harry on the floor and hands him a bottle of milk, from which he starts to guzzle and slurp. She looks up to me and then turns to Max and Ashley. The tension is impossible to miss. The warmth of the sun through the glass of the conservatory has been replaced by a simmering frostiness.

I know I shouldn't but I can't help myself. 'What?' I say, teenage half-shrug and all. I turn between the two men, daring one of them to actually say what they're clearly thinking. Ashley, especially.

'Nothing,' Max replies. His brother is silent.

Mum looks up from Harry and takes a step forward, putting herself between us. She speaks to her husband. 'I think it's a lot for everyone to take in,' she says, running a hand through her hair. It's a lot for *her* to take in as well. Her more than anyone.

His gaze doesn't leave me as Ashley finally speaks. 'Aye,' he replies, nodding, somehow making it sound like a threat. 'Where've you been?' he growls.

I start to answer but Mum gets in there first. 'She's already been through everything once and I'm not going to stand here and make her repeat it all. We can go over it later if you're concerned.'

There's a spiky spark of annoyance and the sneering look Ashley gives her makes it clear there's little affection between them.

It's Max who breaks the impasse, stepping forward and stroking Mum's arm. 'Of course,' he says, though his brother is unconvinced.

We all sit: Max, Mum and me on the sofa, Ashley in a wicker armchair that rocks slightly. I'm watching Harry and he's back to being a happy delight. His bottle has been discarded as he bangs the Duplo bricks together again, apparently forgetting that he hurt his finger moments before.

'It's weird having a brother,' I say.

'Harry started nursery last month,' Mum replies. 'He's there two mornings a week – it's supposed to make children good at mixing if they experience being around other kids at a young age.'

It seems like such a happy little life at that age. Toys and food on demand, unconditional love and affection, somewhere warm and safe to sleep.

As Harry plays obliviously next to the window, it's easy to imagine that he'll never be allowed into the back garden by himself. I wonder how long it took Mum to be able to let him go to nursery, to let him out of her sight, even.

'We can go to the police when he's settled,' Mum says. It's matter-of-fact, as if this is the natural thing to do.

I turn to her. 'Sorry…?'

'They might come here if that's easier.'

'Who?'

'The police.'

'Oh…'

For the first time since we met in the café, she frowns at me; disappointed as if she doesn't understand.

'Is that what you want?' I ask.

'Isn't that what *you* want? Someone committed a crime. They took you and effectively kept you prisoner. Unless you've already been to the police…?'

I shake my head and Mum looks to Max for support, even though he doesn't say anything. We're interrupted by a loud belch from Harry. We all turn to look and there's an orange splurge on the front of his dungarees. He stares at it and then licks his hand before continuing to play with his bricks.

'Oh, Harry…' Mum sighs his name and then dashes out of the room. Her footsteps disappear along the hall and then there's quiet except for the clink of plastic brick on plastic brick.

The brothers are watching me again and it's impossible to ignore them this time; Max on one side, Ashley on the other. Considering he seems marginally the kinder of the two – and he's family – it's Max I look to.

'So… you're back,' he says.

'Something like that.'

'Are you back for good?'

'I've not thought any of that through. I didn't know if Mum would want to see me…'

Max nods but there's an under-the-breath snort from his brother. The conservatory doesn't feel like a very welcoming place any longer. I want to leave but then remember that I didn't come in my own car. I don't know the way back to the village and I'd have to walk anyway.

It's only a minute until Mum returns, cloth and clean pair of dungarees in hand. Harry grumbles as he's plucked away from the floor and wiped down. Mum unclips what he's wearing and tosses it to the side, changing him with the ruthless efficiency of someone who's dealt with more than enough baby sick in her time.

Nobody speaks until she lifts herself back onto the sofa, patting my knee as she does so.

'If you've not been to the police, then we should let them know as soon as possible. You're still a missing person.'

'What do you want me to say?'

She tilts her head, as if she's misheard. 'The truth. What you told me.'

'It's just… I can – if you want – but what then? I left more than a year ago. I don't know where my – where *the* – other family is. They could be in Ireland or Europe, or anywhere.'

I'm looking to Mum but she glances sideways to Max and then across the room to Ashley. I know they're both watching me and shiver under their attention. I don't like this at all. I can't believe there's a right or wrong thing to do in this type of situation, that someone's written a manual for it all.

'Don't you want them punished?'

Mum has tried to tone down her words but there's steel there. Anger at what she's been through, perhaps fury on my behalf as well.

'I know what they did,' I say, 'it's just… they sort of looked after me as well. I was never hungry; they didn't hit me. I think I want to forget it all – for now at least. Can we do that?'

She bites her lip and I'm unsure if she's angry, disappointed or both. I think she wants me to understand what it's been like for her over the past thirteen years, that she wants someone to answer for all that. There's a big part of me that wants to ask – but knowing that pain, *feeling* it, could change everything.

'I can tell people if you want,' I add. 'It's up to you – but won't the papers want to come? We've got our own catching up to do before any of that…'

She starts to nod slowly and then it's as if the spell has broken. 'You're right,' she replies. 'It's your decision, your story to tell. I'm just glad to have you back.'

FIVE

For a while, we all sit and watch Harry play. He's wonderfully oblivious, happy in his own world and unaware of how his family has changed. One day he might ask about what happened today.

I'm jealous of his innocence.

Ashley is shuffling in his seat, probably wanting to say something, though seemingly not *to* me. I risk a glance up to him and he's not looking at Harry at all; he has eyes only for me. There's a big part of me that wants to challenge him, pump my shoulders up and ask what his problem is – but it doesn't feel like the time. Not yet. I keep reminding myself we're related now – step-uncle and step-niece. How very twenty-first century. Broken Britain and all that.

I stand and ask where the bathroom is. Mum says there are two: one by the front door, the other up the stairs. With a smile for Harry, I head out of the room, following the hall until it reaches the intersection with the kitchen. There's silence from the conservatory, so I continue to the front door; opening and closing the toilet door loudly and then padding my way back along the hall silently on the tips of my toes.

The only sound from the conservatory is the gentle clamour of Harry playing on the floor, interspersed with his calm gibberish.

It's only a few more seconds until the conversation begins: 'How'd you know it's her?'

I'm not sure who's speaking out of Max and Ashley. Max has hardly said anything but what little he's said has been growled with the same gravelly tone as his brother. It's like they swallowed glass as children.

'What do you mean?' Mum replies.

'It could be anyone, couldn't it? Not hard to figure out that Olivia would be, what, eighteen? Nineteen? Twenty? Anyone could claim to be her.'

I suppose this is what I expected all along. How *does* my mother know it's me? She talked about remembering my eyes, but is that enough? Is it even true? I expected to have to prove myself, but nothing today has gone as I expected.

'I know my daughter's eyes.'

There's a snort, which makes me pretty certain it's Ashley who's talking. I'm standing by the kitchen door but the sound is echoing along the wooden floors and amplifying. I might be able to hear them even if I was by the front door.

'*Eyes?*' he says. 'You're believing all this based on the colour of her *eyes*?'

He's sneering and indignant but, in some ways, he's echoing my own thoughts. *Eyes?* Is that what it means to be a mother? If there were ten kids lined up, each inside a full-length box with only a pair of eyeholes cut into the cardboard, could a mother pick out her own child?

Could she do it after thirteen years?

'It's not only the colour,' Mum replies. 'It's more than that. You wouldn't understand.'

'Why wouldn't I understand?'

'Because you've never given birth and you never will.'

It's definitely Ashley who has been speaking. There's a short silence and I can feel the tension from along the hall.

'You need to take a step back and think about this rationally,' Ashley says, changing his tone. He's tried force, now he's onto logic.

'Think about what?' Mum says.

'You're being scammed.'

'I know you used to run a garage – but not everything is a con.' She sounds fed-up, perhaps ready for an argument.

'What do you mean by that?'

The snapped, snarled reply has a definite undercurrent that's hard to judge without being able to see his face. It sounds dangerous.

Mum replies instantly, cutting Ashley off. 'Nothing. All I'm saying is that she's *my* daughter. Call it intuition, whatever you want. I know who she is.'

'Sounds more like naivety to me.'

'It's not. Olivia knew things. She remembered a dress I had. Natalie had a birthday party at a bowling alley when she was young and Olivia knew about that too. She remembered her father and me playing rounders on the beach one time.'

There's a pause and I wonder if this is the end of the conversation. At least I've managed to get something across competently today. I can't remember everything I said to Mum, only what I *meant* to say. It's all a blur. I was supposed to be clinical and logical with my words but seeing her was too sentimental.

The next voice belongs to Max. I realise now that there is a subtle difference between the two brothers. Ashley speaks more slowly and deliberately. There's a suggestion of menace to almost everything he says. Max is far more nuanced. He doesn't sound angry or annoyed, more worried – probably out of concern for his wife and son.

'You know there could be an explanation for that,' he says.

'For what?'

'For her memories.'

A chill licks my back and I can't stop myself shivering. My ears tingle, straining to hear what's next.

Mum speaks now: 'What do you mean?'

'All that sort of stuff was in the papers at the time. I remember the photo of Olivia at the beach. Lots of people will. Anyone could've seen that. I'd bet there was one of her at the birthday party, too. They were released to help people identify her. Some of that will have ended up online, but there are newspaper archives in libraries. If you wanted to go looking for things, you could find everything out.'

It feels like a lamp has been switched on, when there's that fizzing buzz of electricity in the fraction of a second before the bulb illuminates.

There is a short gap before my mother replies: 'Are you saying you don't believe her?'

'I'm saying this is the problem with putting yourself out there. People can find things out and use them against you.'

Logic, not emotion. When I played this day out in my mind, that's what I wanted. It's what I told myself: logic. Explain who I am and where I've been.

Except that's no good when there are real people involved; when there are tears in another person's eyes, when their bottom lip wobbles. I think I said everything I wanted to but I don't know for sure. I want to be my mother's daughter and yet there's still a part of me that wants to leave the village and not come back. I thought I'd be fine with everything but it's simply too weird.

There is another pause. The only sound is the gentle bash-bash-bash of Harry playing on the floor. I lean against the wall and slowly lift up one leg, then the other, alleviating the cramp. How long can I get away with hanging around here until someone comes looking for me?

'Why don't you say what you really think?'

Mum's tone is scolding and raw. She sounds stung, as if none of this crossed her mind.

'I don't know what I think,' Max replies.

'I do,' Ashley says. 'She's a fraud. Shows up after all this time. Has she asked for money yet?'

'No.'

'She will – mark my words.'

'Is that what you think? She's an imposter?'

'That's all I've got to say – but I wouldn't go leaving my kid with her if I were you.'

Another chill ripples along my spine and there's a large part of me that wants to stomp down the hallway and start wagging fingers. Or worse. The insinuation that I'm a danger around children is beyond offensive.

Mum's voice is barely concealed fury: 'Don't you *dare* talk about her like that. This is still my house and—'

'It's not *your* house.'

'Well it's definitely not yours.'

I wonder what the issue is between my mother and Ashley. Whether his true problem is with me or her. Max doesn't seem to be saying or doing much to calm whatever's going on between his brother and his wife.

Mum's voice wavers this time, cracking halfway through her reply: 'Why would someone do that? We're not rich.'

'It *looks* like you are.' Ashley is dismissive, as if this is obvious. 'Big house, big car, coffee shop. How much do you spend on getting your hair done every month? Your nails? Fake tan? Christ—'

'Hey!' Max finally interrupts. I don't catch what he says next but it's probably along the lines of saying that his brother has gone too far. When I tune back in, he sounds conciliatory: 'I think what Ash is saying is that there are all sorts of nutters out there. You see things in the papers all the time. You should ask her something hard.'

'Like what? How much do you remember from when you were five? She's been honest enough to say that there's a lot she doesn't remember. Do you really think someone's going to go through all *this*, to fake everything, just for the takings of a coffee shop or some cab fares?'

'Cab fares!' Ashley shouts his reply and then lowers his voice. 'You're always talking us down. Up on your high horse—'

He's shushed by Max and I can sense them turning towards the hall, listening in case I'm near. I push up onto my toes again, feeling another cramp in my left calf.

When Max – when my *stepfather* – talks next, he speaks quickly, knowing it can't be long until I return. 'You can pay for a DNA test,' he says. 'There are all sorts of companies online who do it. If she is who she says she is, ask to swab her mouth.'

'No. How would you feel if your own mother asked you to do that? It's offensive to me and her.'

It's Ashley who replies: 'We could steal some hair, send it off and—'

'Don't you dare.'

'If she's got nothing to hide, then—'

I've been resting on one leg for too long and press back onto the other, making one of the floorboards squeak. There's a moment of silence and there's no turning back now. I stride along the hall back into the conservatory, keeping my head high and at least pretending to be full of self-assurance. Ashley is staring at me and I return it with as much interest as I can manage. I read a book about confidence recently and it all seemed very easy in theory. Stand or sit tall; speak slowly and clearly; smile – even if it is a shit-eating 'up yours' grin; make eye contact and don't look away.

'Nothing to hide about what?' I ask.

The silence booms and even Harry has stopped playing on the floor. I can feel him looking up towards me with those huge eyes but it's no time to turn away from my step-uncle.

Ashley pushes himself up from the chair, now ignoring me and losing the staring battle.

'I'm going,' he says.

He doesn't wait for anyone to object or follow, spinning on his heels and stomping away down the hall. The front door slams and then there's quiet once more.

'How much did you hear?' Mum asks quietly. She sounds hurt.

'Not much. What did I miss?'

She takes a breath. 'Nothing, it's just… this is all very new and different. It's a big shock. People don't know how to react.'

She grips my knee and squeezes. I'm real. I'm definitely real. When I look to her, she's smiling sadly and she looks years older than she did a few minutes ago. Now I'm looking for the things Ashley mentioned, I can see the darker roots starting to show, the wrinkles around her eyes and mouth. A pale blob or two underneath her ears where's she's missed the fake tan. She suddenly seems very tired.

'There's so much I want to ask you,' she says. 'So much I don't know. Like whether you've got a boyfriend… or girlfriend, I suppose. Whether you've got qualifications, the places you've seen, the things you've done…' She tails off. 'Where are you staying?' she asks.

'The Black Horse in town. There's a room above the bar.'

She glances towards the ceiling. 'There's a spare room upstairs…'

I look over to Max, whose arms are crossed. He's watching Harry on the floor, not committing to anything. I wait for him to glance up to me, catching his eye and keeping it.

'I don't think that's a good idea,' I reply.

SIX

The Black Horse is a mix of cosy country pub and bit-of-a-hole. It has the quaint grey stone interior like something out of a British guidebook. I can imagine American tourists heading inside to take pictures of the thick wooden beams and tranquil fireplace, then becoming bemused at the warm frothy beer and lack of ice with everything. There's no fancy cocktail list or extravagant food menu. It's all fish, chips and peas; steak pie, chips and peas; or half-a-chicken with chips and peas.

If someone doesn't like chips or peas, they're pretty much screwed.

The tables and bar have a slightly tacky feel, not full on gecko-like stickiness but enough that the beer mats hold firm as if they've got a bit of double-sided tape on the underside.

It's typical Britain that there's a bed and breakfast room upstairs – after all, who could possibly want to rent a room that didn't have a pub at the bottom of the stairs?

Peter, the landlord, seems friendly enough. He's late-thirties or so, apparently single and running this place by himself. When I pass him at the base of the stairs to head towards the bar, he's balancing a box of smoky bacon crisps on his shoulder. He asks if everything's all right with my room, which it is.

It's early evening and the bar area is quiet. A pair of blokes are feeding pound coins into the quiz machine in the corner and there are a couple of older men leaning on the furthest end of the bar. From their minimal conversation and glassy-eyed oblivious stares, I suspect they spend a lot of time here.

Peter is still busy carrying boxes from one part of the bar to the other, so I'm served by another bloke. He's older, squinty-eyed to the degree that it's hard to tell what he's looking at. His strange demeanour is made worse by the fact that it looks like he's only shaved one half of his face. One side is pock-marked and covered with a pimply purple rash; the other is peppered with thin stubble.

It's all very odd.

He asks what I want but it takes me a second to realise he's looking at me. I order a Guinness and wait on one of the stools, trying to avoid the stickiness of the actual bar.

Obviously this is subjective, but Guinness is one of the marvels of human achievement. A roast meal in a glass: no need to eat beforehand because it covers all bases.

The barman pours the first part and then leaves it to settle. He keeps glancing up to me – or near me – it's hard to tell, and the more he does it, the more unnerving it becomes. In the end, I take my drink over to one of the corner booths and hide behind my phone. The greatest function of a mobile isn't the ability to call or text, nor the Internet connection; it's the wall it puts up. Staring at the screen is an instant message to would-be botherers that their attention is unwanted.

Or that's what it *should* do.

I'm busy searching for the name 'Ashley Pitman' when a shadow falls across the table. There's a builder-type standing over the table, pint of Guinness in his hand. It looks like he's not long got off work, with dirty fingernails and a smear of plaster, cement or something similar on his cheek. His sleeves are rolled up, showing off thick forearms, and his hair is a ruffled dark-blond nest. It's the sort of style that seems like he's actually tried to make it look that way.

'All right?' he says, not that he's asking if I'm all right, of course. I sometimes wonder what other English-speaking countries think of the things we say. How 'all right' can be anything from 'hi' to 'get out of my seat before I rip your ears off'. He's actually asking who I am.

'Hi,' I reply, non-committal smile and all. It's good to switch off for a few moments, like I've had a long day at work, even though I haven't.

'I've not seen you around before.'

'Nope.'

He bobs awkwardly and then nods at the other side of the booth. 'Mind if I sit?'

I glance past him towards all the empty tables and chairs.

'I'm Rhys,' he adds, slotting into the space without waiting for a proper answer. He nods at my drink. 'Nothing quite like one of these to finish the day.'

He's persistent, I'll give him that. I put my phone on the seat and look up to take him in properly. He's a few years older than me – mid-twenties at the most.

'What's your name?' he asks.

I snort: 'You really don't want to know.'

'Ah, like that, is it? Mysterious stranger walks into a bar…'

He grins and it's hard to remain stony-faced. He has an infectious enthusiasm.

'Who's the guy behind the bar?' I ask.

Rhys turns to look and the bloke who served me quickly turns to pretend he wasn't watching us.

'That's Chris,' Rhys says. 'He's, well… I don't want to say. He's got issues. Let's put it like that. I think Pete gave him a job out of pity. He used to hang around the park all day.'

Rhys checks his shoulder again. Chris is still watching us but he's being a little more careful about it now, wiping some of the glasses clean with a tea towel while glancing over to our booth every few seconds.

When he turns back, Rhys has a sip of his drink, leaving a sliver of foam on his top lip. 'Is Chris causing you trouble?' he asks.

'No... not really. When I booked into the room upstairs yesterday, he watched me go up the stairs and I thought it was a bit weird. Pete seems nice enough.'

'Pete's a good guy. Been running this place for years. If Chris gives you any trouble, tell him.'

I have some of my drink and then motion to Rhys that he's got some on his lip. He wipes it away with his hand and then leans back into the soft chair.

'So... you're staying upstairs, then?'

'Right.'

'Any particular reason? You're not on holiday, are you?'

'What if I am?'

He shrugs. 'It's just... there must be better places than this. Half the shops still do half-day opening on Thursdays – or they're closed completely. I didn't realise that was weird until I went to high school and realised it's only this place that does that. It's some weird throwback to a law from the early 1900s – *that's* how out of date this place is.'

'You're still here.'

He laughs and gulps a mouthful of his drink. 'True – but I was born here. I work at a builders' yard, but I wouldn't *choose* to be here on holiday.'

'I'm not on holiday.'

Over in the corner, the men have finally given up on the quiz machine. One of them bangs his hand on the side as if it's screwed him over and then they head to the bar. The pub has started to fill up without me noticing. A family of two-point-four children is at the table in front of the unlit fireplace, browsing through the menu. I hope they like chips and peas.

'Are you going to tell me your name?'

I turn back to Rhys, who has his eyebrows raised expectantly. I didn't come here to make friends and yet... there's something pleasant and normal about the attention. The *right* attention.

Chris is now serving the quiz machine pair at the bar but I still keep catching him looking in my direction.

'Are you sure you want to know?' I ask.

'I wouldn't ask otherwise.'

'I'm not sure you can handle it.'

He laughs: 'Try me.'

'How old are you?'

'Twenty-four.'

'And you've lived here all your life?'

'Right.'

'I'm going to blow your mind.'

Rhys presses his lips together and it's clear he very much does not expect that to happen. He's enjoying the game, though.

'Go on,' he says.

'I'm Olivia Adams.'

Rhys stares at me and then his eyebrow twitches. I can almost see the cogs turning, the memories rearranging themselves. Then it's there in his eyes and he knows exactly what it means.

'*You're* Olivia Adams?' he says.

'I told you I didn't think you could handle it.'

His pint is halfway from the table to his mouth and he hasn't moved his hand in a few seconds. He presses the glass to his lips but doesn't drink, instead returning it to the table. Then he turns, leans around the back of the seat and calls towards someone I can't see.

I have a momentary panic that he could have called over anyone but, a moment later, the waitress from the café arrives at our table. She's in a short red skirt with a tight white T-shirt. Her long red hair hangs to her shoulders. She looks between us and then focuses on Rhys.

'What do you want?' she asks.

'This is Nattie,' he says before nodding to me. 'You'll never guess who this is.'

Nattie turns to face me, screwing her lips up into an O. She doesn't seem that bothered. 'You were in the café earlier,' she says.

'Right.'

'Left your drink.'

'Sorry about that.'

Nattie twists back to Rhys. 'Go on.'

He grins: 'Well, your café is named after her…'

Nattie does the slow turn back to me, eyes widening. 'No freaking way…'

SEVEN

Nattie drops onto the seat next to Rhys and stares at me. It's like I'm something she's never seen before. A new, undiscovered colour. 'Olivia?'

I glance past her towards the rest of the bar. 'I'm trying to keep it quiet for now.'

'But you're her? You're back?'

I smile and give a small shrug as a reply.

'We knew each other as kids,' Nattie says. Her words come so quickly that they run into one another. 'We were in the same class at school. We used to play together. My mum has the photos.'

'That's what my mum said earlier.'

Nattie nods as if it all makes sense now. '*That's* why you were asking who she was in the café earlier. You were checking you had the right person.' She takes a big puff of breath. 'I can't believe it's you. You were like this bogeyman when I was a kid.'

'How'd you mean?'

'If I was ever naughty – which, of course, I never was – Mum would say that if I didn't behave, I'd end up like Olivia. If I ever ran ahead or anything like that, she'd say I'd disappear like you. You were like this myth growing up. Everyone at school knew your name, even though most people didn't know you. When someone was off sick for a day, we'd say they'd been Oliviered.'

'Nice – you know you've made it when you become a verb.'

Nattie isn't listening, she's counting on her fingers. 'How long has it been? Twelve years? Thirteen?'

'Something like that.'

Nattie looks to Rhys, who's full of amusement. She slaps his arm. 'You could've said something.'

'I called you over as soon as I found out.' He downs the rest of his pint, asks Nattie what she wants and then heads off to the bar.

Nattie watches him go and then leans forward, eyes narrowing as she focuses more closely on me. 'Do you remember me?' she whispers.

A shake of the head. 'It was a long time ago.'

'You used to come over after school. I think your mum had work or something like that. We'd play in the garden…' she tails off and then adds: 'I was never allowed in the back garden after that. Mum would make me play inside.' She rubs her temples, as if caressing out the specific memory. 'I still remember the day you went missing really vividly… it's probably my clearest early memory. I know odd things before that – us playing – but those almost feel like I remember them because Mum told me. She'd say we used to play together and it's like the memory formed from that. With this, it's so clear. It was a Saturday and I remember Mum asking me if I'd seen you…'

Rhys interrupts by returning to the table with a cider for Nattie. He hadn't asked if I wanted another drink, let alone what I might want, but he nods to the bar where two Guinnesses are settling.

I'm not going to complain.

He slides into the booth, swapping places with Nattie and then looks between us.

'Were you talking about me?'

Nattie laughs. 'You wish.'

He ruffles his hair but it barely moves from the just-out-of-bed wax.

'What happened?' Nattie asks. 'Where've you been? We thought you were, well… *dead*. Everyone did.'

I finish the final third of my first pint in one go. I've only told the story once out loud and I'm already sick of it.

'I might need a drink first…'

Nattie is right on it. She fetches the two pints from the bar and then I tell them much of what I told my mum. Or, more to the point, much of what I *think* I told my mum. It's better this time. I remember everything I say and, beyond that, I'm not nervous. Nattie and Rhys are like me. They react with shock and awe in the way I assumed my mother would. They don't interrupt. They don't cry. Perhaps there's even a small part of me that enjoys it, like I'm a grandmother in a big ol' rocking chair telling stories to her grandkids. The Guinness helps.

I talk about the man, the caravan, being kept inside, moving around, the name Karen, eventually feeling like I belonged, escaping on a train…

It's more natural the second time but it helps that I have an engrossed audience of two. It feels strange yet satisfying to have people hanging on every word I say.

Neither of them speak until I'm finished. Their drinks are untouched. After I've told them about checking into the Black Horse last night and looking for Mum this morning, I shrug as if to say they're what comes next.

There's a pause where they stare at me, wondering if there's more. As if I might pull off a mask and reveal this is all a prank for some TV show.

'Didn't you ever want to come home?' Nattie asks eventually. Her throat sounds dry. 'When you were younger, I mean. Like when you were nine or ten and you were allowed out to play…?'

'What would I have done?' I reply. 'When I was nine, I'd already been away for four years. Say you don't really remember anything before you were four years old, that means I only had vague memories a year or so from being in Stoneridge. By then,

I already had four of being away. You don't have much concept of time at that age.'

Nattie nods in agreement. 'Like with the school holidays,' she says. 'It seems like forever when you're a kid but then, when you're fourteen or fifteen, the six weeks fly by.'

She gets it.

'Right – it was like having two lives. It was only when I got older that I started to realise what might have happened. Before that, it was like watching a TV show. As if it had happened to someone else. Plus, you believe what adults tell you when you're little. Like Santa, or the tooth fairy. It's all real until you grow up and realise it's not.'

There's a pause and Nattie gulps down some of her drink. 'How old were you when you started figuring it out?'

'Thirteen or fourteen, I guess… but it wasn't like I had a Eureka moment. It was gradual. Flashes of memories. I'd wake up and wonder if I was dreaming or if something had actually happened. I remembered names and places.'

Nattie leans back, taking it in, and Rhys speaks next. 'Have they ever come looking for you?'

'Who?'

'The other family. The travellers.'

'I've never seen anyone.'

'Do you think they could come here…?'

'I doubt it… I guess I've never thought of that.'

A couple drift past us and slot onto the table closest with a bottle of wine and an ice bucket. They're twenty-somethings, set for a night out as a couple, not remotely bothered about who we are.

So much of today hasn't gone as I'd thought – and yet, I suppose, the main things have. What's different is how it's left me feeling. I wanted to keep things small, to tell my mother and no one else, yet here I am telling two other people everything as well. Beyond that, there's a small part of me that wants this stranger couple to overhear us and make a big deal. To stick me on some throne and adore me as the village's prodigal daughter. I want that fame but I know I really don't.

Nattie lowers her voice anyway: 'What did the police say?'

'I've not spoken to them.'

'Oh. Is that tomorrow…?'

'I'm not sure. This is all new for me. It's not like I've got some grand plan for what happens next. There's no guidebook for everything.'

They both seem to agree with this.

Nattie nudges Rhys with her elbow. 'Do you remember the search?' she asks.

He nods. 'Like it was yesterday – I wasn't allowed out for the whole summer. I guess I was ten or eleven. I wanted to go out and play football with my mates but our mums kept saying no.'

'I remember everyone going crazy,' Nattie says. 'We were at Ridge Park and there were loads of people. Some sort of village meeting, I think. Your mum was at the front, crying and thanking people for coming to search. I was with my mum at the front and remember looking up at her, not quite understanding.'

The other couple are gazing longingly into each other's eyes, whispering and giggling about who knows what. They couldn't care less about what's happening barely a few metres away.

'I remember the cameras,' Rhys adds. 'It was the first time I connected cameras to what was shown on TV. There were all these news people here and I think I was scared of them. I'm not sure why – probably that it was so many new people. None of my friends were allowed out either, so if we wanted to go round anyone's house, we had to have one of our parents walk us over.'

'I think that's what made it scary,' Nattie says. 'It was bad enough what happened with you but because we were kept inside, it made everything feel much worse.'

'Like a prison,' Rhys concludes.

There are a few moments where we stop and listen to the buzz from the rest of the pub. That's the thing with small communities – everything that happens has a knock-on effect to everything else. A child going missing is a scar on the lives of every other young person in the area. They even invented their own word – Oliviered – for when someone went missing. It's a lot to take in.

Nattie glances across to the couple who are closest to us but they're still busy making goo-goo eyes to one another.

'Your mum must've flipped out,' she says.

'Sort of,' I reply. 'Her husband wasn't too happy, let alone his brother.'

Rhys and Nattie exchange a sideways glance.

'What?' I ask.

It's Nattie who answers: 'It's just… in this village you either like the Pitmans or you don't. It's not your mum; she married into it. No one has a problem with her. It's the brothers.'

I barely have time to think that over before she's moving on.

'What now?' Nattie asks.

'With what?'

'Are you back for good?'

It feels like I should have an answer for that but I don't. 'I'm not sure,' I say. 'It's all a bit odd. Everything's happened really quickly. I didn't have a real mum this morning, now I do.'

Rhys picks up his pint and clinks the glass into mine. 'You should hang around,' he says.

'I thought you said there were loads of better places than this…?'

He leans back and laughs. 'Well, yes… but Nat and I make it better just by being here. Besides, I can't keep carrying her home when she's too pissed to walk. I could do with a hand.'

He gets a playful elbow for that.

'You'll have to come and meet my mum,' Nattie says. 'She still talks about you. She's best friends with your mum, or she was at one point. I'm never quite sure. She's got all sorts of photos and things. She'll lose her shit when I tell her you're back.'

Nattie's mother is apparently in every morning, so I get the address and say I'll head over tomorrow before noon. The three of us swap numbers and it suddenly feels as if this place could become home after all. It's not just weird sets of brothers, creepy barmen and shops that close on Thursdays; I could make friends here.

'You free tomorrow afternoon?' Nattie asks.

'I guess so. It's not like I've got a full diary of things to do.'

'Good – there's something you should probably see.'

EIGHT

The post office might be closed on Thursdays but it was open today and they sell village maps. I'm not particularly sure why as I can't believe this is a haven for holidaymakers but I'm not complaining.

It's dark and the pub is quiet as I lay the map out across the bed and mark the places I know. There's the Black Horse, of course, then the coffee shop, Via's, on the High Street. Figuring out the location of Mum's house is a little more difficult, largely because I didn't drive there or back. There are half a dozen roads out of the centre, two of which are easy to ignore because they're too big. Of the other four, two head south and so it's not long before I'm able to trace the route I think Mum took. At first I think the house must be a little off the map, then I realise it's in the top corner, a few miles from the village itself.

I find the old house, too, and write the name 'Janet' underneath. I have Nattie's address, so find that and write her name on the page. It feels useful to have the information in front of me and though I'd been online to look at everything before, it's more real now I'm here. The church isn't simply a word next to a patch of green, it's an actual place.

When I'm confident I know enough of the village layout to get around for now, I skim through the bookmarks on my phone, reading the Olivia Adams articles for what feels like the hundredth time. Perhaps it is. Perhaps it's more. I know some of the lines word for word. If it happened now, there'd be so much more content online. Newspapers didn't have such a large Internet presence thirteen years ago but there are still a handful of pieces.

What *is* clear is how quickly people forget. Not those who live in Stoneridge, everyone else. For Nattie and Rhys, the missing girl is part of their upbringing, but for the rest of the country, it was a big deal for a month and then it was gone.

There's one line in the reports that jumps out. It's never meant anything before but there's context now:

> *Ashley Pitman, who owns Pitmans Garage in the village, has been helping out with the search since the beginning and remains hopeful. 'We'll find her,' he said. 'We'll keep searching for as long as it takes. Someone, somewhere must know something.'*

That was a load of nonsense. 'As long as it takes'? They must have given up at some point and he didn't seem too pleased earlier at the prospect of a thirteen-year hunt finally being over.

I search for Pitmans Garage but nothing comes up online. It's not necessarily the type of place that would have a website and neither Max nor Ashley seem techie types, but I'm sure there'd be a listing for it somewhere, if only a phone number. Mum said something about a taxi business – and that does get a hit when I search for it. There's a Pitmans Taxis listed in Stoneridge and I mark that on my map. It's not far from the back of the Black Horse, perhaps a couple of minutes' walk away.

I cross the room to my window, which looks diagonally over a courtyard towards the back and side of the pub. It's hard to see much of anything when I wipe away the condensation to stare out into the darkness.

After meeting Rhys and especially Nattie, it's impossible not to imagine how things might have been if I'd actually grown up here. I liked Nattie when I thought she was a sarcastic slightly two-faced waitress but after spending an evening drinking together, I like her even more. Self-awareness is appealing in people. That sense of being a very small part of this massive world and not worrying about it. Of not taking yourself too seriously.

Perhaps I *would* have been happy here?

I'm distracted by something on the other side of the door. The bar is on the ground floor, I'm on the middle, then Pete lives upstairs. The only other room on this floor is the bathroom. It's not en suite as such but I don't have to share. The toilet is in a small room connected to the bedroom.

I creep back to the bed and listen, wondering if the floorboards actually did squeak. It could be Pete on his way up or downstairs, and yet…

The noise sounds again. A definite creak, as if someone's standing directly outside my door. Perhaps the person is listening to me as I'm listening to them?

Another scrape, louder and longer this time.

I tiptoe to the door and press my ear to the wood. I don't have a lot of experience with hotels but this room was cheap and it feels like it. The door is thin and the whole place is a mass of clanking pipes and screeching walls. It would be a nightmare for anyone who believes in ghosts.

There's a shuffling from the other side of the door. Someone pacing, or…

I swing open the door quickly, expecting there to be someone on the other side but there's not. There is a stack of crisp boxes next to the stair banister and a row of other bar-related merchandise. Packets of nuts stuck to large sheets of cardboard, a box of empty, new glasses, filters for the coffee machine, bottles of cordial.

No point in pretending I didn't have a nosy poke around last night.

The floorboards creak as I step onto the landing and look both ways. The same sound I heard a few seconds ago. I peer over the rail to the floor below – but there's no one there.

'Hello…?'

The paint is peeling from the walls and my voice echoes around the stairwell, unanswered. I tread on the squeaky floorboard again and then return to the bedroom, closing the door, locking it, and listening to the silence. No scrapes now. If there was anyone outside the door, they've gone.

I fold up the map and return it to my bag. The room is small; a bed, dresser and side table is pretty much it. I sit at the dresser and turn on the lamp, staring at myself in the mirror. Today has been a long time coming – and then it was a long day.

'Olivia,' I say, watching how my lips move. It sounds good. It sounds right. I've been living under a different name for a long time but I can get used to Olivia.

'Olivia Adams.'

That sounds good, too. Not Olivia Pitman, that'll never be my name.

'Olivia Elizabeth Adams.'

I like that, too. I wonder where the middle name came from. If it belongs to someone important to my mother, or if it was chosen at random.

'Oh-liv-ee-aah.'

I stretch out the sounds. Six letters, four syllables. That's pretty good. Olivia is *my* name – now I need to get used to other people saying it.

2008: LILY, 11

My dad squeezes my hand and the rough, poky bits of his skin make mine itch. He's not been to work for more than a week and yet there are still dry prickly bits on his palms. There is dirt under his fingernails, too, something for which Mum always used to tell him off. I wonder if that should be my job now.

It's uncomfortable to sit still on the hard wooden benches but Dad fidgets before I do. He lets my hand go for a moment but I'm instantly reaching for him again. Spiky skin or not, I don't want him to let go.

This is my first time inside a church and I really don't think I like it. Everything's so big, the ceiling so high. It's hard to hear people speak because their voice drifts up and away. Dad leans in to whisper something to me but I don't hear him. Then he lets my hand go and, before I can strain for him once more, he's on his feet, heading along the stone floor and up to the stage at the front of the church.

There's a priest or a vicar, I don't know the difference. He's an old man who said hello to me as we came inside but I didn't know what to say then. He looks to me again now and I feel very alone in the front row.

Dad stands behind this large wooden desk thing. He's talking about Mum but I don't really hear what he's saying. It's partly because of the echo but also because he's busy biting his lip and trying not to cry. When he looks at me, his eyes are red and his bottom lip trembles. It makes me want to cry but I don't.

I heard Dad whispering to someone he called a social worker a few days ago. I was in the living room and they were in the kitchen. They thought I couldn't hear but I could. Dad said I hadn't cried and he asked if that was strange. He asked if *I* was strange. The social worker said people deal with loss in very different ways and then Dad started to cry.

He's still crying now, still looking straight at me as he talks about Mum. He says she was a good mother, a loving wife.

This is the first time I've seen him dress in a suit like the men on TV. He spent the morning pulling at it, saying it was too tight and that it didn't fit any longer. I've had to wear the black skirt I usually have for school and a new black jacket he bought me because I didn't have one. Mum didn't like dark colours – which is why it's so strange that everyone in the church is wearing black.

With my skirt, jacket and hair, I'm completely in black. Dad spent ages combing my hair earlier, asking if I wanted it down or in a plait. He's nowhere near as good as Mum at knowing how to tie it together, so I ended up plaiting it myself. While he watched me do that, he took really long, deep breaths to stop himself crying.

He's done a lot of crying recently. I hear him at night when he thinks I'm asleep. One time he came into my room and watched me as I pretended to doze. After a while, he said he was sorry and then he closed the door. I heard him sobbing to himself in his own room a little after.

Dad's still talking, though he's stopped watching me. At home, he's been saying 'the C-word', but he says the *actual* word here.

Cancer.

With Dad, the social worker and the other people who've come round, the C-word is like Voldemort. People don't want to say 'cancer', so they say 'C-word' instead.

What cancer really means is that Mum isn't here any more.

Dad finishes speaking and then the organs sound and everyone stands. It only takes a moment before he's at my side again, rough hands scraping at mine. His are so big, so safe.

I stand at his side as we turn to the back of the church and watch all the other people in black start to walk outside. I think they're leaving for good but that's not what happens. When we get outside into the light, everyone is waiting for us, standing on both sides of the path and creating a tunnel. It feels so heavy as they all watch us move towards the cars.

Dad is walking slowly, thanking people for being there. He's still holding onto me, forcing me to move at the same pace as him. I want to run ahead, to get away from the wall of black. I focus on the path instead of the people because all I can hear is them whispering my name, along with things like 'so sorry' and 'here if you need me'. A lot of people have said the same thing in the past week. The social worker sat down with me and said I could tell him anything I wanted, that I could trust him if there was anything I felt I couldn't talk to my dad about.

I tug on Dad's hand and, when he ignores me, I pull him harder until he's forced to stop and crouch at my side. The sky is so bright and everything – *everyone* – else is so black that it's hurting my eyes.

'Are you okay, sweetie?' he asks.

'I want to go home.'

'We've got to go to the wake first.'

He's speaking quietly, so that nobody else can hear.

'What's that?' I ask.

'It's where people go to tell stories about your mum and remember what she meant to them. There's food—'

'I'm not hungry. Can we go home instead?'

'I'm sorry, sweetie but we have to go. This is what people do. They want to remember your mum. Don't you want to remember her, too…?'

He says that as if I don't. As if I've forgotten her just because of the C-word. I don't reply but I squeeze his hand instead and he lets me go for a moment. He wipes his hand on his trousers and then offers it again. He's smiling down at me but it's sad and, for a moment, I think he's going to cry again. His eyebrow is twitching and he looks so very unhappy.

I take his hand, hoping it will make him feel a bit better. I don't want to go to the stupid wake and I'm not hungry – but if it will stop him crying, then it's probably the best thing to do.

We continue along the path, still walking *really* slowly until we finally get to the road. We didn't bring our car. We came in a really shiny, long black one and Dad didn't drive. Someone I don't know is driving instead. He's old and wears a grey cap that he took off when he said hello to me.

I watch out the back window as a row of other cars follow us until we reach this big hall that I've never been to before. When we go inside, there's a long table at the end that's full of food, just like Dad said. He tells me he needs to speak to some people and then, just for a minute, I'm alone. The hall is cold and the floor creaks when I walk across it. There are TVs on the walls but they're blank except for the small red dot at the front. I wonder if someone's lost the remote control. Dad's done that before.

Dad is waiting by the door as the people from the church enter the hall. He's saying hello to them all again, thanking them for coming, even though he's already done that.

I head to the table of food by myself. There are sausage rolls and sandwiches, plus little sausages on sticks. There's jelly and cake, with a whole tray full of Bourbon biscuits and custard creams. I told Dad I wasn't hungry but now I am. There is a stack of paper plates and I take one of everything, piling it high. I look around for somewhere to sit but people are already walking towards me, giving that stupid weird smile that adults do. They're not really smiling, they're not happy. It's this fake lie they tell with their faces when they want to ask me if I'm all right. They do it all the time now.

Along one of the walls is a row of tables, the tablecloths hanging low to the floor. I move quickly towards them before too many people can see me and then I get underneath, using the cloth to hide away from everyone else.

I sit still for a moment, wondering if any of the adults are going to follow and ask me what I'm doing. It *feels* like I'm doing something I shouldn't. When nobody comes, I start to eat, cake first; then the biscuits. Mum always said savoury first but I've been able to get away with a lot more this last week.

I'd still rather she was here to stop me.

It's as I start on a sausage roll that there's a flutter of tablecloth. Dad is crouched low, squinting and smiling that sad smile for me. 'There you are,' he says.

I think he's going to tell me to come out, either that or tell me off for eating sweets first – but he doesn't. Instead, he slides along the floor until he's sitting next to me. His head bonks on the table above, which makes me laugh.

'You're too big to be under here, Daddy,' I say.

He stoops his neck so that he can just about fit and then places his warm hand on mine. 'I love you, Lily,' he says.

'I love you, too, Daddy.'

2009: LILY, 12

As soon as I get through the front door, I know Dad is at home. He doesn't say anything and there's no other sound – but there's something in the air. It's hard to describe. Or perhaps it's because he's *always* at home when I get in from school. He says he's going to work each morning and then he doesn't.

I drop my bag in the hall and head into the kitchen. I'm probably going to have to cook tea for us both again tonight, so I open the fridge. Except… there's hardly anything inside. A half-finished bottle of Coke, a bottle of milk that has only a few drops in the bottom, some soggy lettuce leaves in the salad drawer that have started to go brown, four or five slices of bread wrapped in a plastic bag and a row of beers on the top shelf.

'There are crisps in the cupboard.'

Dad makes me jump as he appears on the other side of the fridge door. His eyes seem heavy, as if he's not had much sleep.

'How was work?' I ask.

He frowns slightly but he never gets angrier than this any more. Sometimes I wonder what I could say or do to actually make him mad.

'Tomorrow,' he replies, before opening the cupboard and taking out a multipack of crisps. Twenty bags, apparently – smoky bacon, salt 'n' vinegar, ready salted and cheese and onion.

'You can't have crisps for tea,' I say.

He looks at the multipack and then returns it to where it came from before opening a few more cupboards. There's a jar of mustard that has been in there for as long as I can remember; some herbs and spices, a tube of tomato puree, a tin of chicken soup and a couple of cans of tuna.

'Tuna on toast?' he suggests.

'Is there anything else?'

He pulls open the drawers of the freezer and hunts through the thick crusts of ice until he pulls out a packet of frosty-looking sausages.

'Sausage on toast?'

That's definitely better.

'Okay… are there any beans?'

A shake of the head. 'I'll go shopping tomorrow,' he replies.

I don't point out that he's supposed to be going to work tomorrow, nor that he promised to go shopping a couple of days ago.

Dad digs a frying pan out from one of the lower cupboards and sets it on the stove as if he's about to cook but he's glancing to me the whole time. We've been here before.

I say I'll do it and he doesn't object, shuffling to the back of the kitchen and yawning loudly as I crack apart the frozen sausages with the biggest knife in the kitchen. It takes a couple of goes before they snap away from each other, sending a couple crashing into the wall and the rest spiralling onto the floor. I wash them all off in the sink before putting them into the pan and setting the heat on low.

After another yawn, Dad asks if I have any homework to do.

'Not much,' I reply.

'Can you be a good girl and stay in your room later?'

'What's going on?'

'It's the Champions League final. I've got some of the lads coming over to watch it.'

That explains all the crisps. Dad must've been out to the shops at some point today, which also makes it clear where the beer came from. We've developed our own codes over the last year. It took me a while to realise that being a 'good girl' involves being out of the way and not making any noise. It does work both ways, though. Dad never bothers to read the letters from school, he simply signs them. When I got double detention, he didn't bother asking why, he scrawled his name to say he'd seen the letter. I can keep up my end of the bargain if he can.

'I've got books I can read,' I reply.

'Good… it won't be late.'

The sausages have started to fizz and I give them a poke with a wooden spoon.

'Can you get cereal tomorrow?' I ask. 'Milk, too.'

He nods and then yawns again.

I give the sausages another good poking and then pop a couple of slices of bread in the toaster.

'We need bread as well,' I say.

'Can you make a list?'

I point towards the fridge, where there's already a list stuck to the front with a magnet.

'Oh,' he says, as if it's a new thing. We've been keeping shopping lists on the front of the fridge for as long as I can remember. Mum used to take it down every Thursday and do a 'big shop'. I used to write 'cookies' on the bottom every week and she'd laugh, telling me I was cheeky. She'd buy them anyway but there's no chance of that any longer.

'Do you want any sausages?' I ask.

'No – you eat them. You need it more than me.'

'Have you eaten today?'

'Yeah, I had… er… something earlier.'

I don't turn to look at him because I know he's lying.

'You can watch telly down here for a bit if you want…?'

That does make me turn, if only to see if Dad's making some sort of joke. He never makes this offer, in fact it's rare that he gets up off the sofa. I hardly ever go into the living room any longer. The television is on almost non-stop, either showing sport or the news. I don't think Dad's that bothered about what's going on in the world, but he likes having the voices in the background. He stopped doing any amount of tidying a long time ago and the photos of Mum are too hard to look at for me. Then there are all the empty bottles. I didn't realise for a long time that whisky and bourbon are pretty much the same thing. Dad said I could try it one time but a sip was enough to know I didn't like it. I don't know how he drinks entire bottles. How anyone does.

'I'll do a bit of a tidy,' he says. 'You watch what you want.'

'Thanks.'

He moves into the hall, out of sight, and there's the clinking and clanking of him moving things around. I wonder quite what 'a bit of a tidy' might mean, then I realise that he's carrying a crate of beer up from the cellar. I wonder if it's new, or if it's been down there for a while. He carries that into the living room and then heads back to the basement for another crate.

After that, he takes a black bin bag into the living room and starts to clear some of the old papers and bottles. As he does that, I continue cooking until the sausages are brown and firm. There's no ketchup in the cupboard, so I add that to the list on the fridge along with beans, milk, cereal and bread. When that's done, I move into the lounge.

I know it's not much but it really does feel important to be in charge of the remote control in the living room. There are so many more channels than I have upstairs. I spend ages hunting through everything while eating my tea. Dad continues to carry things in and out and he has finally cleared out all the empty bottles. I wonder if he's managed to put everything in the right recycling bins. He doesn't usually and I end up moving things from one bin to another.

In the end, I've almost finished my tea by the time I settle on a show about elephants. Dad comes into the living room and stands behind the chair, watching what I am doing for a minute or two before heading out of the room without another word. I hear him going up the stairs and then it's quiet.

Five o'clock comes and I wash and dry up my plate and the frying pan. Then it's six o'clock and I've still got the living room to myself.

I wonder if Dad's finally getting some sleep. Sometimes he doesn't come upstairs at night. He'll stay on the sofa and I have no idea if he's sleeping or watching television. Sometimes a day or three can pass and I wonder if he's left the sofa for any reason other than to go to the toilet. I'll never see him eat or sleep, only watch television.

The elephant show has long finished when I finally hear Dad on the stairs again. It's a few minutes to seven and he yawns his way into the living room.

'Can you be a good girl now?' he asks and I hand him the remote. There's a moment where his hand brushes mine and I remember being in the church, wanting to hold his hand. It was only a year ago but it feels like so much longer. It feels like I was a different me then. So much younger. I didn't understand a lot then, but I do now.

'I'll see you tomorrow,' he says – and that's it.

As I sit upstairs in my bedroom reading, I hear the front door going a number of times. There are men's voices and then the low mumble that always comes through the floor when Dad's got the television on too loudly. Sometimes he falls asleep with it like that and I have to creep downstairs to turn down the volume.

It's not long before there's a loud cheer, which means somebody must have scored. I try to ignore it, putting on some headphones and listening to the radio while I continue to read.

That's probably why I don't realise my door has opened until I see there's someone standing at the end of the bed. I jump slightly and the man puts a finger to his lips as he closes my door. I take off the headphones and shuffle up onto my pillows.

'Hi,' he says.

The man is taller than my dad. He's big but it's not fat, he's more like a rugby player with big shoulders and thick legs. As my eyes adjust to the light, I can see he's wearing a red football shirt and there are tattoos on both of his arms.

'Do you remember me?' he asks.

'No.'

'I'm your Uncle Alan. I remember you when you were a baby.' He smiles, showing off his bright white teeth.

'Are you looking for the bathroom?' I ask.

'Not really… maybe. I thought I'd come and say hello.'

'Hello…?'

He sits on the edge of my bed and it sinks low from his weight. 'How old are you now?' he asks.

'Twelve.'

'That's a nice age. You're a very pretty girl. Does your dad tell you that?'

He shuffles forward and, though I want to move away, there's nowhere for me to go. There's something in the way he's looking at me that I've never seen before. Like I'm a Christmas present being unwrapped. I'm full of mystery and nervous excitement to him.

'Where's my dad?' I ask.

Uncle Alan turns towards the closed door and then looks back to me, smiling thinly. It shouldn't be frightening but it is. 'He's downstairs. We're okay here, aren't we?'

There's a part of me that knows this is wrong. I should bang on the floor and make a noise – but I can't. It feels like I can't move – and it's all about the way he's looking at me. He's frozen me, somehow. It's not only that I can't move, I can't think either. I'm trapped.

'I don't think you're supposed to be in here.'

The words are so hard to get out. Such an effort to think of. It doesn't faze him anyway. He smiles again but says nothing as he stretches a hand towards me.

NINE

WEDNESDAY

It's the sun that wakes me the next morning. The small room in the Black Horse is so bright that I'm surprised I managed to sleep for so long. The curtains are a waste of time and I've never particularly understood why blinds and curtains exist if daylight beams through so easily. Like a bag with a hole at the bottom. It's failed at the one and only thing it's supposed to do.

I reach for my phone instinctively to see that it's a few minutes before eight. There are already a couple of texts waiting from my mother that arrived almost an hour ago. Seeing the word 'Mum' on the lock screen gives me butterflies. It's so simple – three letters – and yet it's a long time since any name has had that effect on me.

In the first message she asks if I have any plans for today. The second came three minutes later and she says she will be at the house all day if I want to come by. 'Would be nice to see you again,' she adds, everything spelled out correctly.

I tap out a text, saying that I'll come over for breakfast in an hour or so, assuming that's fine with her. The message has barely left my screen before I get a reply: 'Great!'.

That's my cue to haul myself out of bed, yawning and stretching my way over to my bag. It's all I came with, packed with a few changes of clothes and shoes. I could probably unpack into the dresser but that would make everything feel a little more permanent, that I'm definitely settling here. I'm not sure I'm ready for that yet.

After fighting away another yawn, I head across to the window and drag the useless curtains open. I can see the yard clearly now and the stacks of metal beer kegs ready for pick-up. There's an alley that runs along the back, which intersects with the High Street. I'm about to start finding clothes to wear when I notice the green car sitting on the far side of the road. It's only just in my line of vision – but it's more the person sitting in the driver's seat that surprises me. A messy mop of dark hair is resting on the window and, although I'm pretty sure it's one of them, I'm not certain whether it's Max or Ashley. Whoever it is shuffles around in the driver's seat and then turns to face the front of the pub before leaning back on the window.

I take a shower and then find some clean clothes but, for as long as that takes, the green car is still waiting on the road when I check the window again.

Peter is already in the bar area when I get downstairs. He's wiping the tables down but I doubt it's going to have much effect on the stickiness. He asks what I'd like for breakfast but I say I'm going to head out, not mentioning my mother. He never asked for my last name when I checked in and was happy to take cash. I get the sense it's the sort of place for which cash is an essential part of keeping the business afloat.

We make small talk about whether I had a good night's sleep but I know it's not worth saying anything other than it was all fine.

He lets me out the front doors and I blink my way out into the bright sunny morning. The sky is blue, the grass and verges a perky, bristling green. What's also green is the car still parked diagonally across the road. The nest of dark hair shifts and turns until I can clearly see Ashley's face. There's a moment where we stare at each other before he looks away and starts the engine. With a chunter and a blasting cloud from the exhaust, he accelerates along the High Street, disappearing around a corner and out of sight.

I wonder why he was here. It's not like he was actually spying because he couldn't see anything. And he clearly didn't want to talk, else he wouldn't have sped away.

I'm on the other side of the road on the way to get my Fiat from the car park by the post office when I realise he was only there to let me know he's watching. He knows where I'm staying and wants me to know that. It was probably a mistake to stand up to him in Mum's conservatory and yet it's hard to regret it.

It's easier to remember the route to Mum's house than I thought. On the map it looks like there are more roads than there actually are. Many of those that are marked are actually smaller, unmarked tracks and it doesn't take that long before I'm pulling onto the gravelly driveway. Mum's 4x4 is there but that's the only other vehicle. Max must be out.

Mum opens the front door before I can get anywhere near it. Harry is at her feet, resting on her legs and staring out towards me. She smiles and tells him to wave at his sister. He does, before turning back to Mum for approval.

'I've been trying to teach him to say your name,' Mum says when I get inside.

There's an awkward moment where neither of us are quite sure what to do but we end up hugging briefly, more touching shoulders than anything else.

Mum reaches down and takes Harry's hand. 'Who's this?' she asks him enthusiastically.

'Egg,' he replies.

I laugh and so does Mum. 'I swear I've not taught him that,' she says.

'Egg,' Harry repeats.

I find out why when we get into the kitchen.

'Wow,' I say, trying to take everything in.

'I didn't know what you liked to eat,' Mum replies.

That's clear, considering she has laid out more food than I've seen in one kitchen before. There are apples, bananas and oranges in a bowl; three different types of jam; a thick, crusty loaf with a bread knife at the side, plus margarine, Marmite and peanut butter. Bacon and sausages are in the frying pan and there is a box of eggs on the side. If that wasn't enough, there are boxes of Corn Flakes, Rice Krispies and Coco Pops – Harry's favourite, she says; plus sugar, a jug of milk and a bottle of syrup.

'I can make pancakes if you want,' Mum says.

'Egg,' Harry says.

'Cereal is enough for me.'

'There's porridge as well, if you prefer.'

'I'll eat Harry's Coco Pops if he doesn't mind too much.'

I reach to pour myself a bowl but Mum gets there before me, shuffling piles of them into a dish, all the while asking if I want more. When that's done, she's asking if I want tea, coffee, juice, water, or something else. Then it's what type of coffee. She has three different blends, an espresso or instant. She asks if I had a good night's sleep, if the bed's comfortable, then about the pillows. Were they firm enough? I get the sense that if I were to say anything was remotely unbefitting, she'd be driving me off to the shop to get something more suitable.

I can't remember the last time anyone fussed over me like this. I'm not sure anyone ever has.

Despite our text messages, the anticipation of being here isn't matched by *actually* being here. We're both floundering. I don't quite know what to say and I think it's the same for her. She's making up for it with food.

Harry doesn't want an egg after all, not after seeing my Coco Pops. Mum pours him a much smaller bowl and it's not long before he's splashing it all over himself, the table, the floor. Everywhere. As Mum tries to help him eat, she continues to watch me.

'I don't know what to talk about,' she says.

'Me neither.'

'It's all really quick.' She clicks her fingers. 'Like that. Don't get me wrong, it's not a bad thing. I've wanted you back since the day you went away but it's been so long…'

She tails off, staring towards the wall, lost for a moment.

It's me who makes the move this time, touching her wrist gently with my fingers and then smiling when she turns back.

'It's the same for me,' I say. 'I've not had a *real* mum in a long time.'

She breathes in through her nose, returning my smile with a gentle one of her own. 'Thank you for coming over,' she says.

'There's nowhere else I'd rather be.'

'I dug some things out for you last night.'

'Like what?'

'Bits and pieces that used to be yours. Some of it was lost when we moved but I kept a lot in boxes. It's been in the attic all this time but I went up there last night and brought everything down.'

It takes me a few minutes more to finish eating and then a little while after that until Harry decides he doesn't want to eat any more. He keeps saying 'egg' and I wonder if that's what he's decided my name is. Could be worse, I suppose.

It's only when we get upstairs that I realise she perhaps had slightly ulterior motives. Mum leads me into what turns out to be the spare bedroom. There's a large double bed that's been made very recently, all neat corners and ironed-out creases. It's far nicer than the room at the Black Horse; the carpet softer, blinds *and* curtains, soft colours. All very welcoming.

There are three boxes against the wall, a thin layer of dust crusted to the top of the cardboard. Mum waits for me to enter and then stands behind me in the doorway as if to say, this could be yours.

'Are the boxes for me?' I ask.

'Of course. Everything in there is yours. If you want anything, feel free to take it.'

She takes a seat on the corner of the bed as I sit on the floor next to the boxes. Harry is busy bumbling around the room, tugging at various things and being tutted at.

The first thing I find in the boxes is a pink T-shirt with *My Little Pony* on the front. It seems impossibly small, the type of thing it's hard to believe anyone could have ever fitted in.

'Do you remember that?' Mum asks. I hold it up, comparing it to the size of what I'm currently wearing. 'You used to love that,' she adds. 'I had to smuggle it out of your room to be washed.'

I snigger but have to shake my head. 'I don't remember.'

She seems disappointed and doesn't ask again as I continue to pull bits and pieces from the box. There's some sort of fancy dress fairy costume, two pairs of dungarees, three pairs of shoes that are smaller than my hands.

The second box is far more interesting than the first. There's a cardboard-backed envelope on top and inside is a birth certificate.

'I thought you'd like that,' Mum says.

The paper is a little crinkled and the writing is slightly shaky and smudged – but it's all there. Olivia Adams, the date of birth and the place.

'You wouldn't have known you were born in the old house,' she adds.

I reread the details and then look up to her. 'Stoneridge really is home…?'

'Born and raised here,' she replies. 'I didn't know if you'd need that for things like a passport. It's yours if you want it.'

I thank her and say I'll take it but she doesn't ask a follow-up about how I got a driving licence, or what name it's under.

The next thing out is a suede jewellery box. The charm bracelet inside has been polished recently and gleams bright. The links are silver and it's like something out of a Monopoly box. There's a small dog, a four-leaf clover, some sort of bird, a heart, a butterfly and a starfish.

'We got you a new charm for each birthday,' Mum says.

I hold up the bird pendant and ask what it is. She squints and smiles.

'It's a chicken,' she says. 'We took you to a farm this one time and you really liked the chickens. That was the day you realised chicken the food was also chicken the bird. You refused to eat poultry after that and cried if your father or I ever suggested it.'

I know she wants me to say I remember but I can't do that.

There's a similar-sized box towards the bottom but there's no jewellery in this: there are teeth. Small, white baby teeth. I hold one up to the light, running my thumb across the sharper edges.

'You got 50p from the tooth fairy for that,' Mum says.

'Is that all?'

She laughs. 'It was thirteen or fourteen years ago. With inflation, that's like two pounds.'

Next is an impossibly small plastic bracelet that holds a slip of paper with Olivia Adams written in faded blue biro. Mum says they put it around my wrist when I was born. It's only a little wider than my thumb.

The final box is really heavy – and not what I expected at all. It's not clothes or jewellery, it is packed with newspapers and clippings. It's only when I'm a few lines into the story on the first paper when I realise it's the one I've been reading over and over. The article I read last night, in which Ashley Pitman says people will search for as long as it takes.

'I kept everything,' Mum says. 'The local papers, the nationals. I used to record the news off the TV but those were all on VHS tapes and I ended up throwing them out. We got rid of the video player years ago. I don't think you can even buy them nowadays.'

She gives that *not like the old days* sigh that people do when they get to a certain age. You talk about streaming movies and get a blank look, or disbelief that being a 'YouTuber' is an actual job. It'll come to us all, I suppose. I'll be romanticising having a phone in my pocket in the days when kids have things beamed directly onto their eyeballs.

The second paper on the pile is a title that doesn't even exist nowadays. It's from the same day as the first document, repeating most of the same details but there's far too much to simply skim. I flick through the rest of the box – and it all seems to be in chronological order, with the oldest articles on the top.

'Can I take this?' I ask.

Mum's biting her lip. She had said I could take what I wanted but now she seems reluctant. It might be because this is something she has kept for so long, or maybe she's suspicious because Max put the idea in her head that I could be mining information.

'There's a lot to take in.'

'I'll return everything – or take one or two things at a time if you prefer. It's interesting to me.'

Mum nods slowly but this is the first time I think I've seen a glimmer of doubt from her. Perhaps I shouldn't have asked. Max sowed the seeds and I'm reaping them.

'Max didn't seem too happy yesterday…'

I leave it there. An absent-minded observation, nothing too accusatory. The truth.

'It's a big change for everyone,' she replies.

'For me too.'

'Of course you as well. You more than anyone. I'm not saying it's easy for anyone – but it takes time to get used to.' She sounds a little flustered and I can imagine she was up half the night arguing about me.

'Where is he?'

'He and his brother run a taxi company in the village. Sometimes they're in dispatch but they drive three or four days a week, so he's doing that. I think he's off at the airport.'

I think about telling her of Ashley sitting outside the Black Horse, waiting for me – except it could be innocent. Perhaps he was waiting on a customer, or killing time before he had to pick someone up. There could be an innocent explanation, so no point in causing trouble unnecessarily. I get the sense Ashley would rationalise it all away in any case.

'They're trying to set up a limo company,' she adds. 'Hen dos, nights out, that sort of thing.' Mum waves a hand dismissively as if to say it's not her thing.

'It looked like they're close as brothers…'

Mum nods. 'You always get two for the price of one with them. I knew that before I got married.'

Re-married, I think but don't say.

Mum turns to Harry, who's playing snow angels on the carpet without the snow.

'I think I want to see Dad,' I say.

It takes her a few moments to turn back to me. When she does, she's biting her lip again. We lock eyes and she takes a breath. 'I'm not saying you shouldn't. You're an adult and he's your father… it's just…' She gulps, searching for the words and then she looks away. 'He's not the man he once was.'

TEN

Nattie's mother swings open the front door before I get a chance to knock a second time. She's the spitting image of what her daughter would be if it wasn't for a bit of work in front of the mirror each morning. Nattie's hair is straight and down; her mother's is a wild puff with tight curls. Wider than it is taller. They share the same scattering of freckles and that permanent upturn of the lips as if they're a step ahead of everyone else.

She throws her arms wide. 'Olivia Adams, as I live and breathe.'

Before I know it – and certainly before I can make any sort of objection – she's grabbed me into a bear hug, shoving my face into her chest and clamping her arms around my back. She releases me almost as quickly as she grabbed me and then takes a step back to look me up and down.

'I can't believe it. When Natalie got in last night saying who she'd met down the pub, I thought she'd had a few too many. You know what it's like. I called your mum and she said it was all true. I wouldn't have believed it if you weren't here in front of me.'

She steps back into the house, holding the door open.

'Come on in then,' she adds. 'Have you eaten? Do you want tea? Coffee? Something stronger?'

She brays with laughter as I edge past, directly into a living room. It's a bit dated – a felt-covered sofa, a carpet square tapestry with a cabinet full of crystal glassware off to the side – but it's homely, too. The walls are covered with photos of various people with ginger hair. Many of them are Nattie.

'You don't remember me, do you?'

Nattie's mum has closed the door and is bounding across the floor, beckoning me into what turns out to be the kitchen. It's all light chocolate brown and plasticky.

'I, um…'

'I'm Georgina, love. Call me Georgie if you want – everyone else does.' She pats a high stool in front of a breakfast bar and I find myself sitting. 'So, welcome home! I doubt Stoneridge has changed that much. This place has only just reached the twentieth century, let alone the twenty-first.'

She laughs again and it's hard not to join in, as if her personality is some sort of infectious disease. She doesn't ask where I've been or about anything that's happened – and I can't believe it's because she isn't curious. Nattie must have told her, which saves me a job. It's not the welcome I anticipated. I expected The Questions.

Where have you been?

Why are you back?

What now?

Everyone has the same things to ask and it's not as if I blame them. I'd be the same. Anyone would be.

'Natalie said you had a right ol' chinwag last night,' Georgie says.

'We got reacquainted.'

'Good for you, darling. She's a good girl, my Nat. You two used to be thick as thieves.' She points to the cupboards. 'So, what can I do you for? Tea? Coffee? Biscuits? I've got some Mr Kipling French Fancies in if you want…?'

'I ate at Mum's a couple of hours back.'

'Oh, that's lovely to hear, darling. She'll be made up that you're back after all this time.'

She speaks as if a child was lost in the aisles of a supermarket and, in many ways, this breeziness is stranger than getting The Questions.

'I was hoping you could tell me a bit about her,' I say. 'I don't remember much about my parents…'

That's all it takes. Georgie leans in conspiratorially and it's clear gossip is what keeps her going. She'll be dining out on this for months. 'What would you like to know? We grew up together, y'know. Same school, same village, all that.'

'I know she and my dad got divorced but I don't know much about Max.'

Georgie takes a moment to fill the kettle and set it boiling. She leans against the kitchen counter and starts to fiddle with the wire of her bra. 'Bloody things,' she mutters, before looking up. 'I've known your mother since school – but we've both known Max since school as well. We were all in the same class at Stoneridge Primary, all the way through to our exams. Your mum started going out with him long before she ever got together with your dad.'

'Was that when you were still at school?'

A nod and then Georgie starts to count on her fingers in the exact way her daughter did last night. 'You're talking twenty years ago and more. We were younger than you. Fifteen, sixteen, seventeen – that sort of age. I guess we were probably sixteen when your mum was seeing Max and I was going out with his older brother.'

'Ashley?'

Her brow ripples but only for a moment. 'So you've met the other Pitman brother, then? No surprise – it's like they're conjoined half the time. Anyway, we used to go around as a foursome. Ashley was older than the three of us. He would've been eighteen or nineteen. The village was smaller then. Everyone knew everyone else. It was a bloody nightmare trying to get up to no good.'

She winks and then the kettle plips off, so she sorts herself a cup of tea.

'Things moved on after school,' she says. 'Your mum started seeing Dan, who was a bit older than us. He was very different to Max. It was a first-love thing for your mum with Max, where you see someone every day and it becomes this sort of natural infatuation. Your mum went loopy when she first met your dad. That was proper love at first sight. They adored each other. She was pregnant almost straight away with you and then they got married a few years later.'

'What happened to Max?'

A shrug. 'No idea, not really. I'd stopped seeing Ashley and met Natalie's dad. I assume the brothers went off and did their own thing. I'd see 'em around the village now and again but that was all.'

She hugs the mug of tea into her palms and stares off into the distance as if remembering fonder times.

'You got a fella?' she asks.

Her question takes me by surprise. 'Sorry?'

'You seeing anyone? Boyfriend, or whatever? You never know nowadays. I asked Nattie that once and she said I was being homophobic.'

It's hard not to smile: 'No.'

She shrugs. 'Not worth it half the time. Still, you're young…'

Georgie doesn't expand on that thought, instead she hunts through the cupboards until she emerges with a giant tin of biscuits. She clicks off the lid and picks out a chocolate digestive. She dunks it into her mug and then sucks on the soggy half. It's somehow equal parts appealing and disgusting.

'I was at both weddings,' she says after swallowing. 'The only one at both… well, aside from your mother, of course. Ten years apart, almost to the day.'

'What were they like?'

'Chalk and cheese, hon. The first one to your father was something special. A proper church affair.'

'In Stoneridge?'

Georgie nods into the living room and I follow. By the time I get there, she's on her knees at the back of the room hunting through a wooden cabinet. There are puffs of dust as she heaves out some frames and then a padded photo album. More dust and then there's a metal filing box, then one more frame. She blows even more dust from it and wipes the glass with her sleeve before holding up the photo.

'Here you are, love.'

I think she's talking about the picture – but her finger is pointing at a blonde girl in a white bridesmaid's dress.

'You were about three,' Georgie says. 'No way you'd remember it but you, me and Natalie were the three bridesmaids. Course, that meant I was a glorified babysitter all day. You two wanted to run off and all sorts. Right little tearaways.'

She laughs to herself as I take the picture and wipe away a few more flecks of dust. Mum looks so different in her wedding dress. Slimmer and taller – though it's probably her heels. She wears her worry now, but in the photo she's so happy.

'How long ago was this?' I ask.

Georgie counts on her fingers again. 'Sixteen years. Your mum would've been twenty-one.'

That's only a little older than me. It seems like such a huge decision for someone that age… but then she gave birth when she was still a teen, so everything came early to her. By the time she was thirty, she'd lived more than some people ever do.

The three bridesmaids are off to the side, all in matching dresses. Georgie's hair is so bright, so big, that it's hard to focus on anyone other than her. Nattie's not looking at the photographer; she's turned to peer up at the married couple.

'Don't laugh at my hair,' Georgie says. 'Christ knows what I was thinking. I'd had this perm and then the sun got to it and it went massive.'

I don't recognise the best man, which isn't a surprise – but he's in a matching suit to my father. Dad is smiling broader than anyone; trim and smart in traditional black with a shaved head.

'The second wedding was much smaller,' Georgie adds. 'That was a register office affair. There were only five of us there: your mum, me, Max, Ashley and the registrar.'

'Mum was thirty-one for the second wedding?'

Georgie's eyes roll upwards and then she starts to nod. 'Right.'

'When did my mum and dad break up?'

She leads me over to the felt sofa, which is far comfier than it looks. 'Pretty much straight after you, er…' She pauses and glances off to the corner of the room. 'After you, um… disappeared.'

'Three years after they got married?'

'More or less.'

'When did she and Max get together?'

Georgie shuffles in her seat and then tugs on her bra again. For the first time, she seems uncomfortable. 'Not long after, I guess…'

She doesn't make eye contact but that's enough for me to know what she feels. There is every chance my mum was seeing Max before the divorce was official.

My brain aches a little but, from what I can figure out, Mum gave birth at eighteen, got married at twenty-one, then divorced at twenty-four. She started seeing Max at around that time and then got married for a second time seven years later. That means she's been with Max for twelve or thirteen years. She also went out with him as a teenager.

'You can have that if you want,' Georgie says, indicating the photo. 'Not doing any good here getting dusty at the bottom of a cupboard.'

'Thank you.'

'I'll have a bit of a dig around and see if I've got anything else you might like. I don't chuck much out, so there's probably all sorts hidden away. Probably got some school photos of you and Natalie together.'

'That'd be nice.'

'Have you seen your dad yet?'

I look away from the photo, surprised Georgie's brought him up. 'No.'

'It's so sad...'

'What happened?'

'After everything with your mum, he went to pieces. I was friends with your mum but I knew him as well. I was caught in the middle. I think he wanted someone to talk to but it turned out most of their friends were *her* friends. He didn't have anyone.' She glances away to the window and then back to me. 'I'm not sure I should say any more.'

That means, of course, that she's dying to say more. I like her, I really do, but I know I'm going to have to be careful with what I say around her. Say something too juicy and it'll be all round the village before I've got out the front door.

'I'd like to know,' I say.

She clenches her teeth, winces. 'He tried to kill himself,' she says. 'He took the break-up really badly and swallowed a bunch of pills. It didn't work, obviously.'

Georgie might be the village gossip – but she's deadly serious about this. This must've been what Mum meant when she said he wasn't the man he used to be.

'Does he still live in village?'

She nods – and so I ask for the address.

ELEVEN

Stoneridge has been postcard-perfect so far. Trimmed lawns, pretty flower baskets, clean streets and a general air of tidiness.

My dad lives in the *other* part of the village. I walk rather than drive, going the other way along the High Street, crossing the bridge over the river and then heading up a hill towards a community housing block.

It must be deliberate that the entire estate is hidden at the back of an outcrop of trees. From the High Street, it looks like a pretty green copse on top of a hill; it's only when I get closer that I realise there is a sprawling mass of red-brick two-storey flats behind. They're like Lego – square and blocky. An abandoned rusty child's tricycle has been dumped in the gutter and there is a long stream of oil stretching from a back yard to the nearest drain. I can imagine some parish-council-types properly losing it over this type of thing. All house-prices this and blight-on-the-community that.

Someone's arseing about with an engine on the other side of an equally ugly red-brick wall, revving and revving until anyone in a half-mile radius wants the perpetrator strung up. The only thing it's really achieving is to drown out the sound of somebody else's dreadful music.

I follow the road through the estate, paying attention to the graffitied signs as I try to figure out where all the paths lead. I find myself in dead ends a couple of times before eventually ending up in front of a two-storey block that's seemingly identical to the rest. It's only the name on the front that gives it away.

Dad apparently lives in a ground-floor flat on a cul-de-sac at the outermost edge of the estate. Any further and he'd be living in the woods. There's a tiny front garden, a square 'why bother?' sort of job. If I were to lie flat on the grass and stretch my arms and legs, I'd take up the entire space. The outside of the flat has a thin crust of weathered grime; not out-and-out filthy but hardly clean either.

I knock on the front door and wait, running through scenarios of what I might say. Mum said 'Olivia' first so that I didn't have to but, from what she and Georgie said, my dad will be another matter entirely.

Nobody answers so I try knocking again. It's a thick double-glazed door and there's no doorbell, so I can't figure out if anyone inside would be able to hear me. The curtains are pulled across the window and I can't see anything through the letter box other than thick bristles.

I try knocking again, palm against the glass this time and then clank the letter box a couple of times for good measure.

Still no answer.

I'm ready to walk away when I figure I may as well try the handle. It needs a good yank but the metal clanks downwards and then the door swings open. As I step inside, I notice a key in the lock that's obviously not been turned.

'Hello?'

The hallway is dark and smells of soggy old socks. It's only because of the light through the front door that I can see there are stairs to my left and two doors on the right.

'Hello? Anyone home?'

Still no answer – and not even the hint of movement anywhere. The thought crosses my mind that I've got the wrong address, or Georgie had it wrong. I've stumbled into a complete stranger's house and this is breaking and entering. I should probably leave, except… something doesn't feel quite right.

The first door opens into a living room, although it's bare to say the least. There's an armchair, a television, a lamp and that's it – except for the man who's sleeping in the chair. His chest rises and then falls as he honks out a large snore like an irate goose. He's wearing a flat cap that's fallen across his eyes and it's hard to make out any more features.

I can smell the alcohol without moving any further into the room. As I start to get used to the light, I can see the empty bottles as well. There are at least three at the side of the chair; vodka or whisky. Perhaps both. There are pizza boxes, too, stacked waist high in the corner.

It's as I take another step into the room that the man splutters, the cap slipping from his head as his eyes blaze open. It's enough to make me jump as well. The only light is coming from the lamp but the dimness doesn't stop him seeing me as he leaps out of the chair to his feet.

'Whuh… uh… what are you doing here? Get out!'

He races across the room and is almost upon me as I throw up my arms to protect myself. In doing that, I lose my balance, falling backwards and landing with a whump on the uncarpeted floor.

'It's me!' I shout. 'It's Olivia.'

The man stops like a statue, arms half up, body arched forward. He has a hipster-like bushy beard, more out of laziness than fashion. The top of his head is bald. He stands up straighter and backs away as he stares down at me.

'No…'

I'm left flailing in the ground, slightly disorientated as I realise there's a pain at the back of my head from where I must have hit it on the way down.

Then he bursts into tears.

He stumbles backwards, covering his face with his hands and flops into the chair as I manage to get to my feet. I cross the room slowly but all he can do is fold in on himself, head to his knees as he continues to sob.

'Dad…?'

I crouch in front of him, one hand on his knee as he slowly raises himself, peering through the gaps in his fingers.

'Olive…?'

I smile weakly as he reaches out and tugs on my hair in the way Mum did. He brushes my cheek with the back of his hand and, much as I try to ignore it, it's impossible to miss the smell. He can't have had a shower in days, perhaps weeks. There are crumbs in his beard and grease stains on his tatty shirt.

'Do you want a drink, Dad? I'll get you some water or something…?'

He nods and I push myself up, heading through the door at the back of the room into the kitchen.

It's a mess.

The sink is filled with grimy, stained dishes; half the cupboard doors are open, showing that they're empty – and then I notice the small pellets of mouse or rat droppings at the back door.

I don't know where to start.

The fridge is empty except for some green and brown gunk at the back and even if I wanted to get him something other than water, it'd be a struggle because there isn't anything. I dig around the sink and find the cleanest glass – which isn't very clean. Something brown and furry is growing at the bottom, so I return it to where I found it.

I check all the lower cupboards and find the bin underneath the sink. I expect a horror show but it's not… or at least it isn't in the way I expected. It's full of empty glass bottles. There's knock-off Smirnoff and Jack Daniel's to choose from, so I take one of the clear vodka bottles, rinse it out three times – and then fill it a third of the way up with water.

That's as good as it's going to get, so I head back into the living room and hand Dad the bottle, telling him it's water. He mumbles a 'thank you' and then I open the curtains at the front and back, finally allowing some light into the room.

In many ways, I wish I hadn't.

There are more droppings around the edges of the room, plus nibbly teeth marks on the pizza boxes at the bottom of the stack.

Dad's clothes are hanging off him, masking what must be a stick-thin body underneath. He gulps from the water, blinking and swilling it around his mouth. There's nowhere to sit and I'm not risking the floor, considering the droppings, so I end up standing in the middle of the room, trying not to touch anything.

He stares up at me, eyes wide. 'I thought you were…'

'That's what everyone says.'

He blinks and then glances away. 'I'm sorry.'

'It's not your fault, Dad.'

His bottom lip is starting to bob again and he clamps down on it with his teeth. 'Are you okay?' he asks.

'Yes.'

'Healthy?'

'Yes.'

'Happy?'

'I'm happier now.'

He nods, bows his head so that he's staring at my feet. This is a different reaction again. Mum, Max, Ashley, Nattie, Georgie have all contrasted with varying degrees of acceptance, scepticism and wonder. This is a mix of grief and relief. I'm not sure how to deal with it.

'Have you had a good life?'

His voice is a croaky whisper, barely there. It's a strange question. Nobody's asked that before – people have asked where I've been, what's happened – but no one wondered if it had been good for me.

'It's getting better,' I reply.

Dad takes a really deep, husky breath and then glugs more of the water.

'They blamed you, didn't they?' I say.

He bows lower and then starts to nod. He's practically burying his head in his knees again.

This is what Mum and Georgie tried to warn me of. He's divorced, single, unemployed, drunk, living in… *this*. No wonder they wanted me to think twice before coming.

I cross the living room and stand next to the chair, resting a hand on his shoulder. He reaches and holds my hand but his grip is flimsier than a child's.

'Is it true?' I ask. 'Did you try to kill yourself?'

He squeaks a low moan and then starts to rock back and forth. I shouldn't have asked but I do eventually get a raspy reply: 'One more thing I failed at.'

I perch on the edge of the chair and put an arm around him, resting my head on top of his. There isn't the spark that I had when Mum reached out to touch me – but there's less of the awkwardness I have with her. It's comforting, even though we're strangers. We sit like that for minutes, so much so that there's a crick in my neck when Dad finally sits up.

'I'm so sorry,' he says.

'Shush…'

'I thought you'd be safe. Nobody ever used that back lane. We'd left you playing in the garden loads of times. You were happy out there.'

'I know, Dad. I know…'

'I should have stayed out there with you.'

'It's not your fault.'

'They said I was watching the football but it wasn't like that. The game was on but I'd only gone in to go to the toilet. They made it sound like I'd locked you out, or something. Like I cared about the game more than you.'

There's snot leaking from his nose, tears pooling in his eyelashes. I want to say it's fine but he's clearly been wanting to say this for thirteen years.

'Then you were gone,' he adds. 'I thought you were playing hide-and-seek. I was laughing, saying I was coming ready or not. I checked the bushes and the shed. Then I went inside and looked upstairs, then down, then I realised…'

'I'm here now, Dad.'

He sputters out a mix of saliva and snot, like a horse snorting. 'I'm so sorry.'

'You don't have to be.'

He shakes his head then holds out his hands. 'Not only that. *This*.'

Oh.

He has me speechless because what is there to say? It's squalor.

'Can you come back another time?' he asks quietly.

'Of course.'

'What day is it?'

'Wednesday.'

He nods. 'Saturday. Come back on Saturday. It'll be different, I promise.'

I rub his shoulder and he snakes an arm around me, hugging me close. I'd love to say it was a heart-wrenching moment, a monumental meeting of father and daughter – but the smell of rotten eggs is so bad that I can taste it. As the stench catches the back of my throat, it takes all I can muster not to gag.

TWELVE

I'm on my way through the lounge area of the Black Horse when Pete waves me across to the bar. I assume news has got around about who I am but it's not that at all.

'You know Ashley Pitman?' he asks.

'Sort of.'

'He was asking about you.'

That takes me by surprise. 'When?'

'Lunchtime. He wanted to know how long you'd been here, how long you were staying for, what name you'd checked in under... that sort of thing.'

Pete seems as confused as I feel. He's whispering so that the blokes at the furthest end of the bar can't hear.

'What did you tell him?' I ask.

'Not much. He's barred for one, so I told him to get out.'

'He's barred?'

'Don't worry about that. Are you in trouble, or something?'

I shake my head. 'Nothing like that. It's complicated, but it's nothing to do with him.'

Pete's eyes narrow, weighing me up. I get the sense he's got enough on his plate as it is.

'I don't want trouble with the Pitmans round here,' he says.

'I don't want trouble either.'

'At least we're agreed on that.' He pauses, looks both ways and then lowers his voice even more. 'You could say I'm not best friends with Ashley Pitman.'

'Why?'

'He and his brother have a legacy around this village. Some love them, some don't. I'm in the "don't" camp.'

Nattie said something similar last night but didn't seem able to give much in the way of specifics.

'Why don't people like them?' I ask.

Pete looks past me this time, making sure nobody's anywhere near us. It's like we're running a drug deal. 'They run a taxi company now but they've had other businesses before. Max and Ashley used to run a garage with their dad. A lot of people thought they were rip-off merchants but they employed some of the locals, so others thought they were heroes. There was some problem with trading standards and they got shut down. That caused a right fall-out because Ashley was going around accusing people of reporting them. They owed a few people money as well – and the people round here have long memories.'

'I didn't know any of that.'

He shrugs. 'Now you do. All I'm saying is that you should tread carefully around that family.'

I start to reply and then realise I'm not sure what to say. My mum is part of *that* family, which means I am as well.

I thank him for the tip and then head upstairs with the box of articles from Mum's house, giving me plenty to read later. The photo from Georgie is inside as well. I change quickly and, by the time I'm done, Nattie is waiting downstairs for me, nursing a glass of wine. She downs it in one and then loops her arm into mine, leading me outside once more.

'My mum loves you more than me,' she jokes.

'She spent most of the time trying to shove food into me.'

'You too?! I don't know what's wrong with her but she's not happy unless she's trying to feed people.'

Nattie tugs me in the opposite direction to the church, towards the darker side of village.

'Where are we going?' I ask.

'You'll see. It's a surprise.'

'I don't think I like surprises.'

'You'll like this… well, maybe. Probably. Definitely.' A pause. 'Probably – let's stick with that.'

When we get to the bottom of the hill, Nattie takes me out along a narrow lane that winds around the back of some cottages. We cross an arched stone bridge over a narrower part of the river and then there are a set of football goalposts in the middle of a field. She leads me around the back of the clubhouse and along another lane until we emerge into a small play park. The sign reads: 'Ridge Park' and there are swings, a roundabout and a pair of climbing frames atop a springy black mat. For a moment I think we're heading for the swings but Nattie continues past, heading for a tree in the far corner of the field.

'Ta-da!' she says.

I squint in confusion. 'It's a tree.'

I follow her closer until I see what she's actually pointing at. There's a large raised knot in the middle of the thick trunk, with some sort of wreath around the edges.

'This is your memorial,' she says.

When I'm close enough to touch it, I can see that the wreath is far more complicated than I thought. It's woven like a wicker basket, with branches and slivers of wood intertwined together to create a sort of crown. There are small beads of paint flecked throughout, like jewel stones.

'It's not an official village thing,' Nattie says. 'Some of the kids made it years ago.'

The name OLIVIA has been carved into the knot of the tree, from which the crown is hanging.

'What do you think?' Nattie asks.

'It's a bit weird…'

She laughs. 'Of course it is now. Everyone thought you were dead. This was where we came to talk about you when we were kids. Like I said yesterday, loads of people didn't remember you properly but you were this myth, so everyone told ghost stories.'

I'm not sure whether to be flattered. I probably should be.

'I visited Mum again this morning,' I say. 'Mine and yours, back to back.'

Nattie lets out a low whistle and then flops to the ground, resting her back against the tree. I follow her lead and we end up staring out towards the empty play park. It's another blue-skied day; warm but not too hot. The tree provides a satisfying shade.

'Your mum's not too bad,' she says. 'Always pays on time, lets me go early sometimes. Doesn't try to cheat anyone on overtime. Doesn't freak out if anything gets broken. I once dropped a whole tray of cups and plates and she said it was fine. Didn't even take it out of my wages.'

'Do you know her well?'

'I wouldn't say that. Our mums know each other – which is why I got the job. They don't hang out as much these days.'

'How come?'

Nattie's fiddling with her phone, fingers swishing across the screen as she hammers out a message. She speaks without looking up. 'Honestly?'

'Honest.'

'If I tell you, you're not going to tell her, are you? Mum would flip if she thought I was telling you stuff.'

'I'm good with secrets.'

Nattie turns to look at me and grins. She likes the sound of that. 'She doesn't like your stepdad or his brother. Calls them Tweedledum and Tweedledickhead.'

'Which one's which?'

Nattie puts her phone down and laughs. 'I have no idea. All seems a bit stalkerish to me.'

'What does?'

'Your stepdad used to go out with your mum when they were fifteen or whatever, then they end up getting married fifteen years later…? It's like a bad romcom. A *really* bad romcom with Adam Sandler.'

She clears her throat and then yawns, before lying back on the grass and closing her eyes.

'Your little brother's cool. He's been over the house a couple of times. He pulled a tea towel off the kitchen counter and brought a massive bag of rice down with it. I almost pissed myself laughing – then Mum made me clear it all up for encouraging him.' She pauses. 'Still worth it though.'

'I think he was calling me "Egg" this morning.'

'*Egg?*'

'Short for Olivia, I guess. Who knows?'

'I went to the christening. It was in the church and then there was a buffet at the village hall. I only went for the food.' She holds her hands out high above her, a metre or so apart. 'Bloody loads. I had about two pizzas by myself. Rhys must've eaten half a pig. There was one of those spit-roast things on the go. Cake as well. I had to throw it all up in the toilets.' She pushes herself up onto her elbows and turns to me. 'That's a joke, by the way.'

Nattie lies back down and it's silent for a minute or so. My bare legs are in the sun and it's wonderfully warm on my skin. I've never had a friend like Nattie, someone with whom everything comes easily. It doesn't feel like she's holding anything back. This is her and people can either take it or leave it. She's so open and honest that it leaves me off-guard. I wonder if I might blurt something out because that's what she does. That could be dangerous and yet I still want to spend time with her.

'Your stepdad got pissed,' Nattie says out of the blue.

'When?'

'At the christening. His brother, too. What's his name?'

'Ashley.'

'Yeah – him. Couldn't stand up straight and fell down the stairs at the front of the hall. All the blokes ended up doing this really lame bro-thing.' She puts on a deep voice. '"*Yeah, bro. You all right, bro? I bet I can jump higher than you, bro.*" They did this standing jump competition out on the grass. Your mum went home on her own and left them to it.' Nattie pauses. 'More cake for me, I guess.'

The afternoon is so peaceful that I feel like I could lie here with Nattie for the rest of the day. There aren't even birds whistling and chirping, no hum of traffic, no constant bustle of people. It's glorious. I close my eyes and stretch out close to Nattie. She brushes the back of my hand with hers and we giggle. People seem to like doing that, to make sure I'm still around and haven't disappeared into thin air.

'Max and Ashley don't have many fans,' I say.

'My mum says Max used to follow her and your mum around when they were at school. They'd be walking home and then he'd be there; or they'd go to the cinema or bowling – and the Pitman brothers would turn up.'

'Didn't they all used to go out together?'

'I think this was before that, when they were thirteen or fourteen, something like that. Mum says Max kept asking your mum out, then she eventually gave in.'

'She *gave in*?'

That's not quite the story I'd heard from Georgie.

'I know. Creepy, huh? Keep on at someone until they give up and say yes.'

'Do you know why they broke up in the first place? My mum and dad were married at twenty-one.'

Nattie nudges my hand again and we both push up onto our elbows. 'I probably shouldn't be telling you all this,' she says. 'Mum only told me after the christening because she'd had too many gin and tonics. Get her pissed and she'll tell you anything you want.

All she said was that your mum disappeared for a summer and then everything changed.'

I sit up properly, crossing my legs and staring down at Nattie. Her hair is starting to curl and fray like her mother's, mixing in with the grass.

'She disappeared for a summer?'

Nattie shrugs. 'Don't ask me. I have no idea. Ask Mum.'

'Do you mind if I do?'

Another shrug. 'Whatever. Your family, innit?'

And she's right. Like it or not, Max and Ashley Pitman *are* my family.

THIRTEEN

It's only when the sun starts to dip below the treeline that Nattie and I head back into the village. We talk about everything and nothing. TV shows and bands, a holiday to Ibiza that she wants to take, a festival she and Rhys have tickets for later in the summer.

It's nice to be normal.

I do a lot of listening because it's been a long, long time since I was able to enjoy things like television, or to imagine going to anything like a festival. It makes me think that perhaps I *can* have this sort of life. Friends and family, sunny days in the park, two weeks in Spain or Greece during the summer. It's what everyone else my age does.

There's something so welcoming about Nattie. In the space of a day, we've gone from strangers to acting like we've known each other all our lives. In many ways, I feel closer to her than to anyone I've met so far. She's full of questions but they're not about where I've been for thirteen years, they're about where my top came from, or whether I have tattoos. She has self-awareness about doing a mundane job in a small village, knowing she might never escape, while at the same time talking about countries in which she'd like to live. She's a dreamer and a realist all at the same time.

We stroll back to the Black Horse and claim the same booth we had yesterday. I've got my usual pint of Guinness and Nattie's on the cider again. I get the sense this is her routine.

She downs the first pint quickly, necks another and then gets back to the wine. I've not even got through my first drink and she's giggly and giddy. Her stomach must be one big pit of mixed alcohol.

Time passes and I'm thinking about heading upstairs to bed – or at least my box of newspapers – when the doors bang open and Ashley strides in. He heads directly to the bar, finger wagging towards Pete as almost everyone stops to watch.

'No,' Pete says before Ashley can speak.

'No, what?'

'I told you earlier and I've told you before – you're barred.'

'Why?'

'You know why – now get out.'

Ashley is hunched, fists balled with energy and aggression. For a moment, I think there might be a scrap but he doesn't argue. Instead, he steps away and turns in a semicircle, scanning the pub until he settles on me. He stares for a second or two at most – and then marches back the way he came, banging the doors on the way out.

There is a hushed moment of near silence and then everything returns to normal as if none of it actually happened. I'm not even sure Nattie was aware of what happened.

She hiccups and then giggles to herself. 'I think I've drunk too much,' she says. 'I might call my mum for a lift home.' She laughs again and then does precisely that as she slumps into the corner of the booth.

When she turns up, I wonder if Georgie might be upset or angry at the state of her daughter – or me for being a bystander – but it turns out she's apparently used to this.

Nattie stumbles out through the pub doors as her mum watches on, one hand on hip before giving me a wink and a smile. 'Did you have a good night?' she asks.

'Not as good as Nattie.'

That gets a laugh. 'See you soon, hon. Don't be a stranger.'

*

It's when I'm struggling to focus on the words of the articles that I realise I've had too much to drink as well. I've only had three pints – but I've not eaten properly since breakfast and I can feel the liquid swilling around my stomach. I'm going to have to be careful with this type of thing. Drinking with Nattie is probably fine – Rhys as well for that matter – but getting full-on drunk has to be a non-starter. I don't want to forget anything I'm told, let alone allow something stupid to slip out.

It's been a good day for information as well. People want to talk to me and I'm more than happy to listen.

I fill a glass with water from the bathroom and drink that, then refill it and return to my room. It takes a few minutes but my vision does return to the point that I can take the words in.

There's an easy chronology to the early articles. Girl goes missing, appeal for witnesses, the police make statements, Mum makes her own appeal... then it goes quiet for a couple of days. There's a definite change to the tone, from hope of being found to acceptance that it's unlikely. After that, there are opinion pieces about Dad. Reckless behaviour, irresponsible, should he be prosecuted and so on. It's all written with the menacing undercurrent that perhaps it was him all along. He killed his daughter and then claimed she'd been taken. It's always a parent, isn't it?

The poor guy.

I believe him when he says he'd only gone into the house to use the toilet. It's something anyone would do, something that probably happens thousands of times every day, where a parent will momentarily leave a child unsupervised to go for a wee, or do any number of other mundane things.

None of the reports say that, of course. It's reprinted over and over that he was inside watching the football while his daughter was busy disappearing from the back garden. It's no wonder nobody believed him, no surprise he turned into... whatever he is now.

As I flick through the publications towards the top, what's also clear is that Max either knew what he was talking about or he made a good assumption about the media coverage. There is a photo from the beach and another from a birthday party at a bowling alley. There are more, too – a family picture from a play park much like the one out by the memorial tree is reprinted over and over.

I continue reading, sometimes venturing a little further into the papers to read the stories of the day. There are more black and white images in the paper than there ever would be now and, strangely, the paper costs a few pence more than it would now. I guess some things get cheaper over time. The hairstyles and clothes bear little relation to what people have now. There are movie reviews of new releases that have long since been relegated to being shown in the middle of the night on TV. There are stories about celebrities who've faded into obscurity, not to mention the Hollywood marriages that collapsed years ago. It's almost as interesting as the disappearance pieces. A snapshot of a different time and a reminder of how quickly things change.

I'm lost in the past but when the creak comes from the other side of my door, I don't hesitate. Not this time. I'm on my feet in a flash and across the room in barely a second. I swing it open and almost fall backwards in surprise as Chris the barman reels away. He's directly in front of my door and my first thought is that he was listening against the wood.

I'm about to start shouting when he topples backwards, narrowly managing to catch himself on the rail before falling down the stairs.

He's still shaky as he gasps with surprise, eyes boggling as he pats his heart with his free hand.

'What are you doing?' I ask. I'm far calmer than he is.

Chris nods towards the boxes of crisps at the other end of the landing. He gulps and pats his chest once more but doesn't actually say anything before heading back down the stairs, empty-handed.

2010: LILY, 13

'Are you going to be a good girl again tonight, Lils?'

I have both hands on my hips as I stare up at my dad. We're in the kitchen, arguing over the countertop. 'Why don't you tell me what you really want?' I reply.

The creases appear on his forehead but he doesn't get angry. 'You know.'

'So why can't you say it? All this "good girl" bullshit.'

Even that doesn't get a reaction. Not a proper one anyway. He stands a little taller and the creases deepen. 'We've had this conversation, Lils. You're not old enough to be using words like that.'

'Like what?'

He sighs and rolls his eyes – which is about as angry as he ever gets. 'Do you want me to cook you tea?' he asks.

That's something which definitely defuses the tension. 'What are you thinking?'

He nudges a cool box at his feet: 'Barbecue? I got about two hundred sausages from the farm shop for tonight. You can have first dibs if you like…?'

We do this. Or, more precisely, *I* do this. Push as far as I can and then we end up friends a couple of minutes later. I follow Dad out to the backyard, where he's done an awful lot of cleaning up. He's laid out rows of garden chairs and has set up a screen against the house, with a projector facing it. It's still warm, even in the shade.

Dad connects up a hose from the gas canister to the barbecue tray and then pulls out a string of sausages from the cool box.

It's hardly health food but it's nice to have him cook for me for a change. If tonight goes well, I might get back onto him about looking for work again.

'Who's playing?' I ask.

'Inter and Bayern Munich.'

'I have no idea what that means.'

'Italy against Germany.'

'So why are you watching?'

'Champions League final – annual tradition.'

I shrug that off. If it stops him moping around the house during the day, then I'm all for it. He talks me through the array of sausages he's bought and, even though he's only going on about different types of meat and herbs, it's nice to hear him enthusiastic about something.

After dragging one of the lounge chairs into the evening sunshine, I put my feet up and enjoy the warmth. Dad hums to himself as he pokes at the fire and then double-checks that his projector set-up is actually working.

I'm busy eating a brown-sauce-drenched sausage in a bun when the first of his friends show up. It's at least an hour before the match starts and he's early, arriving with a box of beer. I don't recognise him but he pays me no attention anyway as Dad talks him through the projector. The screen is at least three times the size of our television and this is apparently incredibly impressive for Dad's friend.

I've almost finished eating when the next pair show up, each with more cans. Dad has seemingly forgotten me at the other end of the garden but I'm feeling incredibly self-aware when one of the men shouts 'hi' and gives me a wave. I don't think I know who he is.

There are four of them fussing over the projector now, each with a bottle or can in hand. Is this really how easy it is to please adult men?

I say 'goodnight' to Dad and he moves away from his friends, rubbing my shoulder and whispering 'thank you' before saying that he'll see me in the morning.

'Can we do something tomorrow?' I ask.

'Like what?'

'Go out for tea?'

'If you're good tonight, I'm sure we can arrange something…'

He pats me on the back but it's more a way of telling me he wants me to go upstairs. I can already smell the bitter beer on his breath that wasn't there before, which means I'll be able to hear him snoring through the walls tonight. He'll sleep in late as well, probably until lunchtime at least.

He doesn't drink like he used to, perhaps a couple of days a week instead of every day. He's trying. I know that.

I head into the kitchen and open the fridge. It's no surprise that the top rack is full of lager but there is also a box of Coke cans. I lever myself out a pair, grab a banana and then step backwards.

Then I see him.

Alan is in the doorway to the living room, leaning on the frame, watching everything I've done.

Uncle Alan.

He's bigger than I remember and he's wearing what I'm pretty sure is the same red football top he had on last year. The hairs on his arms are growing over his tattoos and he has a thin bristle of a beard.

'I didn't know you'd be here today,' he says. His lips twist into something close to a smile.

I take a step away from him – but also a step away from the door to the stairs. A quick glance backwards tells me that it's only us in the kitchen. Everyone else is outside. I don't feel as helpless as I was a year ago but there's still something I can't describe stopping me from shouting for help.

'I, um…'

'You're looking pretty again. Growing up so fast.'

'My dad, he—'

'How have you been? I don't think I've seen you since last year. Are you getting on well at school?'

He takes a step forward and I move backwards.

'Hey… where are you going?' His voice is kindly and soft but I know that's not him. 'I'm only trying to say hello. You remember me, don't you? Your Uncle Alan.'

'You're not my uncle.'

He stops and leans against the fridge, blocking any way I might have of getting to the stairs. I could go outside – but the door is closed. I could shout but what then? What would I tell my dad?

'Not *technically* your uncle, I suppose,' he says. 'Little girls have lots of uncles.'

'I think Dad said the match is starting in a minute.'

He grins, showing those gleaming white teeth again. He's probably had those implants that celebrities do. 'So, how's school…?'

'Boring.'

'That's what all little girls think. School is the best years of your life. You should—'

The back door squeaks inwards and it's the sweetest noise I've ever heard. Alan stands straighter, no longer leaning on the fridge, and then I realise the door isn't the sweetest sound I've ever heard; it's my dad's voice.

'Oh,' he says, surprised. He rests both hands on my shoulders, pulling me towards him. 'You okay, Al?'

'Just looking for the toilet. Couldn't remember where everything was.' He sounds different now, stumbling over his words awkwardly, no longer purring and confident.

Dad points towards the hall. 'Last door on the right.'

Alan turns and then disappears without another word. Dad releases my shoulders and asks if everything is okay. I want to tell him the truth but he's already glancing backwards towards the garden, the barbecue and his friends. I'm not sure if he'd believe me anyway. Every day that's passed without me saying something is a day that brings more doubt. If it was true, why would I wait so long? I can't answer that because I don't know.

I tell him it's fine and then don't wait around, tearing up the stairs and slamming my door.

I get on my knees at the end of my bed and tug it as hard as I can. It is made of thick wood and it barely moves a couple of centimetres. The carpet catches on the legs and the frame is a lot heavier than I thought. My arms feel as if they're going to be ripped out of their sockets as I dig my heels in and pull. It takes a few efforts and a couple of minutes until I've moved the bed enough that I can get behind it and make the final push until the door is barricaded.

There are thick indentations on the carpet from where the bed used to be, plus a trail of bristles angling the wrong way from where I've dragged it. I try opening the door but it instantly bashes into the wooden frame. There's no way anybody could open it. If Dad checks on me later, he's going to get a surprise – but being shouted at is much better than the alternative.

It's only when I'm lying on the bed staring up at the ceiling that I realise there are tears running down my face. 'Not now,' I whisper. 'Not now.'

2011: LILY, 14

The trio of girls are like triplets as they waltz past me, long tanned legs strutting beneath their skirts which must surely break the uniform code. It's a code which is seemingly only enforced when the teachers want it to be. Skirt that's a bit too short: ignored. Lad with dreadlocks: sent home. Girl with dangly earrings: sent home. Boy with white socks instead of black: warned.

It's all about who you are, not what you do. These triplets are in the top set for all subjects and get good marks. They're pushing up the school's average for the league tables, so if their skirts are a bit short, no one cares. Well... the religious studies teacher definitely cares – let's not pretend nobody's noticed the constant sideways glances he makes in their direction when they sit in the front row of his class.

The kids sent home for similar uniform offences are the ones in the bottom sets who get low marks. It's one big corrupt system and everyone here knows it.

But that's not why I give the triplets my best 'what-you-looking-at?'-stare as they sneer in my direction. None of them say anything as they turn forward and continue their march towards their next class.

The hall bristles with students hurrying from one side of the school to the other. Chatter hums back and forth but I'm far from centre of attention. All I'm doing is sitting on a chair outside a door waiting to learn my fate.

It could be bad this time.

A minute or two passes and the hum quietens to near silence. Chairs scrape, classroom doors close and there's a sense of peace that'll last until the next bell in an hour.

Still I wait.

This is probably a tactic: leave me hanging until I've had enough. When I finally get to have my say, I'll be so frustrated by the delay that I'll let everything out.

There's a clock on the wall directly in front of me, one of those that actually ticks for each second. *Tick-tick-tick*, it goes, each one seemingly a little louder than the one before. Why would anyone in their right mind actually create such a thing? Is it so hard to make a clock that counts the seconds without making a noise?

It's probably another little thing to wear students down. The shaming as everyone passes by between classes, the lengthy wait to think over what's been done, the *tick-tick-tick* of the damned clock.

The door at my side opens sharply and I jump to my feet without thinking. Mrs Vincent is standing tall, arms behind her back, chin up.

'Miss Armitage,' she says, nodding into her office and holding the door open for me.

There is a large photo of the school on the wall behind the headmistress's desk, which must have been taken from a plane or hot-air balloon. The entire site is on show and every time I see the photo, I'm surprised at how much green surrounds us.

Around that are certificates proclaiming various school successes, then there's another large photo – this one of all the students lined up on the school field at the end of last year. The photographer had to climb high on a ladder to be able to fit us all into the picture.

I slump into one of the two seats apparently on offer as Mrs Vincent sits in her large leather-backed office chair on the other side of the desk.

'Did I tell you to sit?' she says sharply.

'No, miss.'

'So stand.'

I do, giving it the full rolling-eyes treatment.

'Please sit down,' she says – so I slump with even more force this time, sighing as well, as if the whole thing has been a massive ordeal.

Mrs Vincent looks to her computer screen and taps something onto the keyboard before turning to me. She's sitting up very straight, fingers interlocked with each other. I've never been quite sure how old she is. Her hair is brown and in a neat bun but, though she looks young, she sounds like she's been around for a long time.

'Is it true?' she asks.

'Is what true?'

'Did you pull Jane Binny's hair and then push her head into one of the girls' toilets before flushing?'

She has dark brown eyes that, if I'm honest, are terrifying far beyond anything my dad could manage. It feels as if she can see inside me, know what I'm feeling. It gives me chills and makes it impossible to do anything other than look away.

'Is that what she said?' I reply.

'That's not what I asked.'

'Jane's a bitch.'

A pause.

I know I shouldn't look at her again but it feels as if Mrs Vincent is pulling me with invisible strings. I can't resist and, when I turn back, that stare is still there, willing the answer from me.

'Yes,' I reply.

'Why did you do that?'

'She said my mum killed herself so she didn't have to put up with me.'

The headmistress nods ever so slightly. Not making a judgement, simply acknowledging what I've said.

'I'm afraid the school policy is very clear about this,' she says. 'You'll have to be suspended. That's three days at home.'

'So I don't want to *be* at school – and your punishment is to give me what I want?' I laugh at her but Mrs Vincent doesn't react. She waits for me to stop, pauses for the silence.

'I think you *do* want to be at school,' she says. 'I know you're far cleverer than your grades might say. I know you enjoy books, that you pick things up faster than almost anyone else in your year. I also believe you do a really good job of hiding all that from your classmates.'

She leaves it hanging and it hurts as much as if she'd struck me.

'Shows how much you know,' I scoff at her but it's fooling no one, least of all me.

'Ms Binny will also be disciplined,' she adds. 'I've got statements from everyone present. I know exactly what was said by whom and to whom. Let me be clear, though: violence will not be tolerated at this school – and it is certainly *not* an appropriate response to words you don't like. That's true in life as well as within these walls. Do I make myself clear?'

'It's—'

'Do I make myself clear?'

'Yes, miss.'

She relaxes a little, back not so rigid, shoulders not so tight. Then she types something else into her computer and stares at the screen for a few moments.

'You know you take your GCSEs in two years,' she says without looking at me.

'So everyone keeps saying.'

'That's not long. Your grades are declining at a time when they should be holding steady at the very least.'

I shrug. What's the point in arguing with something I know to be true?

'Is everything all right at home…?'

Mrs Vincent asks the question as if she already knows the answer – even though she can't possibly. There's something about her tone; that smug know-it-all voice she has.

'What do you think it's like?' I sneer. 'My mum died three years ago, my dad's business went bust, we're living off benefits and kids take the piss because I get free school meals.' I get louder, finishing with a shout, almost out of my seat until I realise what I'm doing. I fall back into the chair and return Mrs Vincent's stare with one of my own. I'm not going to look away first this time. No chance.

And I win.

She rests back in her seat and glances to the computer screen before turning back to me. 'Don't say piss,' she says.

'Why? It's a word. Piss-piss-piss-piss-piss.'

A pause and then: 'Are you finished?'

I tug at my tie, undoing the knot and dropping it into my lap. If I'm suspended, the uniform code no longer applies.

'I'm here if you want to talk,' Mrs Vincent says.

I stand and pick up my bag, latching it over my shoulder and taking a step towards the door.

'Lily,' she says.

I turn: 'What?'

'I'm here. Anything you want to say is strictly between us.'

I pull up the hood on my jacket and dispatch the tie into the pocket. I take another step to the door. Pause. Think.

Then I tell her to piss off and walk out without looking back.

FOURTEEN

THURSDAY

Georgie transitions directly from a yawn into a beaming smile as she opens her front door. She wafts her hand in front of her mouth, trying to flap away the tiredness. Her hair is more of a mess than when I saw her yesterday; curly red wisps darting off in all directions.

'Olivia, my love. I didn't expect to see you again so soon. Natalie's at the coffee shop if you're looking for her. She was a right mess this morning, poor dear. Still, she brings it on herself.'

'I was after you, actually.'

This gets an even wider smile. She holds the door wide and welcomes me inside, before leading me into the kitchen.

'It's so lovely that the pair of you are spending time together,' she says – and it takes me a moment to realise she's talking about Nattie. 'Shows you still have that bond after all these years.'

There's not a lot I can say, so smile and shrug instead. She asks if I want anything to eat or drink and then fusses about whether I had a good night's sleep, wondering if the Black Horse is comfortable enough for me. It's suddenly like having two mothers – but I can't pretend it's not nice to be wanted. When she's finally done with that, she asks why I was looking for her.

'I was talking to Nattie yesterday before we went to the pub and she said something about my mum disappearing for a summer...'

Georgie's features tighten, the smiles becoming a concerned grimace. 'She said that?'

'We were talking about all sorts of things. I was trying to figure out what happened between her, my dad and Max.'

Georgie suddenly becomes very interested in scrubbing the draining board. She dips under the sink and grabs one of those squirty surface cleaners, then douses the metal before pummelling away at it with a cloth. I sit on the high stool next to the breakfast bar and wait until she's done. She rinses out the cloth and wrings it tightly, then finally turns back to me.

'I've not thought about that for a long time,' she says.

'I wasn't sure what Nattie meant by "disappear". Did Mum go away somewhere…?'

There's another pause as she continues fiddling with the cloth and then washes her hands.

'It was a strange time… you and Natalie have pretty much grown out of it, but you know what it's like when you're fourteen or fifteen and your hormones are going crazy. Everything feels so big, so important. I think Max always had a thing for your mother, even before any of us knew what those feelings meant. We were at that age where you'd have a boyfriend but it didn't mean anything other than that you might walk to school together. Max and your mum went from that to actually *being* together in a more serious way when they were sixteen.'

She twiddles with her hair, screwing up her lips and glancing up. It's as if she's extracting the memory from the air. 'I remember the four of us had gone out to the cinema and then we got burgers or something like that. We'd been together all day and then ended up in the park as it was getting dark. I was sitting on the grass but Sarah and Max were on the swings. Out of nowhere he stopped moving and waited for her to come to a halt as well. Ashley and me were both there, both listening, and he told her he loved her.'

It takes me a moment to take that in.

'Max said that to my mum when they were sixteen?'

'Right – completely out of nowhere. I remember Sarah's face, this blank deer-in-the-headlights stare, as if she didn't know what to say.'

'What happened then?'

'There was this long silence. I remember looking at Ashley – but he was staring at Sarah – and the pause went on and on. It was like she'd forgotten how to speak. Eventually Max goes, "Aren't you going to say it back?" and there's nothing she can do.'

Georgie stops and rubs her head, shuffling the memories. She then fills the kettle and clicks it on.

'Your mum says it back, of course. She apologises, says he took her by surprise but of course she loves him back. Max says they're going to be together forever and that's that. We never really talked about it afterwards.'

She leans on the counter and waits for the kettle to click off, then fills a mug with hot water and cradles it in her hand like it's a precious newborn.

'What happened with you and Ashley?' I ask.

Georgie snorts. 'Let's say those brothers are opposites in many ways. Max followed Sarah around like a puppy; his brother would flit from girl to girl. Even now I don't remember why I went out with him in the first place. Either way, he moved on – so you could say I dodged a bullet there.'

I'm not entirely sure what she means by that. It might simply be that Ashley isn't well liked around village – but it's probably not worth pushing.

'Was that the summer she went missing?' I ask.

Georgie shakes her head. 'I'm coming to that – but it all kind of fits together. That all happened at Easter time. I don't remember the date but probably April or so. The weather was turning and we used to stay out after school. We'd hang around the park, or sit under the bridge by the river. Sometimes we'd smoke or Ashley would get us a bottle of cider.' She winks. 'Don't let your mother ever tell you she was an angel when she was your age. Neither of us were.'

'She'd already had a kid by the time she was my age.'

Georgie counts on her fingers again. It must be a family thing. 'We both had. My mum hit the roof when I told her I was pregnant…' She tails off and then wafts a hand, brushing the thought away.

I realise I have no idea about the identity of Nattie's father. It definitely doesn't feel like the time to ask – not that it's any of my business anyway.

'Anyway – that day with the swings was around Easter,' Georgie adds. 'It would've been about three or four months later, during the summer holidays – and your mum wasn't allowed out any more.'

'How do you mean?'

'If I ever knocked on the front door, her mum would answer and say she couldn't come out. She was ill, or she had chores, or she was grounded. There was always a reason. Then she simply said Sarah wasn't allowed out with me any more. I remember asking why but she just stared back, as if I was some sort of devil. Told me not to come round again.'

'That's the summer she disappeared?'

'Right.'

'Was she at home the whole time?'

Georgie holds both hands out, palms up. 'I don't know. I remember seeing her in her bedroom window. I was on the street below and waved up. I thought she saw me but all she did was pull the curtains. It was really weird.'

'You didn't see her for the whole summer?'

A shake of the head. 'I only saw her once for the rest of the year. I don't know if she was at home, or if she'd gone somewhere else. The next time I saw her properly was out in the village, shortly after she turned seventeen. It was after new year.'

'She disappeared for six months?'

'I guess…'

Georgie tips away the hot water and then refills the kettle. She gets the biscuit tin out of the cupboard and leaves the lid off as she sandwiches two chocolate digestives together and bites into them. 'It was such a long time ago,' she says.

'You said you saw her once in that time…'

Another bite of the double-decker biscuit. 'Right. I don't think her mum – your grandmother – liked Sarah having friends. There was a time towards the end of the holidays when Max and me decided to go to the house and wait. We figured her mum had to go out sometime, so we'd hide in these bushes over the road. It was really boring – and he used to eat these beef jerky things that absolutely stank. We didn't really hang around together except for when we were both with Sarah – but he talked me into it because we were both worried about her. We were there for a whole day and nothing happened but we went back the day after. We'd been there a couple of hours and then Sarah's mum went out by herself. I think she was going food shopping because she had all these bags. We waited until she was out of sight and then we knocked on the door.'

The kettle clicks off for a second time and this time Georgie makes a cup of tea. She dunks her double-decker biscuits and sucks away the juice.

'It took Sarah ages to answer,' she says. 'When she did she looked at us as if we were strangers – then she told us both to go away. I remember asking if she was going to college because our exam results had just come out. All she did was shrug and say she wasn't allowed to talk to me. She told us to leave and then Max said something like, "Does this mean we're broken up?" – and she looks at him and goes, "What do you think?". That was it. She closed the door and I didn't see her again until the next year.'

I rock back and forth on the stool, trying to take it all in. It's a strange story… except one of my biggest questions might have been answered. Perhaps *the* biggest. Georgie doesn't even know what she's said.

'Did she ever tell you what happened?' I ask.

'No… it was different the next year. I don't think she was so bothered about what her mum thought by then. If she wanted to go out, she went out. She met your dad later that year and that was that. Pregnancy, you, marriage – all that. I guess we grew up pretty quickly.' She dunks the double biscuit and finishes it off. 'Well… in some ways we did.'

FIFTEEN

Mum has a finger to her lips when she opens the front door. She must have seen me coming. 'Harry's sleeping,' she whispers as she steps to the side and lets me into the house. 'He's been up half the night.'

'Why?'

She closes the door and hugs me for the briefest of seconds. 'Who knows? You were exactly the same. You'd sleep when you wanted. Sometimes that'd mean through the night, other times you'd decide you were going to be nocturnal. Used to drive me crazy.'

I leave my bag in the hallway and then head through to the conservatory. Harry is in a rocking crib in the corner, shaded by a hanging blanket that keeps him in something close to darkness. Mum's on edge as I poke my head over the side to check on him. His face is scrunched up like a French bulldog puppy and he's sucking his thumb.

Mum breathes a sigh of relief as I step away without waking him. She yawns long and wide, before apologising.

'How have you been?' she asks.

'I only saw you yesterday.'

'I know… I just…' She tails off and then adds: 'It's nice to see you again.'

'I've been hanging out with Nattie,' I say.

'Did you visit your father?' She speaks breezily, as if this is all perfectly normal.

'Yes.'

She opens her mouth to reply but then closes it again, giving a small nod as acknowledgement instead.

'I visited my grave, too. The wreath thing at the tree.'

Mum's eyebrows rise. 'Nobody knew what to do,' she says. 'You were officially dead… still are, I suppose. I didn't want to get a gravestone because it felt so final. Some of the girls from the school wove that wooden wreath and carved your name on the tree. It became this official-unofficial thing. I go there a couple of times a year and sometimes leave flowers. I've been there on your birthday every year since…'

I wonder if that's an invitation for me to close down any minuscule seeds of doubt that could be lingering. To prove that I know my own birthday.

'Christmas Eve,' I reply.

It's like someone's taken a heavy bag from her. She straightens and breathes out. I'm right. Of course I am. 'Right. It's always so cold. The flowers don't last long. I've thought about taking other things – teddies or whatever – but they'd only get taken.'

'It's the thought that counts.'

She nods and smiles thinly.

It's a nice image of the tree surrounded by small soft toys and flowers. The media might have moved on, a lot of people might have moved on – but there's a small corner of this village that still remembers.

'Can we talk about Dad?' I ask.

Mum stares at me but her eyes are blank, like I've asked about someone who's dead. It feels like a long time passes but then her shoulders slump and she lets out a long breath.

'I loved him once,' she says.

It's so softly spoken that I have no doubt it's true. She eases herself lower on the sofa, needing it for support, then glances off towards a photo of her and Max on a nearby shelf, as if speaking of my dad is somehow cheating on her husband.

'He was a good man,' she adds. 'I'd had the same friends for a really long time – we'd all grown up together, all came from this village and I don't think I realised how small that made everything.'

I'm leaning on a sideboard and she looks up to me, squeezing her hands together.

'It's like there's this trivial corner of the world, this little village, this group of people you know – and that's it. You forget there's a big world out there and Dan was the first time I'd seen that. He didn't come from here and hadn't gone to the same school as the rest of us.'

It is the first I've heard of this.

'Where did he come from?' I ask.

'He's a Londoner – not that you'd know it from listening to him speak. His dad was a dentist and moved here because he was setting up a practice. Dan was eighteen when he chose to come with his father. I was seventeen, maybe just eighteen and he was four years older.' She snaps her fingers and it dawns on me that I do that, too. 'We clicked like that,' she adds. 'One minute we'd never met, the next we were doing everything together. I remember early on and we were talking about going out to eat somewhere. I said we could go to the local burger place, which is where I always used to go, and he asked if there was a sushi place nearby. I stared at him as if he'd suggested something so completely stupid. I only knew it was raw fish, I'd never tried it. It sounded disgusting but he said it was really good – rice and spices and all sorts. It was like he was the most exotic person I'd ever met.'

'Did you ever try sushi?'

She laughs. 'Yes. He had a car, so drove us miles and miles out to this place he'd found. I couldn't use the chopsticks, so they gave me a fork. It was really good, not like I expected at all.' Mum holds her hands out, smiling sadly. 'I still don't think the village will be getting a sushi place anytime soon.'

'You could open one.'

A snort: 'It'd be out of business in a month. You know what they say about old dogs and new tricks. This village is the oldest of old dogs. You should've seen the fuss people kicked up when Tesco wanted planning permission for a new Express store. You'd think they were trying to sacrifice kids or something.'

There's a squeak from Harry's cot and Mum freezes. Her eyes dart sideways, fearing the worst, but the noise is followed by silence. She breathes out in tired relief.

Everything she's said about my dad is the opposite of what I saw. He wasn't particularly exotic as he slept among empty bottles of booze and rodent droppings.

'We'd only been seeing each other for a few months when I got pregnant with you,' Mum says. It's as if she's looking over invisible glasses. 'We didn't plan it – but neither of us were unhappy. We were young, but I don't want you to think you were unwelcome. Unplanned doesn't mean unwanted.'

It's hard to reply because I didn't expect the honesty. There's a stigma about being 'an accident', but she's right: unplanned *doesn't* mean unwanted. The problem is I know more than she realises.

'I understand.'

They are two of the hardest words I've ever spoken – and I'm not sure she'll ever know why. There's a pause, which is good because I need it. She stares off towards Harry and I take the moment to gulp away the words that are on the tip of my tongue. There's so much I could say – but I know I can't.

Mum doesn't seem to notice. 'Sex education wasn't what it is now,' she says. 'We were naïve. Four of us in the same year at school all got pregnant within a few months of each other. Dan and I told his dad that we wanted to have the baby and he was fine.' She pauses. 'Well, not *fine*, I suppose. He accepted it. My mum wasn't so pleased – but I was past caring at that point. Your father and I moved into that old house you know and we made it work. When we'd saved up enough money, we got married and made it all official.'

There's another rustle from the back of the room and this time it's followed by a high-pitched gasp for attention. Not quite a cry – but enough to make it clear Harry is awake and wants seeing to. Mum's face falls and she slowly pulls herself up from the sofa. The crow's feet under her eyes have developed overnight.

'Can I try?'

Mum blinks and stumbles over a reply. 'Oh… um… I suppose. If you want, I mean…'

I cross to the crib, to where Harry is wriggling his arms up above his head, expecting his mother's hands to lift him out. He's gurgling and spluttering, with saliva covering his chin. As soon as I reach for him, he latches onto my hands and squeezes as I pull him from the crib onto my shoulder. I don't know if he's big or small for a two-year-old but he's certainly heavy – not that he cares as he buries his face in my breastbone and flops lazily into my arms.

Within a second or two, he's asleep again.

'I didn't expect that,' Mum says.

I stand, bobbing Harry gently up and down as Mum watches the pair of us, a smile slowly creeping across her face. She tells me to wait and then hurries into the other room quickly before returning with her phone to take a series of photos. She stares at the screen afterwards and there are more tears in the corner of her eyes as she turns the phone for me to see.

It's a good picture: Harry's eyes are closed and he's sucking his thumb, his head directly under mine.

'There's a place in the village that prints photos directly from your phone,' she says.

'Won't Max mind?'

She looks up and mutters something I don't catch. I'm not sure it was meant for me.

'We did have good times,' she says eventually.

'You and Max?'

A shake of the head. 'The three of us – you, your father and me.' She asks if I can continue to balance Harry and then leads me upstairs, back into the spare bedroom. She says she dug out another box of things the previous evening and I sit on the bed as she shows me a crusty-looking photo album. The pictures might only be fourteen or fifteen years old but it feels like a different age. Sepia versus colour. There's a misty fuzz to the edges of the photos, which is likely what comes from being left for such a long period of time – but it goes beyond even that. The clothes seem brighter and looser to what anyone might wear now; any brand logos seem spikier and not as polished as those that adorn high streets all over.

Each photo has a story, however – and Mum seems happy to talk about them. There's the first time Dad changed a nappy, the first family visit to the seaside, ditto for the zoo. And so on.

There's one picture in particular that she stops on. She rubs her finger across the surface of the photo as if it makes the memory clearer. Dad is such a different person to the one I met in that filthy house. He's tall and tanned with a strong jawline. Good-looking by anyone's standards.

'He used to carry you around on his shoulders a lot,' Mum says, pointing to the child clinging onto her father's neck.

'We were in Blackpool when this was taken,' she adds. 'It was the summer before everything happened. We rented this little chalet on the far end of the shore and we'd walk the whole length of the promenade and back every day. He'd carry you pretty much the whole way, then we'd get chips on the journey back. It was our first holiday as a family.' She goes quiet for a moment, then adds: 'And the last.'

She closes the cover of the album and returns it to one of the boxes she's taken down from the attic. The moment has passed and Harry is starting to feel heavier. Mum says he'll probably be fine in his crib. We head back downstairs and it feels as if two arms aren't enough as I lever him over the top of the rails of the cot into his bed. He rolls over, eyes still closed as Mum pulls a blanket over him. She dabs at my top, wiping away the worst of the dried saliva.

'You end up washing clothes every day until your kids get to about four,' she says.

We sit on the sofa and there's a minute or two where neither of us speak. Mum is nervously looking over towards the crib but there is no sign of Harry stirring. Conversation isn't easy because there's only really one thing we can talk about – us. I can't imagine having the same types of breezy conversations that Nattie and I enjoyed.

It's then that it dawns on me that this is what it's *supposed* to be like between a mother and daughter. Thirteen years apart or not, there are meant to be secrets and things that aren't shared. This is probably how we'd be around each other even if there weren't those missing years.

The mothers and daughters who go around as if they're sisters are the exceptions. The *weird* exceptions. Mothers who should know better, refusing to grow up, or daughters who can't find friends their own age. It must be a female thing. There are plenty of dads who refuse to grow up – but none I've met who hang around with their sons as if they're all brothers.

'Do you remember the day?' I ask.

I don't need to clarify which one because there's only one 'The Day'. It's when everything changed.

It takes her a while to answer. She stares off into the distance, back in the moment. 'I was at work,' she says. 'I was doing part-time hours in a supermarket and was on the tills when the manager came over and said there was a call for me. It was the first time that had ever happened and before the days of mobile phones. I didn't really know what was going on. When I got to the break room, it was Dan and he said you'd got out of the garden, that he couldn't find you.'

She clenches her fists and her whole body tenses.

'I remember feeling numb. As if everything was pins and needles and there was a moment where I thought perhaps I was dreaming. That this was the sort of thing that happened to other people. I don't remember what I said to him or my boss – it's all blank. I don't even remember driving home, but I must have done. The next thing I know, I'm at the house and there are police cars everywhere. The neighbours are standing outside their houses and watching me. There was this horrible moment where I knew something terrible had happened. Where I knew you weren't inside, that you'd never be inside again.'

She's speaking really quickly all of a sudden, her hands actually shaking.

'Your father was outside with one of the police officers and I remember someone saying that he'd been inside watching the football when it happened. It might not have even been Dan, it might have been the officer asking a question like, "*Were* you inside?" – that sort of thing. And there was this really strange clarity to my thoughts. I still remember all of that now. I remember where everyone was standing, I remember exactly what went through my head. It's so clear. I started shouting at him in front of everyone, saying how could he do this? How could he leave you alone? How could he choose football over his daughter? The officers were trying to get us to go inside because there were so many people watching, but it was already too late then.'

She pauses for breath – not a surprise given how quickly she's been talking. When she starts again, she's speaking much more slowly.

'The thing is, even if you'd come back then. If it had all been some elaborate game of hide-and-seek, or whatever. Regardless of all that, I think our marriage ended in those few seconds. I ended it because I couldn't help myself… because I wanted someone to blame.'

I take her hand and, for the first time, it feels like I'm a real burden, that I'm bringing up things that might be best forgotten. Mum squeezes my fingers and apologises, even though she has no reason to.

'He wasn't to replace you, y'know…'

It takes me a moment to realise what she's talking about but Mum is staring towards Harry's crib.

'That never crossed my mind.'

I'm not sure she's heard because she keeps speaking: 'I never stopped hoping you'd come back. They declared you dead but it didn't stop me dreaming.' She stops to lick her lips. There's a wistful silence but I don't know what to say any more than she does. 'How have you managed to get things done?' she adds eventually.

'Like what?'

'Drive? Have a job – things like that.'

'I have a national insurance number from the other family. There's a small pack of documents, including a birth certificate. I always assumed they belonged to someone who died. I didn't want to ask too many questions because it's only recently all of this makes sense. I'm still not used to being called Olivia.'

'Olivia,' she says. She smirks as if it's hilarious – which, in some ways, I suppose it is.

'It's good to hear you say it,' I reply – and it's true.

'What did people used to call you? Karen?'

'Something like that.'

Her eyes narrow for a moment but she doesn't press me on the point. In a lot of ways, it doesn't matter any longer.

We're interrupted by the sound of the front door opening. Mum leaps up and hurries from the room, shushing all the way out to the hallway, where a couple of male voices quickly go quiet. She returns by herself shortly after, briefly peering into Harry's cot and then sitting back on the sofa.

'They're so noisy,' she whispers.

'Max and Ashley?'

A nod and then she pats my thigh. 'Have you made any decisions about staying in the village, or…?'

'Not yet. It's still very new. I like hearing all the stories about you and my dad, though.'

I push myself up from the sofa and spike onto tiptoes so I can see Harry without having to get any closer to him. He's sucking his thumb again, eyes closed, chest rising and falling in perfect serenity.

'I'm going to go,' I say.

'Do you want to go for coffee tomorrow? We can meet at the shop.'

I tell her that sounds good and that I'll text her a time when I know what I'm doing. We hug again and, even when I try to pull away, she holds me for a few seconds longer. Her lips are parted when we separate and it looks as if she wants to say something. I hesitate for a moment but if she was going to speak, it's lost as Harry gurgles from the corner. I tell her I'll see myself out and then follow the hall to the front of the house.

Which is when I see Ashley going through my bag.

SIXTEEN

'What do you think you're doing?'

Ashley turns to look at me but doesn't stop hunting. There's no sign of Max. My purse is open and he's flicking through the contents. There's a café loyalty card in his hand which he flips over to look at the back before dropping it on a side table.

I march across the floor and snatch my bag and purse from him, cramming everything back inside. He doesn't try to hold onto it but he barely moves away either, standing uncomfortably close and invading my personal space with the smell of grease and sweat.

'Where's your driving licence?' he asks.

'None of your business.'

'In the name of Olivia Adams, is it?'

'That's none of your business either.'

He finally steps back, sneering with incredulity. '*Really?*'

I realise we're whispering to each other – hate-whispering, I suppose – neither wanting to be overheard by anyone else in the house. In some ways, it's a good thing. This is out in the open between us now. He's telling me outright he doesn't believe me and I'm letting him know I won't be bullied.

'I know you've been asking around about me,' I say. 'Checking up. Spying. Where's it got you?'

He scratches the stubble on his chin, weighing me up. I can't figure out if he's smart or stupid. Sometimes there's a fine line.

'Why are you here?' he asks.

'Visiting my mum.'

'Not the house – Stoneridge. Why are you here?'

'What's it to you?'

There's a massive part of me that really enjoys being obtuse – especially to someone who so badly wants answers.

'What do you want?' he asks.

'None of your business. You're not my dad and neither is your brother.'

Ashley takes another moment to examine me, glancing down to my bare legs, across my midriff and chest and then focusing on my face. He's smirking and it's a proper game of one-upmanship. A battle to prove who's winning.

'My brother is married to Sarah – which means her business *is* my business. We're brothers and business partners. If you're here for money, you're out of luck because there's nothing for you. You might as well piss off to wherever you came from.'

He uses his middle and index fingers to motion a pair of walking legs, as if I couldn't figure it out for myself. No holding back now.

'I don't want money,' I say.

'Everyone wants money.'

'I don't.'

He bites his lip, nostrils flaring, trying to work out what I could possibly mean by that. If I don't want money, what else could I want? He doesn't have a clue. This part of him is easy to read – he's obsessed by money and yet he'll never have any. He will have been taking shortcuts his entire life, running crappy businesses, fiddling the books, haggling over every pound that anyone else spends. There's nothing necessarily wrong with that but nobody gets rich in a place like Stoneridge. It's too small, too inward-looking. The ambition he has is tempered by preferring to be a big deal around the village, instead of a nobody in a big city.

'Why are you here?' he asks with a hiss, repeating himself.

'Why d'you think? Because she's my mum.'

That gets a laugh. His head rocks back. 'You're not fooling me, darling. I've looked you up. You're there telling your gullible *mother* about walks on the beach and birthday parties – but that's all online. I've *seen* those photos. Anyone could've come out with that.'

'Why don't you say it properly, then? Get it out in the open. What do you *really* want to say to me?'

Ashley pumps himself up, standing a little taller – although he isn't that much bigger than me. I wonder if he'll actually do it – call me an imposter to my face. We've danced around it but it's clear that's what he thinks.

'I'm not saying anything,' he hisses, before proving himself wrong. 'Just know that *I* know you're not who you say you are. I'm on to you – and, sooner or later, I'll prove it.'

I grin – because I know that's what'll annoy him the most. 'Good luck,' I say, keeping my voice low. 'How are you going to do that? You don't know anything about me.'

'I know there's no way you're stealing what rightfully belongs to my family. You might have some of this village fooled – but I'm too smart for you, darling. Way too smart.'

He speaks with such cocky assuredness that I wonder if he knows something I don't. It's surely all front: bluster and bravado. I know the type, and yet…

That doesn't stop me, of course. There's no way he's getting the last word. I haul my bag up onto my shoulder and take a few steps towards the front door before spinning back. I don't make any effort to lower my voice this time, giving Ashley my sweetest of smiles.

'Oooooh. I'm so scared. I've seen smeared dog shits that are smarter than you.'

Before he gets a chance to reply, I'm out the door and on the way to my car. I regret it instantly, of course. He's already set himself to make my life difficult and dig around every aspect of my past – and I can't help but feel I've only given him one more reason to find out the truth.

2012: LILY, 15

'Armitage?'

Ever since I can remember, I've always been the first name on the register at school. I used to wish someone named 'Aardvark' might come along to change things.

'Yes, miss.'

'Banner?'

'Yes, miss.'

Our teacher continues to go through the list of names as the cult-like series of 'yes, miss' responses continue one after the other.

When it gets to 'Nurse?', Zoe, who is sitting next to me mumbles her 'yes, miss' and then we sit in silence until 'Young' replies to say that she's also present. It's a full house today... but not for long.

Our form tutor bangs on about something to do with mock exams and the school field being out of bounds for a reason I don't catch. Zoe is busy doodling love hearts on the back of her workbook with the name 'Joe' in the middle. She also has a talent for drawing cats, even though she doesn't own one. She's even told me she prefers dogs but, for whatever reason, it's felines she can sketch. Her books are covered with various biro drawings of hearts and cats, which would be a very curious mix for anyone who didn't know her.

The bell finally rings to shut our teacher up and then the entire class grab their bags, desperate to get out. Zoe and I trail out towards the back, shuffling along with the zombie horde. The school is made up of half a dozen blocks but there's no covered path to get from one to the other. When it's raining, that means mad dashes to get between buildings – but it also means there are blind spots that are out of view of the classroom windows.

Zoe and I wait for our moment, slowing our pace and not needing to speak. We've done this enough times before that it's second nature now. As soon as there's nobody behind us, we calmly head for the hedge at the side of the path and shove our way through. It only takes a handful of seconds and that's that – we're out of bounds.

There's a mushy patch of grass which we hop over and then we're on a narrow lane at the back of a row of houses. If there was anyone in the upstairs window of the nearest house, they'd see us – but, as ever, it's clear. We press up against the fence, using the height to shield us from view, and then Zoe loosens her tie and unbuttons her shirt. She's momentarily wearing only a bra on her top half but then she pulls a T-shirt from her bag. She swaps her tights and skirt for a pair of jeans and then it's my turn. I have jeans and a sweater and then we head through to the rest of the estate.

It probably looks a little odd that we're carrying bags on our back – but out of our school uniforms, we don't instantly stand out as truants. When we were out the last time, a police car drove past. We continued walking as if everything was fine and the car didn't even slow, let alone stop.

There are no such concerns this time and we're at the play park before we know it. Joe is the same age as us but goes to a different school a few miles away. He's already waiting on the swings as we approach, gently rocking back and forth. He's still in his school uniform, minus the tie – although dark trousers and a white shirt could be office wear for him. Not that he seems to care about things like that.

'Where've you been?' he calls as we get closer.

Zoe flings herself at him, dragging him from the swing and pushing him onto the matted floor until she's straddled across his waist. She pecks him on the lips and then leans back, squirming and giggling.

There's another boy sitting on the roundabout, black skin like Joe but with tight braids over the top of his head, dangling to his neck. He's thicker, more muscled, but as soon as I get near, I know they're brothers. They've got the same pouting lips and wide nose.

'State of that…' he says, nodding at Joe and Zoe. 'What's your name?'

I settle on the next triangle of the roundabout and drop my bag. 'Lily.'

He repeats my name, making it sound rougher than I ever could.

'I'm Lincoln,' he says, nodding and winking at the same time. 'Do you go to school with Joe?'

He laughs. 'Nah, I'm eighteen, ain't I? Don't need any of that.'

Lincoln digs into his jacket pocket and takes out a small tin. It takes me a moment to realise he's rolling a cigarette – except he's not doing that. Not quite.

'You on it?' he asks, holding the spliff out towards me along with a lighter.

Zoe and Joe take that moment to pick themselves up from dry-humping on the floor and come to sit on the roundabout with us. Zoe saves me the job, taking the roll-up and lighting it far too casually for it to be her first time. She sucks on it deeply, holding the smoke in her lungs and closing her eyes before passing it on. I'm next – but there's no way I'm saying I've never done it before. I try to copy what Zoe did, spluttering slightly but managing to avoid any full-on coughing.

Not that anyone's paying much attention. Now the spliff has come out, everyone's gone quiet. It makes a couple of laps of the circle before Lincoln finishes it off, mashing the remains into the edge of the roundabout and dropping what's left on the grass.

Joe is on top of Zoe now, grinding against her until his brother tells them to knock it off.

Zoe asks what time it is and when Lincoln says it's after ten, she says we can go back to her house because her mum will have left for work. The four of us do just that, traipsing through the back alleys and narrow lanes that only locals know as we make our way around a couple of housing estates until we emerge at Zoe's back gate. She reaches through a gap in the fence to unlatch it and then we move into the backyard. Zoe unlocks the house and goes in by herself, calling after her mum. When it's clear she's definitely out, she waves us in with a wicked smile.

We've only been inside for a few seconds when she disappears up the stairs with Joe. There's the sound of a bedroom door closing and then a bump on the floor.

Lincoln and I are alone in the kitchen and he opens the fridge door. 'You drink beer?' he asks.

'Not really.'

There's been enough beer-drinking at home, without me getting involved.

He takes out a bottle of Bud and snaps off the lid with the bottle opener that's attached to the cupboard door. There's another bump from upstairs and some muffled giggling. Lincoln ignores it, opening and closing the cupboards until he finds a multipack of crisps. He picks through the selection, asking if I fancy anything and then, when I say I'm fine, settling on salt 'n' vinegar for himself.

I've been to the house a few times before and lead him through to the living room. Lincoln instantly switches on the television, flopping into the lounger chair. He kicks his feet up and starts to flip through the channels.

He has a mouthful of crisps when he next speaks. 'You got a boyfriend?'

'No.'

'You a carpet muncher?'

'I don't know what that is.'

I'm on the sofa and he turns to wink at me before putting down the remote control. 'Whatchu wanna do?'

'I don't know.'

It's true – I really don't. There's a really big part of me that wants to dig my uniform out of my bag and head back to school.

'How old are you?'

'Fifteen.'

He chews on his lip, mulling over what to say next, then turns back to the TV. 'You ever done it?'

It's only four words. A completely throwaway sentence. None of the words have more than four letters and yet there's so much meaning to the question. I bet everyone gets asked it at some point in their lives.

I answer before I've even thought about the consequences. It's like a reflex: 'Yeah'. All casual and grown-up, as if it's nothing. Course I have. Who hasn't? Pfft, why even ask?

The TV is showing some sort of kids' show – all dayglo puppets and bright green background – and Lincoln doesn't bother to change the channel as he puts down the remote. He takes a few steps across the living room and then puts a hand on my thigh.

'Lily,' he says. 'I kinda dig that.'

2013: LILY, 16

Zoe holds her envelope up in the air as I clasp onto mine. 'Want to swap?' she asks. 'You open mine, I open yours?'

'No…'

'Suit yourself.'

She rips across the top of her envelope and pulls out the slip of paper from inside. Zoe blinks at the contents reeling back slightly. 'Wow. I did *not* expect that.'

'What?' I reply.

She nods to my envelope. 'You go.'

This isn't how I wanted things to work out. I would far rather open my envelope by myself. I know what's inside anyway but once I've seen the words, it's final. Like the tree falling in the woods. As long as it remains in the envelope, it could say anything.

There's a shriek from over my shoulder and I turn to where a photographer from the paper is busy lining up the triplets. They're all blonde and summery; shirts too tight, tits half on show. Sixteen years old now, so it's fair game, I suppose. Nothing like a bit of flesh when you're officially legal. The triplets are holding up the papers that show their exam results and I bet it's a string of As for each of them. The photographer is telling them to smile – and the budding models do as they're told, pouting and waving as he snaps away.

I can't avoid Zoe any longer so I carefully slice underneath the envelope flap and pull out the square of paper from within.

'Five Cs,' Zoe says, looking at her own slip. 'Can you believe that? I got a C in maths. How did that happen? Double-C in science, C in drama, C in religious studies. Ridiculous. My mum owes me fifty quid.'

She leaves it hanging there, waiting for me to spill my own results.

'B in English,' I reply.

'You got a B?! Did you blow Mr Garland or something?'

Zoe laughs but I don't.

'What else?' she asks.

'Fs.'

There's a short pause in which she's wondering if I'm joking. 'Oh,' Zoe says. 'I got two Es, some Fs and a couple of Us.'

I turn the page so Zoe can see – and there it is in all its humiliating glory. One B and a row of Fs.

F for fail.

She passes me her results slip and laughs it off. 'Ah, well – there's some cider under the stairs at my mum's house. She's at work if you want to come over…?'

I give her back the slip and shake my head. 'I have to get home,' I say.

Zoe's staring at me and she must know I'm lying. There's a moment of awkwardness and then she shrugs. 'If you change your mind…'

There's nothing else to say, so she turns and walks along the long school driveway. No need to sneak through hedges any longer – we're done with this place. Neither of us will ever be back and there's a part of me that knows I'll probably not see much of Zoe any longer either.

I wait until Zoe is out of sight and then make my own way along the drive. There are small groups of people from my year celebrating on the grass verges. It's a chorus of laughter and joy. An alphabet that consists entirely of As, Bs and Cs. They're talking of A-levels and colleges; the rest of the summer of fun followed by the future.

Nobody calls after me but it's not as if I've spent much time among them over the past year or so. Some of them have probably forgotten my name and, as for the others, why would they care?

I could take the direct route home. It would only take me twenty minutes or so and it's a nice enough day – but that'll mean I have to tell Dad even sooner how much of a failure I am. How he should be ashamed of me.

Without any sort of plan, I find myself drifting through the housing estates that surround the school. It's a summer's day, so there are people everywhere – mums with prams, couples on a late-morning stroll, blokes in combat shorts. There are students from Joe's school drifting around in twos, threes and fours; full of smiles and happiness.

I've almost passed the van when I realise what's on the side. I stop and stare at it, wondering if it's some sort of optical illusion or my mind playing tricks. I touch the side and it takes the warmth of the van's panel to convince me it's actually there.

'JOIN WITH AL'.

I look up and down the street but it's empty and there is no one staring out from any of the house windows. I do a lap of the van and it's when I get to the back that it feels like my eyes really are deceiving me. I knew 'Uncle' Alan was a joiner but here he is: full name and phone number.

I'm standing in the road when I hear the sound of a front door opening. I risk a glance through the driver's side window, all the way through to the other side where Alan is walking down the path of the adjacent house with a plank of wood in his hand. He's whistling absent-mindedly to himself, not paying attention. There's a moment where I think he can't miss me – except he does. He goes to the back of the van, opens the doors and then rummages inside. While he does that, I wait at the front of the van. As soon as he closes the doors, I edge back round to the driver's side as Alan returns to the house.

It feels like some sort of miracle that he's not seen me. A calling, as if this was how things were supposed to happen. I wait until I hear the front door of the house sounding again and then it's hard to stop myself from laughing as I notice what's on the drive directly opposite the van. Instead of being tarmacked or paved, it's covered with a selection of pebbles. I don't bother to check along the street to see if I'm being watched because I somehow know I'm not.

I'm supposed to be doing this.

I take my time, kicking through the mass of rocks until I find one that's close to the size of my fist. It's perfectly smooth, almost spherical. Even though it's heavy, I toss it from one hand to the other and then cross the road once more.

The windscreen doesn't simply shatter, the rock sails straight through the glass, sending a perfect crinkle out to the corners and leaving a circular hole in the middle of the driver's side. I take a moment to enjoy the handiwork – but only that. Then I turn and run.

SEVENTEEN

FRIDAY

I'm dreaming of someone else – another time, another place – when the bang of hand on wood invades my consciousness. There's a moment where they're part of my dreams and then I'm in the room above the Black Horse again and someone's knocking on the door.

It's a man's voice: 'Hello?'

I grumble that I'm on my way and then roll out of bed, grabbing a loose T-shirt from under the bed and putting it on over my flimsy top.

Pete is waiting on the landing – and it looks like he's not long out of bed himself. He's in tracksuit bottoms and a scraggy sweater, his hair wet from the shower.

'Sorry,' he says, stepping backwards. 'It's, um… the police are downstairs.'

'Oh…'

I knew this was going to happen sooner or later and I suppose it's been three days. The village isn't big enough for newcomers to stay unnoticed for long, especially not when they've been missing for thirteen years.

'You're her, aren't you?' Pete says.

'I'm sorry. I should've said, it's just—'

He shakes his head. 'You don't have to explain, but I don't know what to call you now.'

'Olivia, I guess. That's what everyone else is calling me.'

He stares at me for a moment and it's the same look I've seen so often recently, as if I'm a ghost of Christmas past. What is there to say?

'Why are the police here?' I ask.

He shrugs. 'I didn't ask. They're in the bar when you're ready. The doors are locked and I'll wait up here. You won't be disturbed. Take your time.'

I thank him and he waits for a moment too long before realising he's staring. There's a moment where I think he might reach out and touch my arm – check I'm for real like my mother – but he doesn't. He steps back, smiles apologetically and then heads upstairs.

Back in my room, I'm running seriously short of clean clothes. Pete said something about a washer I could use on the ground floor and I'm going to have to take him up on that later. It looks warm outside, so I settle for a skirt from two days ago that looks clean and a fresh fitted T-shirt. I've got some exercise gear but going out for a run always feels like a good idea the night before, never by the time I wake up.

I think about spending a few minutes making myself more presentable but figure the bemused just-out-of-bed-look will probably be more appropriate. I ruffle my hair a little more and then head downstairs, into the bar.

It's eerily empty. Chairs are still scattered randomly, from where drinkers left them the night before; there are beer mats on the floor and empty packets of nuts and crisps scattered into corners. That's not to mention the glasses that are strewn throughout, some on tables, many stacked on the bar. Pete evidently leaves the cleaning until morning, which probably explains the slightly sticky tables everywhere.

It takes me a moment to realise there are two people in a booth around the corner from the door. They're sitting in silence and stand when they realise I've entered.

Classic cliché police, I suppose. There are two officers: an older man and a younger woman, like some sort of buddy movie. Throw in a talking dog and we've got a summer holiday kids' film.

'Olivia, is it…?'

The man has his hand outstretched. He's got grey hair and a matching neat moustache. His suit looks itchy, a light grey almost cream summer job. Something out of a catalogue, perhaps – but a crime against fashion either way.

I shake his hand and then the woman's. She's early thirties at most, over-straightened dark hair and a smart, dark suit, with an officious by-the-book kind of look about her. Either that, or I've watched too many movies.

The first officer tells me he's Detective Inspector McMichael and he's the one who does the talking. The woman does introduce herself but I instantly forget her name. Those are the only words she says anyway, taking notes as her partner talks.

We sit in the booth and then the inspector repeats himself: 'So, it's Olivia, I understand…?'

'Right.'

He nods stoically. 'For the record, could you say your full name out loud?'

'Olivia Elizabeth Adams.'

Another nod from the inspector while the other officer's pen scratches away. I wonder what she's writing.

'I was on the original case,' he says. 'The missing persons search from thirteen years ago. It was one of our biggest failures.'

I'm not sure what he wants me to say, so I sit and wait for him to continue.

He clears his throat and then he's off again: 'The case is technically still open,' he says. 'I suppose it can be closed now but we'd need some details from you, obviously…'

This is a moment I've been thinking about a lot. There was always going to be a time where I needed to talk to someone who wasn't my family about what happened. I've only told the story twice – to Mum and then Nattie and Rhys. I probably phrased things differently on the two occasions I spoke of it.

I ask if I need a lawyer and the two officers exchange a glance that doesn't tell me much.

'It's up to you,' the inspector says. 'If you think you need one…'

There's a definite edge to that and I wonder what he's heard. It occurs to me that it's not only my story that's out there. There'll be whispered versions around. Nattie will have told her mum and Georgie will have told any number of people. Details will change, specifics will blur. Chinese whispers are one, probably racist, thing – but Stoneridge whispers will be another thing entirely. Ashley and perhaps Max will have their versions too – and I doubt I'm painted as the loving, long-lost daughter.

'Is there a law about walking away and then coming home?'

The look between the officers lasts longer this time; a good second or three. That's really confused them. It feels like the temperature of the room has dropped.

DI McMichael turns back to me and his eyebrows are like thick caterpillars that are butting heads as they angle down over his nose. 'Is that what happened?' he asks.

'I don't really want to talk about it any more. I told my mum what happened and that was hard enough. What's done is done. I don't want to keep repeating it.'

Another pause. The inspector licks his lips. 'I'm only asking you to tell me. You don't have to repeat anything after today.'

'I know… but I still don't want to talk about it.'

I'm not sure I can explain why I feel so confident about this particular encounter. I shouldn't. These people are the police. Not some rent-a-cop shopping centre fat bloke in a uniform. It's not like giving lip to an old lady who's offended by a teenager's swearing or smoking. This is important, I know it is, and yet nothing will be harder than telling the story to Mum. I guess it's that which has given me this assurance in what I'm saying. If I don't want to talk, I won't talk. What are they going to do? I'm not trying to do anything that breaks the law.

The inspector presses back in the chair. His mouth is open and his tongue runs along his top row of teeth. Whatever he was expecting from this morning, it wasn't this.

'Obviously, I understand that things might be a little raw for you,' he says, 'it's just I've never heard of a case where a young child might voluntarily walk away from home and not return for thirteen years…'

I leave it there for a moment, thinking about what to say.

'I'm not saying that's what happened,' I reply. 'I'm saying I don't want to talk about it. I've not done anything wrong.'

'But if someone else has, if there's been any sort of criminal activity, then there could be dangerous people out there who need to be prosecuted.'

There's that village grapevine…

A yawn pushes its way up from my stomach and it's almost through me before I can cover my mouth with my hand. I apologise but my eyes are watering and this isn't exactly the impression I wanted to give. I apologise and gulp back a second yawn before wiping my eyes clear.

'I'd rather forget about it all and get on with my life,' I reply.

'If you were taken – *if* – whoever it was might still be out there. They would be dangerous people. Other children could be at risk.'

He waits for me, but I wait for him. I don't have anything to say.

The inspector leans forward, making the crucial error of resting the elbows of his jacket on the sticky table. 'Are there dangerous people out there?' he asks.

'I'm sure there are loads of dangerous people around.'

'Are there any you'd *specifically* like to tell me about?'

I shake my head. 'I really don't want to talk about it.'

He presses back and the material of his jacket makes a soft slurp as it peels itself away from the table. He winces and twists his arms to see what he's done.

'Let me put this another way,' he says. 'If there's someone out there who has snatched a child, that person might be in a position to snatch others. He or she could return here to cause problems for you, your mother, other people you know. Isn't that something you'd like to help us with?'

He's not *actually* put it another way, he's repeated himself. My heart is thundering and it's so loud that I wonder whether he can hear it. I've not had a lot of contact with the police before, let alone stood up to an officer. There's a large part of me that feels in the wrong.

'I don't think I can help.'

The inspector presses his lips together hard and his eyes narrow. I wonder if there's something I've missed. A law I might not know about, something I've done wrong. Even if a person is accused of a crime, he or she is allowed to say nothing to the police. I'm not even being accused of anything, so why shouldn't I remain silent?

'I should tell you that obtaining goods or services by deception is considered fraud. Fraud by false representation could mean anything up to eight years in prison…'

More from the grapevine. He speaks calmly, with authority and the room feels even colder again. There's steel but I have that, too. I make eye contact, force myself not to gulp.

'Surely it's only fraud if you're trying to impersonate someone? If you *are* that person, then what's the crime?'

There's a slow nod and another barely perceptible glance between the officers. 'There isn't a lot of precedence in cases such as this,' the inspector says, 'but a DNA test could put any questions to rest…'

'I wasn't aware there *were* any questions to put to rest.'

It's a long few seconds and then, without a word, both officers stand at the same time. It happens with such abruptness that it makes me jump. I shuffle out of the booth and then stand myself. DI McMichael is taller than I first thought. A good head and shoulders above me. We only shook hands a few minutes ago but he didn't seem so imposing then. He offers me his hand once more.

'In that case, I guess that'll be all,' he says. He digs into an inside pocket of his jacket and passes me a business card. 'If you think of anything else, or you change your mind, you know where I am.'

The two officers cross to the front of the pub and McMichael pulls down the heavy bolts to unlock it. He pauses for a moment and turns. 'Welcome home, Ms Adams.'

'Thank you.'

I get the sense this isn't yet the end but he shunts the doors open with a wooden *thunk*. Sun bursts into the bar and I'm blinking into the sudden explosion of light. From nowhere, my mother's silhouette appears between the officers. She rushes the doors as soon as they open, calling my name and then she's hugging me. I'm still disorientated from the light and it's all a bit bewildering. The officers have stopped on the pavement outside, watching Mum and me on the doorstep.

'Are you okay?' she whispers, her voice cracking.

'How did you know they were here?'

Mum releases me but keeps hold of my hand as she takes half a step away. She doesn't need to answer because it's clear: there are a couple of dozen people massed on both sides of the street outside. A police car is parked a little along the road and word has obviously gone around the village that the prodigal daughter has returned. There's a hushed, collective intake of breath as I squint towards the watching crowd. There are old and young, some teenagers barely younger than me, some bloke biting into a pasty, the pastry crumbs flaking onto the ground as he goggles at me.

'It wasn't me,' Mum says.

'What wasn't?'

'I didn't tell the police you were back.'

I squeeze her fingers. 'I never thought for a moment that you did.'

EIGHTEEN

The two officers don't look back as they get in the marked car and then drive away. I'm not sure what the villagers were expecting but it's like a game of statues. The music starts and they all move at the same time, apparently remembering why they were on the High Street in the first place.

Harry is strapped into a pushchair next to the pub doors. He's been less than a metre away the entire time and yet I hadn't noticed him. He seems perfectly happy, amusing himself by wriggling against the restraints.

'We can go to Via's,' Mum says. 'I'll close it and we'll have the place to ourselves.'

I quickly return inside the pub and shout up to Pete that we're done, then Mum and I head along the High Street, side by side. For the first time since I arrived back in Stoneridge, it feels like I'm being watched. The place is hardly teeming with people and it's still early – yet everyone on the street turns to watch as we pass.

Or it seems like that.

Via's is already open when we arrive but there are no customers and the girl behind the counter isn't Nattie. She's a little older and barely gives me a look as we enter. Instead, she crosses the café and kneels in front of the pushchair, cooing at Harry.

'How is my favourite little man?' she asks playfully as he grabs for her. She looks up to Mum and must read something in her expression. 'Is everything all right?' she adds.

'One of those days, Oona,' Mum replies as the waitress stands. 'I'm going to close up for a few hours. Perhaps reopen for lunch. If you want to hang around, that's fine – or you can head home for a couple of hours. I'll pay you either way.'

Oona again asks if everything's all right but doesn't get much of an answer. She certainly doesn't complain about a paid morning off as she grabs her jacket and heads out.

Mum switches the 'open' sign to 'closed' and then locks the door, leaving us alone in the café.

'I used to work here myself every day,' she says breezily.

'When did you open it?'

'About three years ago. I wanted it to be earlier but there are permits and licences.' She swirls a hand. 'It's only after Harry was born that I got someone in to run the place. The business was doing okay…' She crosses to the large espresso machine and twiddles a few knobs. 'I *think* I still remember how to use all this stuff. Do you want something?'

'Full afternoon tea with a triple-shot mocha skinny latte made with soy milk.'

She laughs: 'Oi! Be nice to your mother.'

'A cup of tea would be good. Normal tea.'

'I'm sure I can manage that.'

I sit at one of the tables and wheel Harry's pram towards me. He's bashing a plastic dangly toy that's hanging over his head but he grabs my finger when I offer it and tries to put it in his mouth. I tickle his chin instead and he burbles a perfect, cherubic laugh.

'He likes you,' Mum says from the other side of the counter.

'I don't think brothers and sisters are supposed to get on.'

'Most are closer in age.'

'True.'

I continue making ooey, gooey noises to Harry as Mum potters behind the counter. It's not long before she's back at the table and we each have cups of tea in front of us.

'Didn't want to risk the cappuccino machine for yourself?' I tease.

'I could make something fancy if I wanted.'

We smile to each other and then stop to watch Harry for a moment. He's not particularly doing anything, more bouncing around, trying to latch onto my hand. Things feel a little looser between my mother and me today. There are only so many times people can look at each other and say how weird things are.

'What are you going to do now?' Mum asks. 'I know you're not thinking immediately about it – but if you want a job, I can help sort something out.'

I sip my tea and it occurs to me that I've done an awful lot of this since arriving in the village. The whole place runs on gossip and hot drinks.

Without thinking, I glance across to the counter. 'No offence – but I don't want to work in a shop. It's not like there's anything wrong with that but—'

'I didn't necessarily mean here. I know other people in the business community. Friends of friends, too. That sort of thing. There are people who'll want to help, especially now that word's out.'

I'm a bit chastened by that. Anyone who starts a sentence with 'no offence' automatically means offence.

At that moment, a woman walks past the café window. She stops as if about to come in and then realises the door is locked. She presses her hands to the glass, cupping her eyes from the glare and stares towards us. It's probably innocent – someone who's after breakfast – and yet I wonder if this is what it's going to be like. Am I the newborn panda cub in the zoo at which everyone is desperate to gawk?

When the woman notices the 'closed' sign, she turns and toodles off along the street. Mum didn't even notice her.

'I've not figured out what I want to do yet,' I say. 'I might go to college and try to get some proper qualifications. Perhaps an Open University thing? I'm not used to having choices.'

Mum's watching me but not saying anything and I get the sense that all she wants is confirmation that I'm staying around. Especially after the police visit, I can't tell her what she wants to hear.

'How are you fixed for money?' she asks.

'I don't want your money, Mum.'

'But how are you managing? You're not working in the village but you must be paying to stay at the Black Horse. Then there's the cost of food and everything else. If you want to study, there's the cost of books and the course itself.'

'I'll figure it out. I don't want your money. That's not why I'm here, despite what your husband or brother-in-law might think.'

She cranes her neck back slightly and I can see that the remark stings. 'Nobody thinks that,' she says.

'Are you sure?'

'Why? Did Max say something to you?'

I think about it, hold my breath, wonder if I should tell her about Ashley going through my bag, about him stomping into the pub or parking his taxi outside and waiting for me to emerge. He *definitely* thinks I'm here for money.

'Olive…?'

The change of name takes me by surprise. 'Is that what you want to call me?'

She blinks, apparently not realising what she'd done. 'You used to like it when you were younger. I let you choose from Olivia, Via, Olive and O. You chose Olive.' She stops and then adds: 'What would you like now?'

'I honestly don't mind.'

Mum doesn't reply because Harry shouts at her and starts actively fighting against the straps of his pushchair. She unclips him and lifts him out but, as she's about to place him on the floor, he clings onto her sleeve and yanks at it like a baby orangutan trying to hang from a branch. She tries to latch him free but only manages to let him pull her sleeve higher – which exposes a series of yellow, purple and black bumps at the top of her forearm, a little below the elbow.

She acts as if nothing's happened, calmly lowering her sleeve and then placing Harry on the floor, allowing him to toddle off towards the other side of the café. It's only then that she turns to me, meeting my eyes momentarily and knowing that I saw the bruises.

'I walked into a door,' she says, not keeping eye contact. 'I was trying to deal with Harry and take the washing downstairs and got all caught up. Silly me.'

A pause and I really do feel lost. There might as well be a neon sign over her head flashing the word 'liar'.

'Do you walk into a lot of doors?'

'I—'

'And are all those doors shaped like someone's fingers?' There's a bristling in my stomach, a flash of protective anger that's completely unexpected.

Mum looks off towards Harry, remaining still for a moment: 'It's complicated,' she says softly.

'How complicated can it be?'

She turns back to me and it feels as if she's my disapproving mother. I've brought some lad home who has a face tattoo and enough piercings to turn a magnet into a dangerous weapon.

'There are things that you don't want to talk about, Olive – and I've respected that. All I'm asking for is the same respect.'

'If you're being hurt—'

Mum snaps a reply: 'Don't you think *I* have questions about everything? I'd love to know what's been going on for the past thirteen years. I'd love you to tell the police everything and get some justice. I'd love to see people arrested, to get a day in court. I'd love to look into the eyes of the man who stole my daughter and changed my life. I lie awake at night thinking about all these things. There's a lot of things *I* want – but I've given you space. I've let things go. If you can have your secrets then I can have mine.'

She finishes with a sharp sigh and there's nothing I can say. She's right.

I find myself staring at her sleeve, under which are her bruises. I consider whether she has more on other parts of her body, wonder if it's something new because of me, or if this has been going on a while. The obvious assumption is that it's been done by Max but I get the sense there's a lot I don't know.

In many ways, the silences between us say more than the actual words. It's in those that we're lost in mutual understanding that there are things about each other we'll never know.

'I nearly walked away, y'know…'

Mum focuses on me once more. Blinks.

'When I was here,' I add, pointing towards the table I sat at barely days ago. 'I thought about leaving and not coming back.'

'Why?'

'I was scared. I didn't know if you'd want me back, if I'd have a home here. I didn't know if rejection was worse than taking a chance. I'd forgotten what it was like to have a real mum. I thought you might blame me.'

'For what?'

'I don't know. It's been a long time. I'm not six years old any more.'

Mum stands and her chair scrapes noisily on the floor. She pulls me to her feet and holds me tight. 'I'll always be your mother,' she whispers. 'Always.'

NINETEEN

Mum and I spend more than an hour together in the café. There are a few soft toys in the staff area at the back and Harry is one of those kids who seems perfectly happy amusing himself.

Despite the two of us avoiding a few subjects, I feel closer to my mother because of it. Our reluctance to reveal certain things is something we have in common.

That doesn't mean I'm going to forget those bruises on her arms, though.

When Harry starts to get restless, Mum and I say goodbye and then I walk along the High Street back to the Black Horse. It's perhaps no surprise that there's a welcoming committee. There are two men sitting on a bench at the edge of the pavement and both jump up when they see me. One is fiddling with his phone and the other accidentally drops his bag.

'Are you Olivia Adams?' one of them asks.

They don't seem the pushy types, more haggard and rushed. The one who spoke has a hole in the collar of his shirt. The other is ridiculously young, a straight-out-of-uni-type.

'Who are you?' I ask.

They give their names one at a time. The guy with the hole in his shirt is from the local radio station, the other works for a newspaper. It's not quite a bristling press pack, more a slightly sleepy duo. If they'd have walked down the road, they might have seen me through the café window, so hardly the hardcore investigative types.

They seem surprised that I'm standing and listening, rather than telling them to do one. The radio journalist asks if I'd like to tell my story, despite the fact I've not confirmed my name.

'This is my life,' I tell him. 'How would you feel?'

The older guy tells me what is probably the truth – that people will always have questions unless I go on the record and get everything into the open.

I'm cautious but not stupid, so I ask what sort of questions they have.

'Is there somewhere we can go…?'

I shake my head. 'I'm not saying I'll do this. I'm asking what your questions are. If I have something to say, I will.'

He pulls a radio microphone from his bag and holds it between us, while the other journalist has his phone out and is presumably recording everything being said.

'How do you feel at being back?' the holey shirt man asks.

That's an easy one: 'Stoneridge feels new to me.'

'Do you remember being a child here?'

'It was a long time ago.'

There's a woman on the other side of the road who's stopped to see what's going on. When she realises I've noticed, she turns and continues walking, glancing over her shoulder to see if I'm still watching.

'Where have you been for the past thirteen years?' the holey shirt man asks.

I shake my head, saying nothing and all, and wait until he gets the message that I'm not answering that.

'Can you tell me what happened?'

'I don't want to talk about it.'

If he's frustrated, then he's not showing it. 'What did the police ask you?'

'What do you think?'

He smirks at that: 'I asked and they said they have no comment to make.'

I smile and shrug.

'What do your parents think?'

'You'd have to ask them.'

That does get a sigh, probably because he knows there's not a lot he can use.

'What now?' he asks.

I nod to the Black Horse. 'Now I go and wait for my friends.'

With that, I take a step towards the pub but there is one final question – this from the young newspaper man.

'What do you say to the people who claim you're an imposter?'

That was something I didn't expect.

'Who's saying that?' I reply, far more aggressively than I meant.

The reporter doesn't want to meet my eye. He looks at his outstretched hand and the phone screen instead. 'That's what people are saying,' he replies.

'*Which* people?'

'I'm not sure I should get into specifics…'

I take another step away but he isn't done.

'Will you take a DNA test?'

There's a moment where I hesitate, unsure whether to reply or walk away. I probably should have ignored them in the first place but that sense of being the centre of attention is so powerful. Even though it's not what I want, there's a power to it; a satisfaction at being wanted. I wonder how people who are properly famous deal with it. There are stories of those who go on massive ego trips and I can sense that even in a small way. I don't want money from my mother and yet I could ask for more or less anything and she'd probably agree. I could demand money from the media; not necessarily this pair, but others.

In the end, I walk away. I definitely made a mistake by stopping but there's not much I can do now. Ego over logic. I do wonder who planted the idea of the DNA test. There's no way the journalist would've come up with it by himself because he'd have no reason to doubt anything. The police mentioned it, too. It's not unexpected.

Nattie and Rhys are already waiting in our booth of the Black Horse when I get inside. The usual crowd of full-time drinkers and fruit machine bandits are in and there is a collective turning of heads as I walk towards the booth.

Chris is behind the bar again and, while the other patrons turn away after clocking me, he stares relentlessly. His pimply rash has spread from one side of his face to the other, the sort of severe acne with which only teenagers usually have to deal. I can't work out if he has a lazy eye, or if it's that he's never quite gawking *at* something, more around it. He's watching a spot close to me but not actually staring directly.

I stop a few paces short of the booth and stop to stare back at him. 'Can I help you?' I ask.

When he realises he's been clocked, Chris shakes his head and turns to the row of glasses behind the bar. I stay where I am until he makes another sideways glance in my direction and I hold my hand up and out. *What are you looking at?* I don't need to say anything because he scurries away into the back room, leaving the bar temporarily unattended.

Nattie and Rhys slide around to let me sit. They each have a drink in front of them and then Nattie asks if everything's all right.

I point a thumb towards the bar. 'That Chris guy keeps staring at me.'

'It is out who you are,' Nattie replies. 'I only told my mum, so don't blame me. You could possibly blame her.'

'Not that – he was staring a couple of days ago, before anyone knew. What's his deal?'

The two of them exchange a brief pouty-lip glance. Nattie shrugs: 'He was accused of touching some girl a couple of years ago. I don't think anything came of it – he was never in court or anything – but mud sticks round this place.'

'What girl?'

'No idea – it was a few years ago. I was too young.' Nattie turns to Rhys but he shakes his head.

'I don't remember either,' he replies. 'I do remember my mum telling me not to talk to him though. I think he was homeless or something like that. You'd see him around the park during the day, hanging around and looking a bit shifty. Pete probably felt sorry for him, or something? I don't know if he's a genuine creep-o, or if he's like those weird kids at school that stay weird forever. The blokes you see hanging around the underwear sections in department stores.'

'Does he ever stare at you?'

Nattie tilts her head. 'Sometimes, I guess.'

'It's not only girls,' Rhys adds. 'It's lads, too. Look.' He nods to the bar and, sure enough, Chris is back behind it, staring towards the men at the quiz machine. Or staring *close* to the men at the quiz machine.

'I've never had a problem with him,' Rhys says.

'Me either,' Nattie adds.

Perhaps because he realises we're watching him, Chris turns to look at the three of us. We quickly look away and Nattie changes the subject.

'Those reporters still outside?' she asks.

'Did you see them out there?'

'No – but Pete booted them out about half-hour ago.' She waits and then adds: 'Did you tell them anything?'

'They were asking about DNA tests…'

It's almost imperceptible but there's another quick glance between Nattie and Rhys. 'It does sounds a bit OTT,' Nattie says. 'Like some trashy talk show.'

I pause, unsure if I should say it, and then reply: 'Did somebody say something about a test?'

The glance between the pair is no longer imperceptible. They each fully turn their heads, giving me an answer.

'One of the journalists mentioned it when he was in here,' Nattie says. 'They knew you'd been staying upstairs and were asking around. That's why Pete threw them out.'

'Someone must've mentioned DNA tests to them...'

Neither Rhys or Nattie reply but something's changed and they are each suddenly reaching for their glasses.

'What?' I say.

Nattie chews on the inside of her cheek before answering: 'It's just... this is what people are like. *We* believe who you are. Your mum believes you – but not everyone will. It's that sort of village. People love their little rumours and whispering campaigns. Someone starts gossiping to someone else and the next thing you know, some guy from the newspaper is asking about DNA tests. That's how things go.'

Rhys continues: 'If you end up staying in the village or even you don't, you'll always have this. People want everything to be a conspiracy. Like with those nine-eleven nutters, or the people who think the Tube bombings were done by MI5 or whatever. I guess if you have a DNA test, it shuts everyone up.'

There's a pause and then Nattie sums it up in a way with which I can't argue: 'Isn't that what you want?'

2014: LILY, 17

There's a moment where I wonder if Dad has changed the locks. A grey haze scratches at the edges of my eyes and there are intermittent swirly things that rush towards me until I blink them away. The street lights behind aren't helping – partly because they're not producing much light but mainly because the orange is burning into the colour of the swirly things and making me even dizzier.

The key scrapes along the lock and it's suddenly very funny. Swirly things. Heh. Swirly things are funny.

My forehead is on the glass of the front door. I don't remember resting there but it's really cool and the sharpness makes me incredibly thirsty. There's water inside, of course, except that my key's not working.

Actually, where is my key?

It was in my hand a minute ago except—

Heh, swirly things. All pink and green and orange and swirly.

I wobble slightly as I press away from the glass and the path hurtles up, making me rock back and away from it. A few seconds pass while I try to steady myself, one hand on the door, the other—

Oh, there's my key. It's still in my hand. Did I put it down or something?

This time it slips seamlessly into the lock and, though it feels stiff, the key eventually turns and I fumble inside.

The hallway is dark and I nudge the door with my shoulder, waiting for it to click back into place. I should probably lock it, but when I reach for the catch, the small button in the centre leaps towards me and I can only make it go away by screwing my eyes tightly shut.

That's when the swirly things appear again. They're not so friendly this time. The colours aren't as bright and, rather than dancing for me, there's a red swish that burns angrily.

My head is thundering as I get into the kitchen. The cold of the fridge gives some respite but the light is too bright and I can't focus properly on anything inside. In the end I stick my face under the kitchen tap and sup from it like a dog. The cool water makes everything feel better, evaporating the swirly things and somehow making it easier for me to see through the gloom of the kitchen. I also realise my key is still in my hand.

The slurry of confusion clears from my head almost instantly from the water and I'm suddenly aware of what's happened over the past few minutes. I'm in the kitchen, having fumbled my way into the house. The red digits from the clock on the oven burn 03:17 through the gloom and it feels every inch as if it's three in the morning. I've been awake for far too long. I've drunk way too much. My feet, legs and hips hurt from dancing and generally being on my feet.

I head into the living room without turning on any lights. The lounge chair is calling, if only to help me get off my feet. It's dark, the only light coming from the clock on the cable box and the vague orangey glow of the outside light through the curtains.

'Hi.'

It feels like I jump so high that my head scrapes the ceiling. I'm sure I yelp, possibly scream but everything happens in such a fraction of a second that I'm not entirely sure.

Dad is sitting in the lounger, apparently wide awake.

'Have you been up all night?' I ask. My voice is croaky but firm enough. It doesn't betray my evening.

'I could ask you the same.'

I move onto the sofa, resting my head against the comfortable corner cushion and curling my legs up. The room is so dark that I can only vaguely make out his outline.

'Where've you been?' he asks.

'Out.'

'You're seventeen, Lil. That's all. I'm still responsible for you.'

'I was only out with Zoe.'

'How'd you get home?'

'In a taxi.'

'Where'd the money come from for that? You don't have a job and it wasn't from me.'

There's an edge to his voice and it's obvious something has changed.

'Zoe paid.'

It's the first thing that falls into my mind but an obvious lie.

'Zoe?'

'Right – she got some money off her mum.'

'So Zoe bought you drinks all night? Paid for your taxi? Paid for entry, or whatever else you spent…?'

From nowhere, there's a pneumatic drill going off at the front of my head. There's a dull throb underneath as well. The double whammy of drunken headaches.

'Can we do this another time?' I say.

'What's wrong with your head?'

'Tired, that's all.'

With a flick of his wrist, he flips something across the room, which lands on my lap. I have to pick it up to realise it's a small ziplock polythene bag.

'Sure it's not something to do with those…?'

I run my thumb across the half-dozen disc-shaped tablets in the packet. There's no chance of riding this out.

'What were you doing in my room?'

'*That's* your answer? I find drugs in my daughter's bedroom and she's worried about how I found them, not why she has them. If you want to know, I was emptying your bin and – as you clearly know – they were taped to the underside of your desk. I wasn't snooping, though perhaps I should.'

He sighs long, waiting for an answer I don't provide.

'What are they?' he asks eventually.

'It's just a bit of E, Dad. Everyone does it.'

'*Everyone?* Who are you hanging around with?'

I have no reply. What's the point in saying Zoe's name when he already knows that?

'Are you taking them yourself?' he asks.

'I've tried it. Not really my thing.'

'Are you dealing?'

This time he waits and waits. We sit in the darkness for what feels like an age.

'Does it matter?' I reply.

Even longer passes. Dad doesn't move and neither do I. The night is filled with his disappointment and it hurts so much more than the headache.

It's a really long time until he speaks again. When he does, it's more of a sigh than a statement. 'I don't know what's going on with you, Lil. Do you think your mother would be proud of you? Of your school results? The going out all the time? Now this?'

The breath catches in my throat and it feels as if my tonsils have swollen to twice their size. There's a massive lump that I can't swallow.

I can't speak, so Dad does. 'I'm not saying I've covered myself in glory,' he says. 'I've made mistakes. I know what I've done… but this. C'mon, Lil… what were you thinking?'

We sit in the dark for another long while. The only clock in the living room sits high on the wall and is shrouded by shadow.

'I wanted to get caught.'

The words are out before I can take them back.

'Why?'

'So somebody would ask me why.'

'*I'm* asking you why.'

More silence. I'm trying to think of the words and then they come. The sentences I'd practised in bed over and over but never spoken. Dad can do nothing but listen in increasing horror and fury as I tell him about Uncle Alan.

2015: LILY, 18

The police car stops me dead. I'm at the corner of our road, facing the house and it's parked directly outside: one single white vehicle with fluorescent stripes along the side. The word POLICE blazes bright along the street.

Dad.

I race across the road but in the handful of seconds it takes for me to get to the other kerb, the front door opens. And there he is: my father is fine. He's smiling and happy, cracking a joke with a pair of police officers who are a little in front of him. The three of them all shake hands and then the officers return to their car and pull away as I watch on.

Dad is about to head back inside when he spots me a little way up the street. He hesitates, the door in one hand as he waves with the other. My heart is still racing as I try to calmly walk to the house but Dad must see it in my face.

'You all right, Lil?'

'I… um… I saw the car and I thought…'

It takes him a moment to realise and then he's apologising, even though it's not his fault. 'Oh, Lil, come here…'

I do and he hugs me close. We've not done this for a long time and it's only now that I realise how much I've missed it. I might be eighteen but sometimes there's nothing better than being that little girl.

He releases me and then we're in the house. 'They were asking about shed thefts,' Dad says. 'Someone broke into the one two doors down and they wanted to know if I'd heard anything. There have been a few in the local area.'

We move into the kitchen, where there are three upturned mugs on the draining board.

'I should've thought,' Dad says. 'After everything with your mother. Did you think I was...?'

He tails off, unable to say the word 'dead'.

The problem is, that's not what I was thinking at all. It should have been. One time it would've been.

Dad realises and then he slumps back against the fridge. 'Oh, Lil...'

We stare at each other for a moment and there's a moment of absolute clarity where it feels like he can read my mind. He knows what I'm thinking.

'What happened, Dad?'

He shakes his head and moves into the living room, switching on the television and slumping into the lounger. I follow, putting myself between him and the TV and then snatching the remote control from the armrest.

'Lil...'

'It's been nearly a year, Dad.'

He scratches his head and then pinches the top of his nose. All of a sudden, he seems very old. The wrinkles in his face are deeper, the muscles on his arms that used to bulge when he spun me around have shrunk.

He's very, very human.

'Why do you want to know?' he replies. He didn't before, but he sounds tired now. 'You've turned it around, Lil. Retaken your exams, you're doing what you always should've done. What does it matter?'

I squat down and sit on the floor in front of him, almost like it's story time.

It feels as if he's ageing in front of me. He squeezes his nose again and the folds of skin on his knuckles almost crinkle back on themselves. There's something bone-shiveringly horrifying when it becomes clear that parents are mortal. To most kids, mums and dads are superheroes; the fountains of all knowledge and wisdom. They can do anything… until they can't. I learnt that when Mum died and now it feels like I'm learning it all over again.

'Do you really want to know?' he says quietly.

'I do.'

'Because there's no going back afterwards.'

'I want to know.'

He nods crisply and that's that. He jumps up and tells me to get my jacket. A couple of minutes later and we're in the car. Dad doesn't say a word as he drives off the estate and heads for the ring road. It's not long before we're surrounded by green, the roads narrow, the hedges high. The soundtrack is some play on Radio Four but all I hear are voices talking at one another. The words don't go in and I don't risk saying anything.

It's around fifteen minutes before Dad checks his mirror and indicates, before turning off the road. He stops on a gravelly lay-by next to a wide metal gate between two hedges and then switches off the engine.

'Is this it?' I ask.

Dad doesn't reply, opening his door and rounding the car until he's standing next to the gate. I follow, but it feels as if we're in the middle of nowhere.

'Where are we?' I ask.

Dad puts a foot on the lower rung of the gate and hoists himself over, then he starts to walk along the hedge line. It's much more of a stretch for me to get over and I narrowly avoid a puddle on my jump down as I follow. For every one of his strides, I'm taking at least one and a half and am almost jogging to keep up as he continues relentlessly until he reaches a stile between a pair of overgrown hedges that connects two fields. He waits for me to go first and then tells me to stop when I'm standing at the highest point.

'What can you see?' he asks.

I stare out into the distance towards half a dozen large four- or five-bedroom houses and a larger expanse of mud.

'Some random houses,' I reply.

'It's called Queen's Landing. One of the companies I used to do some work for are building an exclusive estate.'

'We're in the middle of nowhere.'

'Not exactly but… that's the point. The people with the money to buy those homes are the ones who want to live in the privacy of a small private estate in the middle of nowhere. They're building it in two stages. The first set of houses were finished a couple of months ago and the next lot are about a year off. It should be quite nice when it's all done.'

I slouch down so that I'm sitting on the rail at the top of the stile. 'I don't understand why you've brought me here.'

'They were laying the foundations for the first set of houses about a year ago.'

I don't understand at first what the house-building has to do with Uncle Alan. Then it hits me.

'Oh…'

It's all I can say. Nothing, really.

Dad reaches up and lifts me down and then we both lean on the stile, looking out towards the housing development. If someone ever goes digging deep down beneath their patio, they might get a surprise.

'I love you,' Dad whispers.

I wrap my arm around his waist, tucking my head underneath his armpit and waiting for him to put his arm around me.

'This isn't who I am,' he says.

'I know.'

'It's just… sometimes people need to be put down like dogs. I know that sounds awful. I know, I know, I know. There's a huge part of me that doesn't think that – but it's true. I wish it wasn't, but it is. People will never say it. They refuse to think those things but, honestly, some people in this world are bad. There's no better way of putting it. They're bad people, Lil, and rehabilitation will never work. They don't deserve another chance. They deserve to be put down like the dogs they are.'

He squeezes my shoulder.

'I let you down, Lil. A father's supposed to look out for his daughter but I didn't do that. I can never say sorry – but all I *can* say is that he won't do it again.'

I allow myself to be pulled closer. I can feel Dad's heartbeat through his top, racing and spiking. I've made him this, turned him into a person he wasn't.

And it's so hard not to wish I'd never said a word about Uncle Alan.

TWENTY

SATURDAY

The scientist from the lab doesn't look particularly sciencey in the sense that there's no white coat or glasses. I realise that sounds ridiculous but sometimes the cliché is comforting. She's mid-twenties at most, her hair is down and she's in trendy tight jeans. Police officers should be big burly blokes that ooze authority; dentists should be evil – and scientists should wear white coats and glasses.

Her name is Cassie and she turns from my mother to me and holds up a pair of giant cotton buds that must be fifteen centimetres long. 'All it takes is a mouth swab from each of you,' she says. 'You rub the soft end into the inside of your cheek, get it nice and moist and then put it into one of these tubes.'

The tubes are long and thin – and there is a separate bag for each to be stored within.

Mum is handed her swab and I take mine. It's an extended version of the type of thing I've used to clear out my ears in the past. Not a pleasant thought.

Things moved ridiculously quickly after talking to Nattie and Rhys in the Black Horse. I called Mum to say I wanted to do a DNA test with her to get rid of any doubt. She was surprised and said it wasn't necessary – but I made the same argument Nattie, Rhys, the journalist and DI McMichael had. If we didn't do this, there will always be doubt. The whispers will never go away.

I thought it would take a while to set up. Days, for sure; perhaps a week. It's the next morning and here we are. Through Mum's 'friends of friends', she knows someone who manages a laboratory. Among other things, one of their specialities is analysing DNA. It's a booming thing on the Internet, apparently, largely with fathers wanting to check for sure that their new baby is indeed their own. Broken Britain again, I guess.

It feels murky, that if somebody doubts that sort of thing, there's probably something wrong with the relationship regardless of what any test might show.

We agreed to meet at Mum's house the next morning and it's turned out to be something of a sideshow. As well as Mum, myself and Harry; Max and Ashley are both here. It seems the two brothers are rarely apart. When I first met her, Georgie said they were practically conjoined and that's proved to be true. Max was dealing with Harry when I got to the house but Ashley had watched me in the way a fox stalks a hen. His skin is so brown that it looks like he's been sleeping on the sun. He's not shaved for a few days and his stubble is becoming sharp, with grey pepper-pot specks eating into the black.

Luckily for me, it's not the Pitman brothers against just me. Nattie is at my side and it feels like everyone is on their best behaviour because of her. Not counting Cassie from the laboratory, Nattie is the only person in the conservatory who isn't a member of this family.

Mum holds her swab up a little higher. 'You don't have to do this,' she says to me.

'I want to.'

I speak to her but look towards Max and Ashley, who are both focusing on me. Ashley in particular looks as though I've given him a quadratic equation and asked for an instant answer. He doesn't understand what's happening. It's probably him who started talking about DNA tests and the like. *Whispers*, as Nattie and Rhys said. It's what the village runs on, and who better to start those whispers than a taxi driver?

Have you seen the new girl in the Black Horse? Have you heard who she is? Do you think it's her? Do you really *think it's her? It's been thirteen years. It could be anyone. What do you think?*

That's all it takes. One person tells another, who tells another – and suddenly police officers are knocking on the door and journalists are asking about DNA tests.

If it was Ashley, then he got what he wanted – or he thought he did. He thought I'd find a reason to avoid this, guilty until proven innocent, and yet here I am, swab in hand.

Mum is more nervous than me. This is the seventh or eighth time she's told me I don't have to do this. The swab doesn't go near her mouth as she turns back to the scientist.

'What happens next?' she asks.

If Cassie senses the tension in the room, she doesn't show it. 'I can get as technical as you want but, in essence, we extract and compare the saliva from the two swabs. Every cell in the human body contains a complete set of DNA. Most of the DNA between all human beings is the same – but we look for specific genetic markers that vary from person to person. A child receives half of his or her DNA from a mother and the other half from the father. Your DNA is what we'll start with. Let's call that DNA Sarah. After that, we'll check Olivia's. If Olivia is Sarah's daughter, we would expect to see her make-up to be half DNA Sarah and half DNA Dad.'

'How long does it take?' I ask.

'My boss says this is a special case, so we'll be working on it straight away. I'd imagine you should have an answer by Monday.'

'Is it accurate?' I ask.

'It's very close to one hundred per cent. There are more than seven billion people on the earth, so there might be a chance someone else shares an identical DNA sequence – but the chance of that person knowing about it and then tracking down the person with whom they share an identical genome... well, that's about as close to zero per cent as you can get.'

It doesn't get a lot more conclusive than that. I grip the swab tighter. 'So if our results come back as a match, there's no doubt we're mother and daughter?'

'No question at all.'

I open my mouth ready to collect the saliva but Mum puts a hand on my wrist and locks me into a stare. 'You don't have to.'

It's only with the gaze that I realise she doesn't know what she believes. There might be a part that wants to trust everything I've said but there's a voice in there somewhere saying it can't be true. *Whispers.* Perhaps from Max, Ashley or others around the village; perhaps her own internal monologue.

She prefers the *idea* of her long-lost daughter returning to having that wrecked by science.

Losing a daughter once is soul-destroying, losing one twice is something from which not many would be strong enough to recover.

'I want to do this,' I say.

I don't break the stare as I swish the cotton end around the inside of my mouth and drop it into the tube. Cassie plugs the top and then places it into the bag. Mum hesitates, holding the swab in front of her mouth.

'You can do it,' I say. 'Trust me.'

There is a second of hesitation but then she does. She twirls and swishes the swab around like a toothbrush and then the scientist does the rest.

I know in that moment that she actually does trust me. It's a burden I know I can't betray.

'That's that,' Cassie says cheerily and then she packs her things away. She wishes us well before saying she's going directly to the lab.

There's an unspoken malaise after she's left, as if there are two tribes ready to clash, with Mum in the middle as referee. There's also a sense of disbelief. At the absolute least, Ashley did not think

I'd go through with it, yet I wonder if the person who is most surprised is Mum. She's watching Harry toddle around but there's an emptiness about her expression.

Max is harder to read. He sits on the sofa next to his wife, hand on her shoulder, and asks if she's okay. 'Won't be long,' he assures her, but I don't know if he's talking about the length of time for the results to return, or some apparent confidence that it 'won't be long' before I'm exposed as a fraudster.

'Can we talk?' I ask.

He looks up to me and there's a moment where it feels like everyone else is staring between us.

'*Me?*' Max replies.

'Just us. Somewhere else for a couple of minutes.'

'What do you want to say?'

'I'd rather we could talk alone…'

Mum is frozen as Max looks to his brother blankly and then pushes himself up from the sofa, leading me through the house until we're in the kitchen. He closes the door and rests against it. His features are nowhere near as hardened as his brother's and, now I'm able to see them apart, I can understand a little of what Mum might have seen in him. He has a strong jaw and set-back eyes that make his cheekbones almost angular. His voice is a little softer than Ashley's and I wonder if he's one of those siblings who ends up browbeaten by the older brother; who feels constantly in the shadow of the child who came before.

'You're going to be my stepdad,' I say.

'You sound very sure.'

'I know what the test will show.'

He nods shortly. It's hardly welcoming but it's better than outright hostility.

'I want you to know that it means something to me,' I add. 'I hope we can get on and have some sort of relationship, if only for Mum's sake.'

He takes his time, breathing in and staring into my very soul. It's like he's trying to see me for what or who I am. 'Is that right?'

'Isn't that what *you* want?'

His nose wrinkles, as if there's a bad smell in the room. He takes a long breath and glances away towards the door, perhaps wondering if there's someone listening on the other side. His voice might be softer than his brother's but he knows how to turn it on. When he replies, it's with a low growl. A wolf warning off a potential predator.

'Whoever you are, whatever your name is, however that test comes back: one kid is more than enough for me.'

His eyes burn into mine, making sure I understand and then, with that, he turns and opens the door.

TWENTY-ONE

The front door swings inwards and Mrs Winter – Janet – stands staring at me. It takes her a moment to place who I am and then her face brightens.

'Olivia, my dear. You're back. I've been hearing all about you. I did wonder if you might return. You should've said who you were when you were asking about your mother.'

The woman who now owns my parents' old house is excited, like a rock star has turned up at her door. Given her age and the fact it doesn't look like she gets out much, it's more testament to how quickly news spreads around this place. She turns to the man at my side and clearly doesn't recognise him.

'How can I help?' she asks.

'I was hoping my dad and I could have a look around the house. Nothing intrusive, nothing you're unhappy about, I'm trying to jog a few memories…'

Mrs Winter looks to Dad and gawks. She can't believe it's him and, in many ways, neither can I. All the facial hair has gone, as have the baggy old clothes. Now he's in something that fits, he looks trim and in shape. I doubt that's the truth underneath. He's underweight and undernourished – but the impression is enough. He looks at least ten years younger than since I last saw him and, more importantly, he no longer smells. It's possible to stand next to him and not want to gag.

'Good afternoon, Janet,' Dad says politely.

'Daniel… you look very, um… different.'

She holds the door open and says we're welcome to look around. As soon as we get into the kitchen, Dad is saying how nice everything is. Turning on a bit of the charm Georgie told me about from when he was younger. Everything has been refitted with stainless steel taps and thick, solid worktops. He talks about where things used to be, the thin patchy linoleum from the floor; the plastic appliances and the time when the sink leaked and he woke up to a mini flood.

The living room is full of ornaments, tat and framed photographs, but Dad talks about where the television used to be and the old battered pair of sofas that took up one half of the room. He's very complimentary to what Mrs Winter has done to the place and the pride beams from her face.

She asks if we'd like to see the garden and it's only then that Dad hesitates. As I head outside, he stands on the precipice of the door watching. Mrs Winter has disappeared back into the house somewhere.

'Are you sure?' he asks – but I'm already on the lawn. It's bowling-green perfect and the whole space is meticulously looked after. Flower beds run along both sides and there is a small apple tree in the far corner. At the furthest end is a metal gate that's taller than me and connected to a tidy hedge that runs the full width of the garden.

'Come on,' I say, offering him my hand. Dad steps tentatively forward and takes it. We head along the lawn together until we reach the metal table and chairs. It's surrounded by green, like something Alice might find on the other side of the looking glass. A proper English country garden.

We pass the table and chairs, continuing on to the gate and pressing against the bars to look both ways along the narrow lane. It's crumbling and dank, surrounded by hedges or fence panels on both sides, the type of land that will never quite dry out.

'I've not been out here in thirteen years,' Dad says quietly. He shivers as if someone's walked across his grave. His confidence and charisma has slipped.

He doesn't say anything else but then he pulls on my fingers, leading me back to the table where we sit. He gulps and it looks like he might start to cry, though he just about holds it together.

'This was our first house,' he says. 'We thought we'd be paying the mortgage on it forever, but I guess things didn't work out quite like that.'

Small beads of sweat are forming above his eyebrows. It's a warm day and he's bald. He should probably be wearing a hat. It's odd to find myself concerned for him.

'How did you meet?' I ask.

He turns back towards the house and blinks, then he's focused on me once more.

'We were at a house party,' he says. 'I was twenty or twenty-one, something like that. Sarah was a little younger. I'd only moved to the village a couple of weeks before and one of the neighbours had a lad who was about my age. It was a friend of a friend thing. I hardly knew anyone in Stoneridge and thought I'd end up sitting in the corner by myself all evening.'

He curves his lips into an O and scratches his chin. 'Most memories fade,' he says quietly. 'There's a time when you're not sure if what you think happened is what actually happened. It doesn't help that I spent so long… well, you know… but I remember the moment I saw Sarah. It was like, *ping!*, as if someone turned on a light or something. There were no awkward introductions. I said "hi", she said "hi" and then we spent the whole evening talking about everything and anything. She liked hearing about places other than here.'

'She told me that.'

His eyes widen. 'Did she?'

'I think she remembers it, too.'

'Oh… I didn't know that.' He stops and stares back towards the house. 'She used to talk about how she felt trapped here because she knew everyone and everyone knew her. We'd go for these really long walks, following the river out of the village for miles before turning around and coming back again. We didn't have any money to do much else. It wasn't long and then she was pregnant.'

'She told me unplanned didn't mean unwanted.'

Dad looks to me and then nods slowly. 'That's a good way of putting it. It sounds horrible, like it was some massive accident and there you were – but it didn't feel like that. We were young. It's not like we sat down and talked about having children, getting married and all that. Things happened and they felt right. We thought we were going to live here forever.'

'Didn't you and Mum ever think of moving away?'

He raises an eyebrow. 'Why would we?'

'You said Mum liked hearing about other places and different things – and yet she's lived here all her life.'

'Oh…' He frowns and runs a hand across the top of his head. 'I suppose it never came up. I don't know. Everything changed so fast that I don't think it occurred to us to move. Stoneridge felt like home.'

'Do you remember the day I was born?'

Dad doesn't answer at first because Mrs Winter toddles down the path with a plate loaded high with sandwiches and cakes. 'I thought you might be hungry,' she says. 'There are tuna and cucumber, or egg salad.'

She puts the plate on the table between us and then returns a moment later with a jug of what she calls 'home-made fresh ginger beer'. Ice cubes are bobbing on top and I'm not sure I've ever felt more British.

'It's lovely to see you both,' Mrs Winter says, 'you can drop round any time.'

We each thank her and then she heads back into the house, leaving us alone in the back garden. Dad takes one of the egg sandwiches and I leave him to it. There's no question he needs the food more than me. I wonder when he last had a proper meal.

'You came exactly on your due date,' Dad says. 'Everyone has a story about babies who come really early or late; or perhaps there's a complication with the birth. Not you. You were out on time, average weight, perfectly healthy. Everything was fine.'

There's quiet for a moment. Distant chirps of birds, the buzzing of bees and flies in the flower beds. A gentle hustle of breeze.

'Why do you believe me?' I ask, surprising myself.

It's the wrong question – a dangerous, stupid question – and yet I've been dying to ask it of someone. Is it blind faith, like people who are religious? They're not necessarily wrong about the existence of a higher power and yet they can't prove they're right. It's all about belief. Is that what I am to my parents? An idea in which they desperately want to believe because it allows them to make some sort of sense of the past thirteen years?

Dad bites his lip. 'I see your mother in you,' he says.

It's more or less what Mum said when she talked about my eyes. It's recognition – and I don't think I fathom it. Is it a parental thing? There *are* physical similarities between my mother and me but how is that enough?

I'm completely ambivalent. I want people to question me and probe and yet I would rather say nothing. I don't understand how both things can be true.

'It's not physical,' he adds and I blink, stunned that my father has somehow read my thoughts. 'There's an essence of her in you. The way you speak, the way you walk, the way you... *are*.'

That's my answer, like it or not. I *am* my mother's daughter.

'I submitted for a DNA test this morning.'

Dad stops, sandwich halfway to his mouth. 'You what?'

'People were suspicious, so Mum and I had our cheeks swabbed. The results will be back on Monday.'

'Did she make you?'

'No. It wasn't her decision. It was mine.'

'Oh…' The sandwich hangs in limbo for a moment before he takes another bite.

Neither of us speak for a while and I wonder what he's thinking. There's bravado in what I've done. Confidence. Willingly taking that test – having it be my idea – was a statement.

'I had a job with the council,' he adds, moving on. 'Sarah was working at a supermarket. It's not like now where house prices have gone crazy. We were doing okay and we saved up enough to get married. Sarah's mum, your grandmother, didn't want much to do with us and it was only a few months after the wedding that she passed.'

He digs into his pocket and takes out his wallet, flipping through the sections and then passing it across to me. There's a small version of the wedding photo that I've seen before. Mum, Dad, Georgie and two three-year-old bridesmaids. I don't ask why he's still carrying it all these years after the divorce.

'It was a nice day,' he says. 'Sunny, straightforward. The vicar at the church did the whole thing for free because he'd known Sarah since she was born. I think she'd been christened there. That meant we didn't have to spend too much. I wish I had more stories to tell you, but everything was so smooth. The only controversy was your grandmother not turning up – but Sarah told everyone she was ill, so that wasn't even a problem.' He pauses, then adds: 'She wasn't even lying.'

'What about your father?'

Dad finishes the sandwich and reaches for another. If it was up to me, he'd eat everything on the plate. Now his beard has been shaved away, it's clear that his cheeks have hollowed inwards. He's like one of the old photos of prisoners of war.

'He died within a week or so of Sarah's mum. It came from nowhere. He was seemingly healthy and working at the practice. He was always really clean-living – didn't smoke, didn't drink, ate well, ran every morning – but then he had brain cancer. One day he was fine; six or seven weeks later, he died.'

I let out a long, low whistle. It's hard not to. It must have been devastating.

Dad seemingly reads my mind again. 'It could've been worse,' he says. 'A long, slow, painful death would've been awful. At least this way he didn't have to gradually fall apart. I think it was probably for the best.'

He finishes his second sandwich as I sit and take it in. He's right. I suppose I've never thought of it like that before.

'Mum said you argued...'

It doesn't need any further explanation because Dad knows I'm talking about the day of the disappearance.

'She never forgave me.'

'She was upset...'

He shakes his head. '*I* never forgave me. I shouldn't have left you alone. Your mother and I said the most awful things to each other. Every day you didn't come back was another day we got more and more vicious. I don't think there was any way back after that. Even if you'd reappeared a week later, we'd gone too far. We stayed married for another year or so but we were done.'

Dad finishes another sandwich, tuna this time, and reaches for a fourth.

'What about Max?'

I suppose I expect a hint of defiance or resentment, but there's nothing. Dad simply bites into his sandwich and chews. 'There was always something between them,' he says. 'Childhood sweethearts, you know? A first-love thing. It wasn't a problem, but I knew she always had a soft spot for him and he for her. I understood it and didn't mind. Living here, it was impossible not to run into one another. I'd see Max and his brother out and about but there were never any problems.'

'They didn't give you a hard time?'

Dad shakes his head. 'No… but they were around a lot when the search started. Everyone in the community knew the Pitman brothers and Ashley sort of became the centre of that. I didn't think he'd ever met you – certainly not in any way other than perhaps seeing you out and about with your mum. But, afterwards, when the police were around, when the papers were here – with everyone watching – he was somehow a spokesman for the village. I suppose I don't blame him. Your mother and I were too busy arguing among ourselves to notice but I think that's when it started. Ashley and Max would be out as part of the search team and then Sarah would be interacting with them through that. There was a time where I guess it all became inevitable. Sarah and I broke up and then she started seeing Max.'

'Didn't you mind?'

He holds up sandwich number five, offering it to me, though I shake my head. There's only one left and I hope he eats that, too.

'I'd found another companion by then.'

I almost ask 'who?' but it dawns that he's not talking about a person.

'I wanted her to be happy,' he adds. 'If Max makes her happy, then great. We were never going to have that.' He looks up and smiles sadly. 'I'm glad you're back,' he says.

TWENTY-TWO

It's not even been a week and yet it feels like I've slotted into a routine of spending each evening drinking with Nattie. Rhys is with us this time, our trio slumped into the usual booth in the Black Horse. Even the rounds are identical: two Guinnesses for Rhys and me; cider for Nattie.

Nattie had an afternoon shift at the café after the mouth swab at Mum's house this morning. She hasn't asked what I talked to Max about in the kitchen but she is interested to hear about the time I spent at the old house with Dad. We talk for a while but there's not a lot to report. She asks if it brought back memories but I have to say no. Nattie says she doesn't really know my dad – but that's no particular surprise. It sounds like he's only had one relationship of note for a long, long time.

The pub is the busiest I've seen it, with almost all the tables occupied and many more people standing in the various corners. There's a constant chirp from the various fruit and quiz machines, not to mention the buzz of conversation.

It isn't simply paranoia, there's no question I've been noticed. As people pass on the way to the toilets, they glance in our direction. Others stare over their pint glasses or around their friends. I see some muttering to their friends and then turning in our direction before quickly spinning away again. People are trying to watch in a not-watching kind of way, but it's so overt that Nattie and Rhys have both noticed.

'We have a famous friend,' Nattie says with a nudge to Rhys.

'You've put the village on the map once,' he says, 'now you're doing it again. You won't forget the little people, will you…?'

Nattie slides a beer mat across the table, though it sticks to the surface halfway between us. 'Do you do autographs?' she asks. 'Or selfies?'

They laugh and, though I join in, it's all a little too close. I'm not sure what I expected.

Time to change the subject: 'What do people do around the village?' I ask.

Nattie and Rhys reply at the same time: 'This!'

'Go to the pub? Is that all?'

'We sometimes visit the city,' Nattie replies, 'but it's a lot of hassle getting in and out. No buses, taxis are really expensive and there's no point in driving if you want a few drinks. Most of the time we hang around here. We go to the park if we're skint, but sometimes the police move us on even if we're only sitting and talking. It's like we're fourteen or something – but there's a lot of coffin-dodgers around and they've got nothing better to do than complain. It's like living in an old people's home half the time.'

'You're not saying much to make me want to stay…'

Nattie laughs and finishes her drink. 'It's different,' she says. 'Not bad, not necessarily good – just different. Stoneridge is all family and neighbourhood. Most people born here end up living sixty or seventy-odd years on the same street.'

'Do you like soaps?' Rhys asks.

'I shower if that's what you're asking.'

He grins. 'Soaps on TV. That's what it's like living here sometimes. You end up with these really silly feuds. Families who hate other families because of something that happened thirty years ago. Nobody even remembers what the original spark was, they just know that they hate one another. There were these two lads in my school who were always fighting and that was back when they were six or seven years old. They didn't have anything against each other specifically but one of their dads claimed the other one's dad had sold him a dodgy bike when *they* were kids. It was some old BMX thing, probably a rust bucket – but they'd been arguing over it ever since. *That's* what Stoneridge is about, if you ask me. It looks like a sleepy, quiet place to be until you actually live here. Then you realise it's constant drama.'

'You lived in London,' Nattie says. 'What was that like?'

I hide behind my drink for a mouthful. 'Big,' I reply. 'Lots of people all the time. It never stops.'

'I guess you either like that or you don't,' Nattie says. 'If you're a city person, then fair enough. Sometimes I think I might be, but every time I go shopping somewhere big, I always want to kick off with people for walking so slowly. They should have fast lanes and slow lanes on the pavement. It's like all the slow walkers are drawn to the cities. I can live without that. I'd end up on a manslaughter charge.'

'You'd get off,' Rhys said. 'Any jury would accept that as a reason.'

We laugh and then Rhys collects the empty glasses before heading off to the bar. I tell Nattie I'm off to the ladies' and am in the hallway when I remember the toilet in my room upstairs is much nicer than the communal one for the bar. The box from Mum's house that's filled with articles and photos is up there, too – and a trip to the toilet is the perfect opportunity to have a quick skim of whatever's next in the stack. I feel drawn to the information.

The stairs are particularly creaky, each step squeaking angrily as I head up. I fumble with my keys, unlocking and pushing open my door in one crisp movement.

I freeze as soon as I enter the room. Instinct screams there's something wrong but it takes my eyes a moment to catch up.

And there it is.

Chris is crouched next to the bed, hunting through the box that's filled with articles and photos, oblivious to the fact that I'm watching on.

TWENTY-THREE

'What the hell are you doing?'

Chris jumps, having apparently not heard me entering the room. He falls backwards from his crouching position, landing on his backside. His eyes widen as he turns to stare in my general direction. It's hard to tell if he's actually looking *at* me. I have no idea what's going on with the rash across his neck, chin and cheeks, but it's grown even more since I last saw him, like the bruised bobbly surface of a smushed blackberry.

'That's my stuff,' I say. 'What are you doing?'

He opens his mouth but only a croak escapes.

I march across the room and grab the box's lid from the bed. I check the first few layers of articles but it doesn't look as if anything has been moved. I jam the lid on the top and then push the box back under the bed to where it was in the first place. Chris is still on his backside, shuffling around like a tipsy crab and I'm on my feet standing over him.

'What are you doing?' I repeat.

'I… um… cleaning.'

The door to the toilet is open and there's a bucket and mop in there. There's also a basket in the corner of the bedroom that's filled with folded sheets. It's not quite a hotel's cleaning cart – but then this isn't quite a hotel.

Before I can say anything else, Pete appears in the doorway. He looks between us and it must seem like quite the sight. Chris is shuffling backwards away from me, still on his backside.

'I heard shouting…' he says, still looking between us.

I'd not realised I'd raised my voice.

'Is everything all right?' he adds.

'He was going through my stuff.'

Pete frowns towards Chris but there's something about his conflicted expression that makes me feel as if he doesn't believe me.

'Cleaning,' Chris says.

I nudge the box with my foot. 'He pulled this out from under the bed and was going through it.'

Chris shakes his head. He's staring at his feet, rocking back and forth. 'Pulled it out to change the sheet. The lid came off.'

My stomach feels like it's sinking, as if I've not eaten all day.

'Is that what you saw?' Pete asks me.

'I don't know… maybe.'

'Chris got in late,' Pete replies. 'He had a few problems, so it was fine. He does the guest room cleaning for a bit of extra money. He's cleaned your room every day you've been here.'

'Oh. I didn't know that.'

'Because he was late, he hadn't had a chance to clean in here yet. I figured since you were enjoying yourself downstairs that it wouldn't be a problem. That's my fault – I didn't mean for anyone's privacy to be invaded.'

He's spoken so calmly and sensibly that I've gone from bristling with righteous anger to feeling like a complete idiot.

Pete glances down to Chris, who has hooked his arms around his knees and is continuing to rock back and forth. He crouches and rests a hand on the man's shoulder, whispering that it's okay, that he's safe and he's done nothing wrong. I sit on the bed and watch, willing the floor to open up and swallow me. I feel *tiny*.

When Chris stops rocking, Pete offers him a hand and helps him up. He says he should go downstairs, where he can take his break or return to the bar. Chris says 'bar' and then he shuffles out of the room, not risking a look back before I hear the creak of the stairs.

Pete stands and motions towards the bed, asking if I mind. When I say it's fine, he sits. I'm at one end by the pillows, he's at the foot.

'I know that look,' he says.

'What look?'

'People have told you things about Chris, haven't they?'

'I, um…'

He relaxes a little, shoulders slumping. 'It's okay. I see it a lot around here. That's the problem with Stoneridge. Mud sticks. Whatever people say you are becomes the truth. It takes a lot to escape that.'

He sighs again and then adds: 'It's not true. If you've heard he touched some girl, it never happened. He was attacked – *he* was the victim – and instead of getting any sort of justice for what happened, all these rumours started.'

If I was feeling small before then I'm subatomic now.

'There's no reason for you to know this,' Pete says. 'I should've said something.'

'Who attacked him?'

Pete shakes his head a little. 'The other person thought it'd be funny. When the police got involved, he said Chris had touched his girlfriend somewhere intimately, but it was an excuse to get off the assault charge. Chris never touched anyone.'

He turns away a little, breaking eye contact: 'I don't say this to be mean but I don't think he'd know what he was doing if he was alone with a woman, let alone touch her somewhere like that. He ended up with a double insult. Not only did he get a kicking, everyone in the village then thought he was some kind of sex pest.'

'Why did the police believe whoever beat him up?'

'Because there were apparent witnesses. Two or three people all had the same story – and you can see what Chris is like. He can barely speak up for himself as it is, let alone when there are police there.'

'Who were the witnesses?'

Pete doesn't speak for a while. He looks to me and then clamps his lips closed before standing. He paces to the window and back again, before pushing the door fully closed and lowering his voice.

'I shouldn't really say.'

'It was Ashley Pitman, wasn't it? That's why he's barred from here. He beat up Chris.'

Pete bites his lip and nods. 'Look, I know he's your family now. Uncle, or whatever, so I don't want to say much more. I'm not trying to stir up trouble. It was a while ago.'

'You can say whatever. Ashley basically told me to leave the village and not come back.'

Pete paces again and then stops by the bed. He looks to me as if trying to decide whether that's true. He doesn't seem completely surprised that my uncle wants me gone.

'Max was one of the witnesses, too, wasn't he?' I ask.

A slow nod: 'Right.'

'Who else?'

'You wouldn't know her. One of Ashley's ex-girlfriends. She moved away not long after that.'

'But you're saying Ashley beat up Chris for no reason…?'

Pete nods.

'Were you there?'

'I didn't need to be. I believe him and I've known Ashley Pitman for a long time. We were at school together. You could say we've got history.'

'What sort of history?'

There's a creak from the landing and Pete glances back over his shoulder towards the closed door.

'Is someone out there?' I ask.

'It's an old building. The pipes hiss and clunk, the stairs and floorboards squeak even when there's no one anywhere near them. I've woken up in the middle of the night convinced there's someone downstairs but there never has been. It's like the pub itself is talking. Used to scare the crap out of me. It takes a while to get used to.'

He goes for another pace to the window and back, then he stops and rolls up his top, turning side on for me to see the area around his left kidney. A purply-brown scar that laces from his lower back around his side.

'What's that?' I ask.

'It was a long time ago but that's how I know the type of man Ashley Pitman is.'

He lets his top drop back into place and then rounds the bed.

'I don't want to get involved in family stuff and, in fairness, it's not like any of this happened recently. You're talking a few years back. All I'm trying to say is that Chris is all right. He's got a lazy eye and isn't very confident at talking to people but it's a self-fulfilling thing. He hears people saying mean things about him, so he doesn't want to engage – but, because he's not engaging, people say more mean things. Just know that you don't need to be wary of him. If you say "hi", you'll get that back. If you catch him staring, smile back and he'll move on. He doesn't even know he's doing it.'

I feel like a playground bully.

'What if I want to know about the family stuff?'

'How do you mean?'

'You said you didn't want to get involved in the family stuff – but what if I want to know about the Pitmans? This is supposed to be my family but I don't know anything about them.'

He turns to the door and then back again. It's hard not to wonder where the scar came from. Deliberately provoking Ashley feels like a silly thing to have done.

'I'll give you a name,' Pete says. 'Someone you can talk to who'll have a story or two to tell.'

'Thank you.'

He sighs and shakes his head. 'If anyone asks, you didn't get the details from me.'

TWENTY-FOUR

'Did you fall in?'

Nattie laughs as I slip back into the booth and it's only then that I realise I completely forgot to do the one thing I left the bar to do – use the toilet. A full pint of Guinness is waiting for me but Rhys and Nattie's are already a third empty. I've been away for the best part of twenty minutes and, now I think about it, my bladder feels like an overinflated balloon ready to pop.

I mumble something about getting a phone call that distracted me and then apologise, saying I need to go again. They probably think I have some sort of urinary tract infection but I *really* need to go.

It's not long later that I'm at the sink in the ladies' washing my hands, bladder finally empty. Another trip upstairs felt like too far.

Every time I look at myself in the mirror, I feel the need to say my name. It's like a reflex: 'Olivia Elizabeth Adams.'

A pause as I curve my lips into various forms, watching how it affects the shape of my face.

'Oh-live-ee-ah.'

My face fits the name but I still can't quite react to when someone else says 'Olivia'. I'm so used to a different name and it doesn't feel like my own.

As well as that, my darker roots are starting to show and I wonder if it's worth getting them bleached again. Mum's hair is dyed and I didn't realise until recently that most kids have hair that darkens over time. Being blonde at six doesn't mean the child will have the same colour hair at sixteen.

'Olivia,' I say. 'Oh-liv-eee-ah.'

I like the 'oh' part at the beginning. It sounds like the word is being announced, as if 'Livia' is the actual name. 'Oh, Livia...'

The door clunks open and I jump back to where I actually am at the sink. The woman who's entered is somewhere in her fifties and totters in with small steps as if she's a cartoon criminal trying to sneak around. She heads for the stalls but then stops and does a double take when she notices me.

'Oh,' she says and I almost expect her to continue, 'Livia'. Instead, she hums under her breath and adds: 'It's you.'

I smile weakly as I dry my hands on a paper towel. I've read about celebrities being accosted by fans in toilets – men who've stood next to footballers at a urinal and asked for a selfie; women who've asked actresses about their boyfriends through the wall that separates toilet stalls. It's all a bit strange and I never thought I'd be the one getting recognised.

'Olivia Adams,' she adds. 'You're Olivia Adams.'

'Right.'

'I'm Pamela.'

She stands and stares as if that's a name I should know. I drop the paper towel in the bin and am ready to leave but she continues talking.

'I was part of the search,' she adds. 'We all were on my road. Some of us were out all night on the Saturday, then we slept for a couple of hours and got up to do it all again. I remember it like it was yesterday.'

I know I should leave but it's hard to ignore the tug of having information so easily available. The articles in the box upstairs is one thing – but they're written by outsiders observing what was going on, not insiders who lived it. This is what Ashley and Max were worried about: bits and pieces of a story can be used to create a whole that isn't real.

People *like* to tell their stories – and what's wrong with that? Everyone is the hero of their own tale.

Pamela leans against the edge of the toilet stall and, though she's not particularly large, the thin frame wobbles.

'Are you back for good?' she asks.

'People keep asking that but I don't know.'

'Where did you go?'

'I don't really want to talk about it. It's a long story.'

She stares at me as if trying to will the information out before relaxing, allowing her knees to bend slightly.

'I've got a daughter,' she says. 'She was in the year above you at school. Joanie. Do you remember her? One of a kind.'

I shake my head. 'There's a lot I don't know.'

'I guess you were only five…or was it six…?'

She tails off and we stand in silence for a moment or two. I don't confirm or deny. It's all a bit awkward. Having this sort of conversation in any public toilet would be odd but the Black Horse's smell as if someone or something might have died here at some point in the not too distant past. There is mould in the corners of the ceiling and, though it's warm outside, it's cold in here. Some sort of microclimate.

For a moment, I wonder if the conversation is over. Pamela pushes open one of the toilet stall doors but then she turns back to me. 'They arrested my husband. Did you know that?'

'Arrested him for what?'

'They thought he took you.'

It takes me a while to realise what she's talking about but there was always a line in the original article that I failed to follow up on.

… *a 27-year-old man was helping them with their inquiries*…

The mysterious stranger was only mentioned in the first couple of days of reports and then he disappeared from the coverage. There was never a name that I found, no further article to say what he was helping the police with.

'I didn't know…'

Pamela nods slowly and then stands up straighter. 'I'm not annoyed or anything like that. It's not like I tried to corner you. I don't want to argue or shout, but seeing as you're here, I thought you should know.'

'Do you mind if I ask what happened? Nobody's told me any of this.'

There's a moment where I can see that she wishes she never started the conversation. If everyone's the hero of their own story, that means there has to be a villain – and I wonder if I'm the villain of hers.

'It wasn't just him,' Pamela says. 'The police talked to a few people at the time. I don't think it all got reported but my husband was the first and so everyone knew.'

'What's his name?'

'Mark. His car was parked along the road from your house.' She stops. 'Your *old* house. Mark told me he was working and that's where all the problems started. He'd left the car on your road and then walked into the village to watch the football. As soon as everything happened with you, the police were checking anyone who'd been seen in the area. His was a strange car that shouldn't have been there. He didn't want to tell the police he'd been in the pub in case it got back to me, so he said he was working. Meanwhile, I thought he *had* been working. He was trying to avoid an argument with me and ended up talking himself into getting arrested for kidnapping.'

We look at each other for a moment and I know she wants me to apologise. I can't, though… not yet, at least. 'I'm not sure I understand.'

'We both told the police he was working but his office said he wasn't. If he'd only said he was on the piss, someone in the pub would've vouched for him. By the time he did, news had already gone round the village that he'd been arrested. Then you had a ridiculous situation where half a dozen of his friends knew he was definitely in the pub with them at the time you went missing – and yet loads more thought he must've been involved. Mud sticks and all that.'

I've heard that a lot about this place.

'That all happened because his car was parked along the street from the old house?'

Pamela snorts a sad laugh. 'Precisely. If he'd parked a few streets over or caught the bus, none of it would've happened. It was like that, though. Everyone was paranoid their kids would be next.'

I'm suddenly feeling very exposed, not wanting to hear the story after all. I've got a horrible feeling of where it's going.

'He couldn't leave the house,' Pamela adds. 'Neither of us could. We were in the supermarket and this woman dragged her kid away from me. She didn't say a word, just grabbed her son's collar and hauled him away as if I was going to stick him under my arm and run away or something.'

She sighs.

'Mark and I broke up and he moved away. Last I heard, he was in Wales. Knocked up some girl and they moved to the middle of nowhere. Can't say I blame him.'

I wonder if I should apologise. It feels like I should but that's probably British guilt. If there's anything we do well as a people, it's say sorry. That and queue, I guess. And talk about the weather.

Before I can say anything, Pamela spins and bounds for the door. She bangs through and her footsteps echo back from the corridor that leads to the bar. Then she's gone.

There's a moment where I'm stuck staring at the bouncing door, not quite able to believe what's happened. It's not like I thought the village would have forgotten what happened thirteen years ago but I had no idea the legacy of one event would stretch so far. The disappearance has changed so many lives. That Saturday afternoon was the stone being dropped in a pond. My parents were the thick, steep immediate ripples, but the waves continued all the way to the edge of the water.

I turn back to the mirror and tug my hair straighter, stare into my own eyes.

'Olivia Elizabeth Adams.'

It doesn't sound any more real.

2016: LILY, 19

Willy Loman has just been fired when the knock comes on our classroom door. Everybody stops as our teacher cranes her neck up like a meerkat and turns, ready to scowl at the interruption. We are all left hanging as she crosses the room purposefully and opens the door before poking her head into the corridor. After a second, she steps outside and closes the door with a solid click. That causes a ripple of muttering from around the class and everyone is suddenly on their phones, checking to see what's happened on Instagram or wherever else in the past twenty minutes.

I'm a couple of years older than most of the class but it's not that which stops me from checking my own phone. The hairs on the back of my neck are tingling and when the door reopens, our teacher takes only a second to focus on me.

She smiles sadly and says my name. Everyone turns to look and somehow I know. I pick up my bag and bang my hip on the desk, weaving between the tables as every set of eyes follow me. My teacher places a hand on my shoulder and squeezes ever so gently. She says nothing as I head into the hall. It's when the door closes behind that I know I'm not returning anytime soon.

There's a police officer sitting on the wooden bench that runs along the wall. I've never been quite sure why it's there. This is a purpose-built further education college and yet, if there were coat pegs on the wall above, it would be like something from a primary school.

'Lily Armitage?'

I don't actually think I reply but there's an understanding that goes beyond words. I find myself on the bench next to him. My knees are hugged to my chest as I lean on the wall. It feels as if the world is caving in.

'I'm very sorry to have to tell you this, Lily, but your father was in a car accident a short while ago.'

He continues speaking after that but I only hear individual words: 'hospital', 'ambulance', 'did all they could', 'sorry', 'sorry', 'sorry', 'sorry'.

After that, nothing matters. Nothing will ever matter again.

TWENTY-FIVE

SUNDAY

Harry is a little too young for the swings but he's happy enough on the roundabout. He's wedged himself into a small alcove in the central pillar and is giggling away as Mum gives it a gentle push. Each rotation is slow but whenever he sees us, he shouts 'Boo!' at the top of his voice.

'You didn't have to do all that yesterday,' Mum says.

'I know.'

There's a constant sense that she wants to add something. To ask if I know what the result will be, if she can *really* believe in me. To ask if she can have faith.

'I saw Dad yesterday.'

Mum pats the roundabout to set Harry off on another rotation. 'How is he?'

'Better. He says he's getting clean. He's had a shave and a shower and it's not a bad start. We went to the old house.'

Her raised eyebrows give away the shock. 'Why?'

'Jog a few memories, tell a few stories. Dad said the whole of the inside has been remodelled.'

She laughs. 'It needed it. It was outdated when we lived there but we couldn't afford to upgrade much at the time. You should've said you were going. We could've…'

The sentence tails off, unfinished, but I'm pretty sure she was going to say she'd have come too. I can only imagine the storm a family reunion would have caused around the village. Whispers and all that.

'I don't know what last name I should have.'

She rests a hand on my knee. 'Adams is your father's name.'

'I know – but it isn't yours.'

'I'm a Pitman now. Used to be Hanham. That was my maiden name. I don't know if any of that helps.'

Harry shrieks 'boo!' once more but this time Mum doesn't push the rails. The roundabout clicks around and takes him out of sight but it's moving ever more slowly.

'I don't know a lot about my grandparents,' I say. 'Dad talked about *his* father. He said he died about the same time as your mum and that she didn't come to your wedding but that's it.'

As Harry comes past this time, the roundabout is almost at a stop and Mum grabs the bars to halt it. Harry grumbles but Mum picks him up and we head over to what is, essentially, an oversized metal chicken on a giant spring. Harry is apparently familiar with it and clambers on top, screeching 'boo!' over and over as he bobs back and forth.

'Your grandfather died when I was only eight or nine,' Mum says. 'He was a lifelong smoker and got lung cancer.'

'What about your mum?'

'We fell out.'

She leaves it at that for a few moments but when I don't reply, there's nowhere else to go.

'It goes back a long way,' she says. 'I'm not sure we ever got on that well. I was a daddy's girl when I was very young. All my earliest memories are of doing things with my dad. I remember being on his shoulders one time down by the river. It's like a photo, a specific moment. I can't remember why we were there or what we did before or after but it's so clear that I can picture him now.'

Harry stumbles off the chicken and grabs the mini football from Mum's bag. He then kicks it ahead and sets off towards the climbing frame.

'I think my mother always resented that,' Mum adds. 'I've tried to think of things we did together – either me and her or as a family – but there's nothing. Either we didn't do them, or I've forgotten. After Dad died and it was only us, we lived largely separate lives.'

'Didn't you say you were only eight or nine?'

'Yes – but I used to be out a lot. I'd be over at Georgie's house, or we'd go somewhere. Even if I was at home, my mother and I didn't do a lot together.'

'That's not the same as falling out…?'

A nod and a long, wistful pause. We watch Harry kick his ball around, stumpy little legs unable to move as quickly as he's trying.

'It was before you were born,' Mum says. 'I guess I was sixteen or seventeen. It sounds young – and it is – but I'd raised myself in some ways because we never talked about anything important. I felt older. Anyway, I was seeing Max and she didn't like him. I'm not sure if it was specifically *him*, or if she would've had a problem with any boy I started seeing. Although we hardly did anything together, she thought women should be stay-at-home types. You marry up, preferably to someone with money; then cook, clean and have babies. She had always been a housewife and thought women with careers were trying to show off. I guess she was the ultimate anti-feminist.'

It sounds like the type of attitude from the nineteen-thirties or forties, not anything that feels relevant now. I find it hard to imagine why someone would think like that. Mum must read that.

'It was a different age,' she says. 'Times have moved on quickly for your generation. You can never know how much things like the Internet have changed everything. It would have blown her mind. She thought women should be looked after and that men should go out and do the work. She didn't want me to stay on at school after doing my exams, let alone go on to have any sort of career. She'd have hated the idea of me owning a coffee shop and going on to marry a taxi driver. It's all the wrong way round. I think that's why she didn't like Max. He was a village boy. Everyone knew the Pitmans and that was all he was ever going to be. She wanted me to start hanging around with the sons of doctors or lawyers. I'm not sure how she expected that to happen…'

After amusing himself for a while, Harry kicks the ball back in our direction. To me, it always seems as if he's on the brink of falling over. I guess all toddlers are like that. Caring for one must be like looking after a drunken friend after a long night on the lash. It's mainly trying to stop them falling over and walking into things.

'Ball,' Harry says.

This apparently means a lot more to Mum than it does to me. She boots the ball off towards the sandpit and Harry bundles after it, swaying from side to side like a true alcoholic.

'What did your mum think about Dad?' I ask.

'My mother and I were pretty much done with one another by then – even though I was only seventeen. He was the son of a dentist, everything she wanted, but I kept them apart. I didn't want her poisoning things – and that's exactly what she would have done.'

'What happened when she found out you were pregnant?'

It's a simple question and yet it's this that is perhaps the key to everything. But if I was expecting a big moment, it doesn't happen. Mum continues to watch as Harry brings the ball back with a series of kicks. He hunches in front of us, like a puppy waiting for the stick to be tossed, and this time I give the ball a boot. It kicks up over the edge of the sandpit, spinning and bouncing onto the grass on the far edge of the playground. Not that Harry cares. He toddles off after it, full of joyous glee.

'When I told her Dan and I were expecting, she told me to "do something about it" – that's a direct quote – or move out. I chose to move out. Dan was great in those days. He borrowed some money from his dad. We'd paid it all back in a year, but we ended up in the old house where Mrs Winter now lives. I hardly saw my mother after that. I'd visit but she wouldn't answer the door. She didn't want to know anything about you and I figured that was on her. I wasn't going to force her to spend time with a granddaughter she didn't want to know.'

'You said Dad was great in those days…'

Harry is back and Mum gives the ball another kick. I never knew kids were this easy to entertain.

She doesn't reply, so I ask what I really wanted to: 'Would you have divorced if it wasn't for what happened?'

It takes another kick of the ball before Mum answers. 'Maybe. I guess you were the catalyst. We wouldn't have argued in the street if it wasn't for that… but perhaps we would've done in the future.'

'It sounded like you were happy…?'

There's another long pause.

Mum's bag must reinvent the laws of transdimensional physics because there is seemingly no end to what's inside. This must be another one of those things about being a mum – when leaving the house, all eventualities must be prepared for. From nowhere, she pulls out a bucket and spade and we head to the edge of the sandpit where Harry starts to build sandcastles. By 'build', I mean he starts to throw sand around.

'I think we *were* too young,' Mum says. 'Your father and I. We had everything really quickly. House, marriage, daughter. I was in my early twenties. He was a little older, so I don't think it affected him the same way but, for me, where was there to go? I was working in a supermarket but didn't have much in the way of qualifications. I neither had the career I'd wanted at one point, nor had I married up to be some super housewife in the way Mum was after. I was stuck between the two and I didn't know what I wanted…'

She tails off but takes a deep breath and it takes me a few seconds before I realise that it's what she hasn't said that's important.

'Max…'

Mum continues to stare stoically towards the sandpit.

'Your father doesn't know… or I don't think he does. I never told him. It was a one-off at the time, a couple of weeks before you disappeared. An accident. It's not like we were ever going to run away together, but I guess I wondered what things might've been like if I'd ended up with him instead of Dan. I wish it had never happened…'

I'm not sure what I should be most surprised about: the fact she cheated on my father with Max – or that she's telling me so openly.

'Does that make you hate me?'

I turn to face her and Mum's bottom lip is bobbing.

'Why would it?' I reply.

'I've never told anyone before. Only Max knows. I think it's probably why I was so angry with your father – I was furious with myself.'

It's the first time I've realised that my parents share the same secret. My father and mother blame themselves for what happened but, at the time, they took it out on each other. They don't know how the other feels.

'I remember when I shouted at him outside the house, wanting to *really* hurt him,' Mum says. 'I was feeling guilty because of what happened with Max and then you. All I could do was try to make him feel it, too. If you'd not disappeared, perhaps we'd have been fine – but maybe I wrecked everything when I spent that evening with Max. Even if your father had known and chosen to forgive me, I wasn't forgiving myself.'

'But you ended up marrying Max…'

She nods, twiddles the wedding ring on her finger. 'It's not like I started seeing him straight away. Believe it or not, except for that one time, we didn't *do* anything until after the formal divorce from your father. I was on my own for a while but loneliness changes people. It changed me.'

From talking to both Mum and Dad about the same incident, it's incredible how little they seem to know of one another from the time. It sounds like she's spent a lot of time thinking things over to the point that she knows exactly what her relationship with Max means. She didn't want to be alone and so she took what was there. It's not the worst reason to end up with someone and it's not like I have the experience to judge but it feels as if my mother and father's marriage was doomed from the moment they got comfortable.

Mum takes her shoes off and stretches out onto the sand. Harry takes this as an invitation to start brushing sand over her feet, giggling the whole time.

'You said your mum told you to do something about it when you told her you were pregnant. Does that mean…?'

Mum sits unmoving for a moment as Harry slowly starts to bury her feet.

'She didn't believe in abortion. She'd have disowned me if I'd even suggested it, let alone had one. That's not what I wanted anyway. I said you were unplanned but not unwanted. Your father and I *wanted* to have a child. I know it sounds strange because we were young – but that's another recent thing, too. Go back to the sixties or before, my Mum's age, and it was common for women to get married and have children before they were twenty.'

'What did she mean by "do something about it" then?'

'Adoption. She'd have seen me give birth and walk away. It was part of the whole marrying up thing. I think she got it from her mum. You're probably a little young to see what the class system is like in this country. It's nothing like as bad as it used to be – but there was a time when, for women especially, the only way to better oneself was to marry a man with a good job and rich family. In her own way, she was trying to do me a favour. She wanted the best for me, but her idea of that was all about patriarchy. She thought nobody important – no man – would be bothered about me if I'd already had a child by someone else.'

Harry has finished pushing enough sand around to bury one foot, so he makes a start on the other. From the way he's laughing, it's the funniest thing he's ever done and there's a part of me that's so envious. He's fed, he's loved. There's somewhere comfortable for him to sleep and he's far too young to understand all the complexities of life.

'Nattie's mum said you disappeared for almost a year...?'

Mum turns so sharply that she accidentally kicks one of her feet out from the sand. Harry tells her off but doesn't seem too bothered as he starts to push the sand around again.

'She said that?'

'She said you weren't allowed out for a whole summer and then a few months past that. It was when you were about sixteen or seventeen. Sometime after your exams.'

Mum twists back to the pit and stares off towards the furthest end of Ridge Park, where there's only shadow and trees. 'I didn't know she remembered that. It's been such a long time.'

'What happened?'

She breathes in and out and then stands, flicking the sand away from her feet and picking up Harry. He grumbles at her as she starts to clean him up.

'Mum...?'

'I don't think I want to talk about that, Olivia.'

She sounds firm but not angry.

Harry is busy fighting against having his shoes put on. Whenever Mum gets one sock on him and starts on the other, he picks off the first. He finds it hilarious and, in the end, I have to hold his arms as Mum slips him into his socks and shoes. That done, she straps him into the pushchair and gives him a plastic beaker with a teat on top. He grabs it and sucks on whatever's inside.

'Juice!' he declares.

'Can I ask you something else instead?' I say.

'Of course.'

'If your mum wanted you to think about adoption, why didn't you?'

I think she's going to say it's because of my father, something about the strength of their relationship at the time – but it isn't that at all.

She's brutally firm. 'Because I was tired of my mum telling me what to do.'

TWENTY-SIX

It's my first Sunday morning in Stoneridge and, as I probably could have guessed, the place is dead. In fact, if there actually was a funeral, it would probably be a bit livelier. At least there'd be a procession of sorts, a few mourners, a buffet at the Black Horse. Instead, there's not even that. Except for Harry and Mum, Ridge Park is empty, as if there's some weird bylaw of which I'm unaware that children aren't allowed out on The Lord's Day.

The High Street is like something out of a zombie movie the morning after everyone's turned. All the living have been eaten and everyone's traipsed off in search of the next meal. I'd have thought there might be some trade but Via's is closed and so is the sandwich shop at the other end of the High Street. The only place apparently open is the Black Horse but I need to be sober enough to drive and don't want the temptation of what 'a quick one' could lead to.

The church bells were ringing at an ungodly hour this morning and there was some service going on when I woke up. That's over now and the rows of double-parked cars have disappeared from the road outside. With the empty streets, the village is more picture-postcard than it was before but it's hard to escape the unnerving sense of being watched as I walk along the middle of the road. There can't be many places in the country where a person can get away with that without having some angry 4x4 driver steaming up behind, mobile phone in one hand, righteous indignation spewing angrily as they pound the car's horn with the other.

With an hour to kill, I don't know what to do with myself. If the pub isn't an option and everything else is seemingly closed, what else is there?

I find myself heading towards the church, mainly because it's the village's focal point. It's only when I've traced the low stone wall and gone through the gates that I realise I'm looking for something.

There's a path that leads to the front of the church, where the stone arch towers high. The church doors are open, though there's nobody in sight. As with the rest of the village, there is green everywhere. Flower beds line the church itself and then its grass is interspersed with gravestones. Some are traditional with a rounded top, others are flat and embedded in the ground.

Some of the older ones have engraved dates back to the 1800s. Many of those are covered with a mossy gloss and there's one I find that has some sort of worm infestation attached to the lower corner.

There seems to be little order to anything. Old graves next to newer ones, clean ones next to stones that don't look like they've seen any attention in decades. The only area that's noticeably different is the furthest corner out towards the woods, which has its own white picket fence. It's the children's cemetery and, instead of similar-looking stones and crosses, there is a host of windmills, lanterns and ornaments. Everything is adorned with multicoloured ribbons and soft toys.

I've drifted past the adult graves but here I stop and look at every one. The first is for a three-year-old boy – 'God took you too soon' – and then there's a six-year-old girl named Olive who died twenty years before I was born – 'Never forgotten.'

There are some for children who have the same birth and death date and I can do little but stare, wondering what happened. Was it a stillbirth? A complication in the hospital? It's like staring into the abyss, picturing the worst that humanity might have to offer.

The final grave is for another six-year-old. Melanie Price died thirteen years ago. She was probably in the same class and yet somehow forgotten to all but her parents. There are no clues as to how she died but, whatever it was, she must have made the mistake of leaving no mystery. Olivia Elizabeth Adams lives forever; Melanie Price is gone.

I wonder if Mum ever thought about adding a grave to this plot and what it would have said on the front. 'Never forgotten' is probably the best it could have got.

After the devastation of the children's area, it's hard to be as affected by the rest of the graveyard. An eighty-year-old had a good innings compared to the baby with the same birth and death day.

I continue on a loop around the cemetery, making cursory glances to each of the names until, almost unexpectedly, I find the one marked Eve Hanham. It's next to Ged Hanham, both horizontal stones tucked away in a dewy corner. The grass around the edges is short – but it's only from a mower; nobody has been around with a trimmer to do a neater job. Mum clearly doesn't spend a lot of time here. Even some of the older graves have flowers on top – but neither of these. A greasy layer of green-brown sludge has invaded the grooves on both stones; but my grandmother's in particular looks as if it hasn't been cleaned anytime recently. It's more green than grey.

My grandmother.

Today was the first time I had a name – Eve Hanham – to go with my dark thoughts.

What sort of person wants their own daughter to give away a grandchild? How is that a thing? It's easy to abdicate responsibility by saying it's a generational thing, but that isn't an excuse, not when other people's lives are involved. If so, where does it end? Slave masters were misunderstood do-gooders trying to give immigrants a purpose? Ku Klux Klan members didn't know any different? Sometimes a line has to be drawn to say that it's not about generations or a change in attitudes. It isn't younger people versus older, men against women or straight versus gay.

It's about arseholes being arseholes.

The witch beneath my feet doesn't even know what she's done.

I poke my head up and look back towards the main area of the church, checking for movement. There's no one there, nor is there anyone mooching around the rest of the cemetery.

It feels wrong and yet it doesn't. I pull my underwear down and loop them over one leg out of the way, then I squat and push, waiting for the fabulously satisfying tinkle of liquid on stone.

When I'm done, I stand and pull my underwear back up, then step away to look at the puddle of piss that's seeping into the grooves of her name.

Up yours, Eve Hanham.

My only regret is that I didn't have more to drink this morning.

TWENTY-SEVEN

I'm not sure I'll ever get used to driving on the constricted country roads that connect Stoneridge to the rest of the world. For some reason, the lanes seem to become narrower and narrower as the sharpness of the bends increase. There are always people banging on about health and safety gone mad – and yet everyone seems to accept that ninety-degree bends with high hedges, single-track roads and sixty-mile-per-hour speed limits are perfectly fine.

According to the details Pete gave me and the route planner on my phone, it is only a sixteen-mile journey and yet it takes me the best part of an hour to drive to Winton Bridge.

It is technically a village, but it's so small that I'm almost through it and out the other side before I realise I'm there. I notice the 'thank you for driving safely' sign while somehow missing the one that reads: 'Winton Bridge welcomes careful drivers'.

Despite only being a few streets, a stream and a postbox, I still end up getting lost as I try to find the address Pete gave me. It doesn't help that the village is the equivalent of the dark side of the moon for mobile phones. Even a single bar of reception is an aspiration and it's as if the whole area is encased in a lead box.

I park on the empty street, figuring I'll have as much luck on foot, and start to walk along the road. There are perhaps only thirty or so houses speckled throughout the hamlet, with various farm sounds and smells drifting on the breeze. There are many more hanging baskets and drystone walls but this is a more condensed version of Stoneridge. Fewer people, smaller area, much more green.

It's on my second lap that I accidentally find the house I'm looking for. The stonework at the front is covered with ivy and there's a battered, unused car on the drive. The wheels are covered with moss and murk and it doesn't look as if it's been driven at any point in the last decade or two.

The door is old, wooden and, if someone was to knock too hard, a knuckle-breaker. I use the palm of my hand to knock, fearing for the skin on my hands if I were try it any other way. It takes a while but there's a vague shuffling from inside, a grunt and then a man's voice mumbles: 'Hang on'.

When the door is opened, there's a man in a wheelchair. It's obviously my own prejudice but it's always a surprise to see a young person in a wheelchair. The man can't be older than mid-thirties, with thick swishy sideways dark hair like something out of a fashion advert.

'Can I help?' he asks.

'Are you Iain?'

He looks up, trying to place me. 'Who are you?' he adds.

'I'm having a few problems with a man named Ashley Pitman and was told you might be able to help…?'

He stares at me for a second or two and then manoeuvres his chair to the side of the hall, pulling the door open wider. 'You better come in.'

The house has been converted for a wheelchair user, with a rail along the hall that's a little lower than would be expected. There are keys, coins, a couple of books and other potentially useful odds and ends scattered along the length. The living room is a similar story, with a dining table that's a few centimetres below the height of what might be sold in a shop and low cabinets that are stacked with papers and more books.

Iain wheels himself in behind me and moves over towards the television. There's a two-seater sofa and I sit.

He speaks first: 'I don't know who you've spoken to but there's no way I can *help* you.'

'But you know Ashley Pitman…?'

He rolls his eyes dramatically: 'You could say that.'

'Can you tell me about it?'

Iain allows the chair to roll forward a few centimetres and then he rocks it back. He does this a couple of times before stopping. 'Why do you want to know?'

I could give him the whole story, of course. Missing girl, thirteen years, old-new family – but the short version is still true. 'I think he might be following me around. I'm not completely sure.'

'Oh.' Iain stops rocking his chair, clamping on the wheel brake and rubbing his chin. 'Pete gave you my details, didn't he?'

'I, um…'

'It's all right. I'm not annoyed.' He nods towards the door. 'Do you fancy a walk?'

It's impossible not to look at the wheels and Iain brays with laughter.

'How about *you* walk, I'll wheel. You can help me on any steep bits.'

I agree and, a few moments later, we are back out in the afternoon sun. There might not be a lot to Winton Bridge but the entire hamlet seems to be perpetually in sun.

Iain wheels himself to the stream and then we start to follow it out towards what turns into an empty towpath.

'I was in Ashley's class at school,' Iain says.

'You look way too young.'

It feels strange to be looking down on someone but I see him smile at that.

'Good genes,' he says. 'Not that I can get into my skinny jeans any more.'

I don't react. I'm not entirely sure if I'm supposed to laugh.

'Did you used to live in Stoneridge?'

'"The place from which you can never escape".' He laughs. 'I used to call it the Stoneridge Triangle. I managed to get sixteen miles down the road – but yes, that's where I'm from. Have you moved there recently?'

'A week ago.'

'Blimey – who'd you kill for that punishment? You didn't *choose* to move there, did you?'

'Sort of.'

'It's quieter than a mute convention in a church.'

'Doesn't look like Winton Bridge is exactly rocking…'

Iain laughs long and it seems like something he does a lot. He's slightly camp with it and it's hard not to join in.

'Touché, touché,' he says. 'Can't argue with that. Still, you don't know what goes on behind closed doors here. I'm pretty sure we've got swingers living at number thirteen. All sorts of couples turning up late on Friday and Saturday evenings and then leaving in the early hours. The lucky bastards. Then there's number nineteen with the constant parcel deliveries. It's three or four times a day. I mean, what can they possibly need so much of? I've heard of Internet shopping but this is ridiculous. I reckon they've got some sex toy business on the go.'

'Is that based on anything?'

'Pure, hard, rubbery speculation.'

This time I laugh.

We continue on for a short distance until Iain speaks again: 'Ashley and I weren't friends,' he says. 'We were in the same year at school and it was a small enough place that you pretty much knew all the other kids in some way, even if it was only their name.'

'That doesn't sound like a lot of fun.'

'You can say that again – especially when you're a teenager who knows you're gay.' He waves a hand through the air, freewheeling for a couple of moments, as if sending the memory off into dust.

'Anyway, a few years later, we'd all left school and I was nineteen or twenty, something like that. How old are you?'

'Nineteen or twenty, something like that.'

He laughs once more. 'I like you,' he says. 'Anyway, you'll know it's the pisshead age. You've got the idiot age – that's like zero to eleven or twelve where you don't know anything and you're this bumbling idiot getting in the way. Then there's the awkward age, which takes you up to about seventeen. You're all elbows, knees and genitals but you're too embarrassed to talk about anything. Then it's the pisshead age, which, if you're lucky, gets you through to your mid-twenties. After that, it's the crushing reality age. Then the lose all the weight stage, then mid-life-crisis, then death. You've got all that to come but, for now: pisshead age. You go to uni or get some shit job, spend all your money down the pub. Great times. I'd recommend it to anyone.'

'I have spent an abnormally high amount of time in the pub this week.'

Iain clicks his fingers. 'See! Can you believe I'm not some expert on human behaviour? I could be the new Stephen Hawking.' He stops and puts on a robotic voice: 'Anyway, where was I?'

'You were nineteen or twenty – something like that.'

Another click of the fingers and he's back to his regular voice. 'Right. I might not look like it and it's not quite the gay stereotype, but I used to play rugby for the Stoneridge team. I was a flanker, or something that rhymed with it.'

A pair of swans descend as if from nowhere, swooping low and landing on the water. It's happened so unexpectedly that we both stop as the birds first dunk their heads and then turn as if to say, 'What are *you* looking at?'

There's no way either of us fancy a fight with a swan, so we continue along until we reach a wooden bridge over the canal. Iain asks if I can help him with the slope, so I push him up and over until we're heading back towards Winton Bridge on the other side of the water.

'It was this really stupid thing in training,' Iain says. 'We had more than fifteen players in a squad, so it was an inter-team match. Twelve on twelve or something like that. Ashley was playing in the centre and I caught him late with a tackle after he'd already passed the ball. It was a total accident but I'd already committed to taking him down. In all honesty, he was too quick for me.'

'What happened?'

'He jumped up and pushed me away. I had my hands up, apologising, but he was in my face. "You want to do this, gay boy?" – all that sort of stuff. I was saying sorry the whole time but he kept coming for me and, in the end, all our teammates got between us. I figured that was it. It wasn't entirely uncommon when you've got a bunch of pumped-up young men charging at each other. We played a game that weekend, then had training the next week and then another match. I'd started to forget about it, but then I was in a pub with a few other non-rugby mates a couple of weeks later.'

Iain has been pushing himself relatively quickly but his pace drops. I find myself a step ahead and have to slow to stay level.

'I was walking home by myself,' he says. 'It was late, maybe one in the morning, something like that. Next thing I know, I'm waking up in hospital.'

I don't mean to do it but I grab the handle of Iain's wheelchair. We both stop and I find myself staring down at him.

'I'm not sure I understand.'

'Neither did I. It's like someone invented teleportation. One minute I was on the road, the next I was in a hospital bed.' Another click of the fingers. 'Like that. The only difference was that instead of teleporting in an instant, I'd lost four days and the use of my legs.'

I'm pretty sure my mouth hangs open. There's a moment where I'm not sure if he's joking. Almost everything else has come with a punchline but not this.

'What happened?' I ask.

'Nobody knows… well, at least one person knows, but *I* don't.' He turns sideways and pulls his hair to the side, showing a thick purple scar that zigzags across the crown of his head. It's so wide that I have the urge to touch it.

'You can,' he says and it occurs to me that there must be times when I'm really easy to read.

'Are you sure you don't mind?'

As he keeps his hair apart, I run my fingers along the length of the scar. It's scaly, like a lizard's skin, and there's a distinct groove where it sinks into his skull.

'You'd never believe how many blokes I pulled because of that scar,' Iain adds, letting his hair fall back into place.

'What caused it?' I ask.

'Not sure. Something sharp – a machete, perhaps the corner of a spade, something like that. Must've knocked me out in one clean blow. I had half a dozen ribs, too. The doctor said someone must've stamped on my chest while I was down.'

'What about your legs?'

'Run over with a car. They were crushed. I'm a medical miracle. Lucky to be alive and all that.' He raps his knee with his fist. 'Like bloody Robocop under here – and not that knock-off new one; the nineteen-eighties version.'

We continue along the towpath and somehow I've ended up pushing the wheelchair. I wonder if I'm being offensive or helpful. Either way, Iain doesn't mention it.

'Are you saying Ashley did this?' I ask.

'He was never prosecuted if that's what you're asking. His brother swore blind they were together all night at his house.' He stops for a moment and then adds: 'I know who it was. I knew then and I know now. I could tell by the way he looked at me afterwards.'

A canal boat is stopped at one of the locks and an elderly man is straining with the gates. I stop and give him a hand as Iain helpfully chirps: 'Put your back into it,' at me, laughing the whole time. The man thanks us both – presumably me for the physical help and Iain for the heckling – and then he jumps back onto the boat.

'Did you say you thought Ashley Pitman has been following you?' Iain asks.

'Something like that.'

He sounds serious now, the comedy act temporarily forgotten: 'Did you end up in Stoneridge for a reason? Friends? Family?'

'Maybe.'

'Well… if you wanted my advice, then here it is. If the Pitmans are showing an interest in you then either run to the police – or simply run.'

2016: LILY, 19

The house is ridiculously empty and yet overwhelmingly full. Everything's still there: Dad's clothes, Dad's old tools, the jar of mint sauce that only Dad liked at the back of the cupboard. The house is packed with *things* and yet there's only me to live in it. This was the type of thing that a silly, stupid fourteen- or fifteen-year-old me always wanted. '*I'll leave home,*' and all that. '*Why can't you leave me alone?*'

What a fool.

I finally got my wish but I'd rather make a new one: To have my dad back.

I don't know what the protocol is for dealing with any of this. The house and everything in it now belongs to me. The mouldy broccoli at the bottom of the fridge: mine. The out-of-date tin of kidney beans in the cupboard: mine. The grime on the oven door: mine. The roll of leftover wallpaper in the nook under the stairs: that's mine as well.

Someone with more patience than me might clinically catalogue everything. Some things could go to charity, others things could be stored somewhere just in case, then there would be a bin pile.

I have no such tolerance – but I do have a very large roll of oversized black bin bags. The downstairs is easy enough to sort as everything except the photographs end up in the bags. There was even an old slipper underneath the sofa.

Upstairs feels harder. All of my father's clothes have their own story.

There's the lost-his-mind red trousers that he wore a few times when he temporarily took up golf. There's a part of me that wants to keep them, that wants to remember him looking like a complete fool. It's not that, it's the laughter I associate with them. Mum laughed at him and so did I. I see red trousers and think of laughing.

They still end up in a bin bag.

He's kept the tracksuit jogging bottoms he wore most days for eighteen months after Mum died. There's a hole in the inner right thigh, another on the left knee. They're horrific and yet, as I dump them into the black bag, there's a part of me that wants to hang onto them. When I think of my father, a lot of my memories are of him wearing those bottoms.

He has two suits, one black; one brown. I'm not sure I ever saw him wear the brown one and, even with the black, I think it was only for Mum's funeral. There is a twenty-pound note in one of the pockets but that's all I get from them as they end up in the trash pile as well.

Of course losing a parent hurts. Probably a husband, wife, boyfriend or girlfriend, too. There's so much more to it than the actual death, though.

When something happened to me before, one of my first thoughts was, 'I can't wait to tell Dad', or 'How am I going to tell Dad about this?' It's instinctive and now that instinct is redundant. I still wonder how I'm going to tell Dad about something – but then I remember I can't. It's like forgetting the urge to put one foot after the other when walking. Every time something happens to me, I have to reprogram the entire way I think.

And then there's disposing of someone else's underwear. No one ever talks about that but a person's drawer that's full of boxer shorts and socks suddenly feels more intimate than anything else. The type of place in which a loved one would never look unless something like this happens.

After everything, it's dumping his socks into a bin bag that sets me off again. I spend the whole time telling myself how stupid it is – how irrational I'm being – but it doesn't help. I have a good ol' cry over filthy socks and then, like some sort of dirty washing miracle, I feel better.

It's when I've dumped the contents of the drawer into the bin bag that I notice the A4 envelope flat against the bottom of the wood. The paper corners are tatty and old but it doesn't look as if the envelope has been disturbed for a long time. There's nothing written on the front or back and it's flimsy.

The flap is unsealed and I pull out the two pieces of paper from inside. The first is a letter addressed to my mum and dad; the second is some sort of certificate. My name is there in clear grey print from an old printer that needed a new toner cartridge.

Lily Armitage, it reads. No middle name. The rest of the information is clear, though, there in grey and white. The key words leap off the page and it's almost impossible to take it in.

It can't be true. It simply can't.

Either my mum or dad would have told me at some point. Why wouldn't they?

It can't be true.

Except, deep down, I know it is.

TWENTY-EIGHT

MONDAY

Rhys and Nattie are both waiting on the bench outside the Black Horse the next morning. For Rhys in particular, it seems strange to see him in anything other than the hazy dim lights of our back booth in the pub. He's dressed in jeans and a checked shirt, like he's off to work on whatever building job he has on. He says he's 'waiting on a call' – whatever that means. Nattie's either off work, or not going in until later. She's in a short summer dress that works for her even though it's cream with purple flowers as if someone's cut up a curtain. She lifts her thick-rimmed sunglasses to look at me as I head out into the sunshine.

'What happened to you last night?' she asks.

'Places to go, people to see.'

She shrugs and hops up from the bench, linking her arm into mine. 'Right,' she declares, 'we've got a treat lined up for you.'

'What is it?'

'That's a surprise.'

'I don't think I like surprises.'

'You'll like this.'

The two of us start along the High Street, heading towards Via's with Rhys half a step behind. I've got a reasonable idea of where everything is now but, even though it's still classed as a village, Stoneridge is a fair bit bigger than most. The edges are surrounded by newer housing estates as the sprawl spreads outwards.

Instead of heading up the hill towards the estate where my dad lives or along the river towards Ridge Park, we go in the opposite direction. There's a charity clothing shop and another café, followed by a long row of thatched-roof stone cottages.

We soon end up outside Stoneridge Primary School. There's a sign with a rainbow and painted images of two children playing with a ball. Schools, especially primary schools, are like elaborate illusions. Everything feels so big as a child and yet, by the time a person grows into an adult, the exact same stretch of playground seems a fraction of the size it once did.

The three of us stand at the railings, looking across the playground towards the school itself. Bright posters and paintings are on show through the windows and the tarmac in front is covered with painted swishes and swirls. It's a kaleidoscope of colour.

'Do you remember anything?' Nattie asks.

'No.'

Rhys digs into his back pocket and passes across a faded photo. There are two girls playing hopscotch: one is balancing on her left leg and has a blonde ponytail, the other has long red pigtails and is clasping a stone.

Nattie points towards the corner of the playground, where there's now an L-shape of benches.

'That picture was taken right there,' she says.

I compare the two and there's no question it's the same spot. The shadow of the wall is hanging in almost the exact same place and I can see the corner of the wall in the picture.

'Mum found it last night,' Nattie adds. 'She reckons we were both five years old when it was taken. She couldn't remember who took it but it was probably one of our mums.'

The school is enveloped by an eerie emptiness. It's the holidays and kids are off playing in back gardens or fields; else sitting inside on Minecraft or whatever it is they do now. There's nobody here, but the playground holds thousands of ghosts of futures unfulfilled.

'Give us a bunk up.'

Rhys does as he's told, cupping his hands into a step for Nattie and then lifting her up and over the railings. She lands with an 'oof' but wipes her hands down and says she's fine. Rhys crouches again and I follow Nattie over and onto the concrete, stumbling forward when I land but managing to get away unscathed. He then heaves himself up, narrowly avoiding impaling his crotch on the metal bar as he levers himself over. Rhys lands with far more gymnastic grace than either Nattie or myself.

'Show off,' Nattie says with a smile.

We head across to the corner and sit on the low, low benches, giggling to ourselves at how ridiculous we must look.

Nattie has the photo and holds it up, turning so that it's clear we're sitting in the precise spot where the hopscotch once happened.

'Remember anything now?' she asks.

'I wish I could say yes...'

She puts the photo on the bench. 'It'll come back one day, I'm sure. You'll be walking past and it'll suddenly be at the front of your mind.'

'I've enjoyed the discovery. Talking to people, hearing the stories. I've got a real sense of what's going on.'

Nattie looks at me and, only for a moment, there's a flicker of her eyebrows as if she doesn't know what to make of me. I shouldn't have said it but it's only taken a week and I really think it's true.

She pushes herself up and moves over to the snake that's painted on the playground. The long length of the animal is separated into squares, with numbers in each. Nattie crouches and picks up a stone from the floor.

'Come on,' she says. 'For old time's sake.'

And so we play hopscotch. Rhys sits and watches and he makes us pose for a photo. I balance on my left leg and Nattie holds the stone. After he's taken it, we rush back to the bench and compare the two pictures. Aside from longer hair, more flesh on display and our height, it's not a bad effort.

Rhys jokes about selling the photo for a fortune to some dodgy magazine or newspaper, but Nattie's threat that she has a key to his house is enough to shut down that line of joke. I don't ask why she's got a key. I've assumed since I first met them that there was something going on but they've never shown anything other than platonic friendship when I've been around.

Nattie stretches out on the bench, lying along the length, her arms high above her head, legs flat. I copy on the adjacent bench and Rhys sits unfazed on the tarmac between us.

'You worried?' Nattie says.

My eyes are closed and the brightness of the sky is singeing through my eyelids and it's only when she says 'O' when I realise she's talking to me. The 'O' hit first time, too.

'What about?' I reply.

'The test results. Aren't they due today?'

'I don't need to be nervous. I know what they'll say.'

'I didn't mean nervous about the *results* – I meant nervous about what comes next.'

The insides of my eyelids are a burning orange, with bright green shapes spinning in circles. I allow my arms to flop down on either side of the bench and breathe in the warmth of the morning.

'I suppose I've not thought that far ahead.'

'It's all going to change though, isn't it? You'll have a mum and dad. A stepdad, too, and a little brother. It'll all be official. It'll only be a day or two until the news channels turn up, then you'll be on TV.'

'I'll tell them I'm not interested.'

'But you'll still have a mum, dad and brother.' She pauses and sounds a little shakier when she continues: 'I was thinking… if you're hanging around, perhaps we can get a flat together, or something? I'm still with Mum because I can't afford anywhere by myself. It doesn't have to be in Stoneridge. We can find somewhere a few miles away. Far enough away to do our own thing and make sure we don't get the dreaded drop-in; close enough that you can visit Harry and your mum…'

Nattie's been thinking about this, perhaps even checking prices and looking for vacant flats. I screw my eyes closed, pushing and desperately trying to force myself not to cry. Tears feel close.

'It was only an idea…'

She sounds slightly aggrieved and I reply instantly, even though my voice is suddenly a croaky sob-filled shambles. 'It's not that.'

My eyes are still closed but there's a shuffling and then my hand is in Nattie's. Her skin is warm. 'I didn't mean to upset you, O. I know it's a lot to think about.'

'It's not that either.'

I sit up and slowly open my eyes. Everything is so bright and it takes me a few seconds to realise Nattie is sitting on the playground holding my hand. Rhys is pressed up against the other bench, watching but not saying anything.

'I don't think I've ever had a real friend before,' I say.

The words hurt, slicing my throat like gravel.

Nattie squeezes my fingers and rests her head on my knee. It feels like she's going to say something but then my phone spoils everything by ringing.

Mum.

I swipe to answer and can sense the nervous excitement from her straight away when she says my name.

'Are you in the village?' she asks.

'Yes – I'm with Nattie and Rhys.'

'Can you come over? A courier's on the way with the official letter and the results.'

I sit up straighter. 'Can my friends come?'

'Of course.'

'What about Dad?'

There's a pause and a moment in which I think the call might have dropped. I take it away from my ear but there are still three bars of reception and 'Mum' on the screen.

'Are you still there?' I ask.

'Yes,' she replies. 'Yes to both. You can bring your father.'

TWENTY-NINE

If looks could kill, the conservatory of Mum's house would be a Quentin Tarantino movie. The benefit of bringing Nattie, Rhys and Dad with me is that the death stares are evenly spread.

Rhys is getting his fair share simply for being someone of whom Ashley and Max are largely unaware. If they know anything about him, they're not letting on. Nattie is proving herself to be unpopular, simply for being my friend. As usual, the Pitmans – Ashley in particular – are doing their best to give me the crooked eye but even that's a sideshow compared to poor old Dad.

He's turned himself around – at least outwardly. I picked him up and, when we hugged, there was the faintest whiff of booze under the smell of clean clothes and shower gel. If he *has* been drinking, it can't have been much. He's coherent, fully aware of where we are and why. I haven't asked how he's doing, figuring it's none of my business. If he wants any sort of relationship, which it seems he does, he knows it's up to him. *He's* improved himself, not me.

There was an awkward, amicable handshake between him and Max and a mutual nod with Mum.

How are you, Dan?
Fine, thanks, Sarah. You?
I'm good, thank you.

The silence between them was very polite and courteous, like two business partners having their first meeting in a while. All very hands-off and corporate.

Although Max and my father shook hands, there was nothing similar on offer from Ashley. He's not moved from the single seat in the conservatory, eyes flicking from one of my group to the next.

It's warring cowboys and Indians, with Mum in the middle.

The glass-topped coffee table in the conservatory is clear except for an A5 brown envelope sitting askew in the centre. Everyone converges on the table, standing and waiting.

'It came about five minutes before you did,' Mum says. Her darting glance to Ashley is a telltale giveaway as she adds: 'I thought it would be best that we were all here before we opened it.'

I'm tingling. The hairs on my neck are on end and there are pins and needles in the tips of my fingers.

Mum picks the letter up from the table and bobs it up and down, weighing whatever's inside. I guess the true weight isn't in the papers but in what they say.

'You or me?' she asks.

'You do it.'

It feels as if everyone breathes in at the same time. Mum flips the envelope around and latches a fingernail underneath the flap. She tears along the seal and then pulls out a small sheaf of folded pages. She takes a deep breath and there are tears in her eyes. It's like slow motion as she turns the papers over and flattens them in her hand.

The tingles ripple down along my back, whispering out to my sides. It's impossible not to shiver because everything has led to this. In more ways than anyone knows, the words printed on the pages will confirm who I am.

It's almost anticlimactic when Mum looks up to me. She doesn't smile, not straight away. 'It's a match,' she says.

Nothing happens for a second and then she grins wider than I've ever seen. Mum grabs me tight, clawing at my back with one hand, clasping the pages with the other.

Nattie whoops but I barely hear it over Mum's breathy gasps in my ear.

She pulls away again, offering the page to Dad.

'There's no doubt,' she says. 'No one can question this. Ninety-nine-point-nine per cent accuracy. It's a match.'

Dad rests a hand on my back and there's a moment that's simultaneously wonderful and horrifying. He leans his head on one shoulder and clasps my waist; Mum has her head on the other and cups her hands around my back. We're a family of three: Mum, Dad and me.

It's only a second, perhaps two, but it's suddenly like being in a walk-in fridge. Everyone must feel it because each of my parents pull away abruptly. Somehow I've ended up with the pages in my hand, though I don't remember Dad passing them over.

'Ain't that nice,' Ashley sneers from his seat. 'One happy little family. You see that, bro? Just like I told yer...'

Everyone has stopped. Rhys and Nattie are looking to Ashley; Mum and Dad are looking at Max. He's looking to his brother – and Ashley is staring directly at me.

It's Dad who speaks first. He steps away, hands up in the air. 'I'm sorry,' he says meekly. 'I didn't mean anything by it. I was excited at the test, that's all.'

Ashley stands and takes a step towards my father. They're more or less the same height but Ashley is bulkier, with thicker arms and a mightier chest. He snatches the pages away from me and scans the front before shoving them at my dad.

'Doesn't say you're her father, *does it?*'

His eyes are narrow and he scoffs with relish. They're eye to eye but Mum moves quickly, pressing herself between them and pushing Ashley away. I'm a little surprised that Dad stood up to him unmovingly.

'Shut up,' Mum says.

Ashley nods towards Max. 'C'mon. Everyone in the village knows you two never stopped playing hide the sausage.' He points at me: 'She could be anyone's.'

Mum steps towards him. 'Don't you *dare* come into my house and say things like that.'

He laughs in her face and Mum turns to Max.

'Aren't you going to do something about this?'

Max is sitting on the arm of the sofa. 'Like what?'

'Stand up for your wife?'

He shrugs and Mum moves away, before turning to my father.

'It's not true,' she says.

'I know it's not.'

'Olivia is yours. I never slept with Max or anyone else at that time.'

There are three crucial words at the end of her sentence and I wonder if Dad knows the truth. Perhaps he always figured Mum had cheated on him with Max towards the end? If he does, then he doesn't say anything.

He looks to me and we lock eyes: 'I've never doubted Olivia's mine,' he says. 'She *is* my daughter.'

Ashley looks to his brother. 'Are you buying this happy family bull? You gonna stand for this in your own house? They're making you look like a fool. Taking you for a right mug and you're gonna sit there and take it?'

Max doesn't look as if he's going to move but there's something about him. He looks genuinely puzzled, as if he can't quite believe everything that's happened.

Ashley's steaming for a fight and seeing as I doubt even he would stoop to smacking a woman in front of others, there aren't many candidates. He doesn't know Rhys and has little reason to go for him, so it's only my father. The test results are now on the side. Ashley's fists are balled, his head arched forward as he takes a step towards my dad. I move quicker than either of them, putting myself between the two men. Because he's hunched over, I'm temporarily able to look down on Ashley and take full advantage of it.

'Big man…' I say.

He straightens, puffing up his chest out. '*You.*'

There's genuine hatred and, though there's a part of me that wants to feel it back, it's not there. I have no obvious reason to dislike him – but there's no way I'm going to let him get anywhere near my father.

'You're a sad little man, aren't you?' I say. 'A pathetic excuse for an existence, following your younger brother around all day. Haven't you got your own friends? Or are the girls around here too smart to look at you twice?'

It doesn't help that Nattie snorts a laugh but there's a vein looping around Ashley's eye that bulges with fury. Before anything can happen, I'm being pulled away roughly, fingers gripping and wrenching at my forearm.

It's Max.

He spins me around and then shoves me towards Nattie, who has stopped giggling as quickly as she started.

'You will *not* talk like that in my house,' he says to me. He's not quite shouting but there's a controlled anger in his voice.

'She's my daughter, Max.'

Mum cuts across us all and then everyone's looking at her. She picks up the letter and holds it up. 'You can't keep saying things are different with Ashley because he's blood. Olivia is blood, too. This proves it. There's no question.'

The two brothers stand united but alone – and it feels as if there's been a shift, like it's them against everyone else. They know it, too.

Ashley steps around his brother, still focused on me. 'How'd you do it?' he asks.

'Do what?'

'Cheat the test.'

I didn't expect that at all and puff out a sigh of exasperation. 'You were *here*,' I tell him. 'You *saw* me swab my mouth. You watched Cassie take everything away.'

'Did you pay her? Something like that? You know someone at the lab.'

'I didn't know the name of the lab until I got here. I only know it now because it's on the letter.' I flash a hand towards the papers in Mum's hand. 'Go on, call them and ask. Better yet, ask them to come out. We'll do it all again. You can hold the swab if you want. Nothing's going to change.'

Both brothers stare at me and it feels like anything could happen. It's like they've watched an illusionist pull off a master trick and they're trying to figure it out. I've walked through the Great Wall of China, flown across a stage in Vegas or levitated next to The Shard.

'There's something going on here,' Ashley says. 'What do you want?'

'I don't *want* anything. I've not asked for anything.'

'You're not having money.'

'I've turned *down* money. I don't want anything from you and I don't need it.'

Everyone's stuck in the moment because there's nothing else to say. It's one thing to get angry at a person but another entirely to be furious with science.

Ashley lunges forward, stabbing an accusing finger in my direction. 'I'll find out the truth,' he says. Before anyone can stop him, he's pushed past Rhys into the hallway. He stops for a moment and turns to Max. 'You comin'?'

Max does precisely that and, moments later, the front door slams closed, sending a booming wave of rage spiralling through the house.

THIRTY

Everyone stands in stunned silence for a few seconds before Mum breaks the silence with an apology.

I'd somehow managed to miss the fact that he was in his cot – but Harry chooses that moment to wake up and start calling for Mum. She sweeps her way across the room and plucks him out, rubbing his head and back, then placing him on the floor. He's oblivious to the open warfare that's been going on around him and toddles off to play with his toys in the corner.

Dad sits on the sofa and rubs his temples, looking at the floor.

Mum refolds the papers and returns them to the envelope before handing it to me. 'I never doubted the test,' she says. 'I can't tell you how pleased I am to have this out in the open.' She turns to Nattie and Rhys. 'Thank you for making my daughter feel at home.'

'Mum—'

She cuts me off with a wave of the hand and turns back to Nattie and Rhys. 'No, I want to say this. I really appreciate that you've welcomed Olivia to the village with your friendship.'

'I am *here*, Mum.'

'I'm your mother and it's my job to embarrass you. I've got a lot of years to catch up on.'

She smiles and it's only then that I realise fully how much her happiness means to me.

Nattie says that it's fine and then I ask Mum what's going to happen with Max and Ashley.

She spends a few moments watching Harry before replying. 'Max isn't so bad when it's just us,' she says. 'He'll listen to me. It's only his brother who gets him riled up.'

'Why are they always together?'

It's a rude question, I know it is. None of my business – and yet, for the moment, it feels like I could ask anything I want and get an answer.

'They've always come as a pair,' Mum replies. 'It's not like I didn't know that.'

It might be inadvertent but it's hard to tell: Mum is clasping the area a little under her elbow where I saw the bruises. She's wearing a long-sleeved top, so nothing can be seen, and she corrects herself the moment she realises she's doing it. Mum knows I've noticed and turns away quickly.

I could say something, especially with Dad here – but what then? It's not like I expect him to protect her honour or anything like that. And the Pitman brothers already have enough reasons, however contrived, to resent him.

Perhaps sensing something not being right, Dad pushes himself up from the sofa. 'I'm going to get off,' he says. 'I have a few things to do. Thank you for inviting me.'

This time, there's the briefest of hugs between my parents: arses out, chests in, touching shoulders, then away.

Dad nods towards Harry, who's happily amusing himself with the Duplo blocks.

'He's a gorgeous little boy.'

'Thank you.'

He tells Rhys it's nice to meet him and says something similar to Nattie, telling her that it's nice to see her again. I'm not sure if he relates her to the red-headed girl who used to play in the back garden, or if he has some other reason for knowing her.

I lead him out to the front door and there's a moment where it's only us.

'Thank you for coming,' I say.

'I wouldn't have wanted to be anywhere else.'

'Is everything all right?'

Dad rests a hand on my shoulder and I can sense the faint smell of alcohol again on his breath when he breathes out. It's masked by mint but it's there.

'I'm working on it,' he says.

'Do you need a lift back to the village?'

He shakes his head. 'I think a walk would be good for me.' Dad unlocks the door and then stands half in, half out. 'I love you,' he adds. 'I promise I won't let you down again. Not ever. You need me and I'm there. I'll always be looking out for you. I have a lot to make up.'

'You really don't, Dad.'

He reaches out and cradles me onto his shoulder. I can feel his heart beating through his top and his short, sharp breaths on my neck. It's not that I'm anti-touching but everyone's been particularly touchy-feely today. I pat his back and he steps away.

'I'll see you soon,' he says – and then he turns and I watch him walk along the driveway, out to the road.

He doesn't look back and then he's out of sight. I wonder if I should do more, or get others involved. I've spent hours in the room above the pub reading the articles in the box Mum gave me and yet I've spent no time looking into how best to help someone with an addiction. Perhaps I need to properly sort myself out first.

Back inside and Mum is busy trying to feed Harry some sort of goo from a pot. He seems to be happy enough with whatever it is and I suppose that sums him up. Given his father and uncle, it's hard to see where the boundless joy comes from.

Mum tells Rhys, Nattie and myself that we should 'go have fun' and I can't help but feel that she needs a little time to herself. There's no reason to argue.

There's only one road that leads to the village centre and I assume we'll drive past Dad on the way back – but there's no sign of him. We're almost at the car park by the post office before Rhys speaks for the first time in a while.

'I told you it's all TV soap opera round here,' he says.

There's a pause where I know he's wondering if he's gone too far – but then Nattie starts giggling and it's impossible not to join in. This is the Christmas special episode that everyone's been talking about.

I park and we're at the corner near the obelisk. I'm instinctively heading for the Black Horse but Nattie has stopped.

'Pub?' I say.

'Let's show you somewhere new. You know there's a second pub in the village, don't you?'

'That's sacrilege,' I reply. 'Pete would never forgive me.'

'Your secret's safe with us. Come on.'

The three of us head in the opposite direction along the High Street and follow the path until the pavement disappears and there's no option other than to walk in the road. It's hard not to think of what Iain told me happened to him when he was walking in the road around here. One minute, he was in one place; the next he was in hospital and had lost the use of his legs.

The problem is that, for everyone else, the story is done. Mystery solved – the missing girl is back and that's that. We all move on.

But they don't know what I know and what no one seems to realise is that there are still secrets in this village. Still questions that people don't even realise they need the answers to.

The only thing is… should I care?

Perhaps I do. I'm not sure – but, if I do, then it's not something for today. Today is for celebrating.

The Angry Sheep is a ridiculous name for a pub – and the inside is the complete opposite of the Black Horse. Instead of stone walls and cosy fireplaces, the ceiling towers high, with varnished bright beams that look far too new. Pete's bar has a grimy homeliness about it, despite the grimness of the sticky tables. Here, the tables have been polished to a gleaming finish. I can't imagine piles of hiking boots next to the door here, let alone wet-through dogs or trampled grass clippings.

We find a booth and Rhys refuses my offer to pay, saying we're celebrating my news and that it's all on him. We have our usual – two Guinnesses and a cider – but Rhys does admit he's down by a few quid per round compared to 'Horse prices'. We all agree that 'Horse prices' is the official marker by which all other financial transactions will be compared.

The afternoon passes in no time as we drink and laugh. I guess 'the call' for work Rhys was waiting on either didn't come, or was ignored. The thirteen years doesn't come up, neither does Mum or Dad or any of the other stuff. I can't even remember what we talk about, not really, not specifics. It's normal things: Nights out, apps for our phones, the best places to go shopping, holidays we might take. All the topics blur into one.

I'm wanted.

I have parents, a younger brother, friends.

For the first time since I arrived, this village feels like home.

The high pub ceiling zooms towards me and away again, the spotlights above blink and spin. I know I've had too much to drink but I don't think that's the only reason that I find myself resting on Nattie's shoulder, telling her she has lovely hair and that we should definitely move in together. Rhys cheers and then he's off to the bar for another round.

We drink more.

The sky is a dizzying swirl of purple, grey and black when we finally leave. It's late in the evening and night is well on the way as Nattie and I dance our way back to the High Street ahead of

Rhys. The cool air sobers me up a little and, though the colours of the sky still thicken my thoughts, I'm able to walk by myself.

A few of the regulars are on their way out of the Black Horse, meaning I'll have to use my key for the back door when I'm ready for sleep. The night still feels young, though, and there's not a thought that we should separate yet. Nattie leads the way, on past the pub and Via's out towards the hill and then along the river towards Ridge Park. She's swaying and singing to herself out in front as I walk alongside Rhys.

He's one of those types who never seems too affected by alcohol. His words slow and sometimes it feels as if he's not quite able to focus completely, but he can continue a conversation and seems largely in control of himself.

Whether it was Nattie specifically or some sort of fate drawing us, we end up at the tree and my memorial wreath. Nattie flops to the ground and rests her head on the tree, while Rhys and I sit a little more gracefully.

'We should take it down,' Nattie slurs, mouth full of saliva.

'The wreath?' I ask.

'Make it official. You're back, aren't you?'

It is completely dark now but the moon is bright, the sky cloudless. It's clear enough that's it's like daytime in the park. I can see from one side of the field all the way to the other.

Rhys stands and unhooks my memorial from the tree. He puts it carefully on the ground at my feet and I run my fingers across the woven strips of wood.

'How did it last so long?' I ask.

It's Rhys who replies: 'The primary school kids used to replace bits and pieces if they got damp or it started to fall apart. That's probably not even the original. I think there's probably been a few over the years. There was some sort of service here for the ten-year anniversary. I guess there's no need any longer.'

He looks up to the knot in the tree and I follow his gaze to the word 'OLIVIA'. It's more than a series of letters scratched with a penknife; someone who knows what they're doing has engraved the name artfully, as if it was a trophy or medal.

'Burn it.' Nattie cackles as she rocks forward and back, bumping her head gently into the trunk.

'The tree?'

She laughs loudly, the sound echoing around the huge open space.

'The wreath,' she says. 'Burn it.'

Rhys stretches out his legs and pulls a lighter from his pocket, flicking the ignition and sending a flame shooting up into the darkness.

'We can if you want,' he says. He's talking to me. The flame dies and he hands me the lighter.

'Do it!' Nattie calls.

I run my fingers across the brittle, interwoven fettuccini-like threads of wood. Someone's put a lot of work into this. Probably more than one person.

'I don't think I want to.'

'But you're back,' Nattie says. She sits up and shuffles across until she's at my side. 'You don't need this now.'

Rhys pockets his lighter: 'It's still a place for people to remember,' he says. 'It still happened.'

Nattie slumps down onto my shoulder and I put an arm around her. 'But you're home...'

'Yes,' I reply. 'I'm home.'

THIRTY-ONE

Rhys and I help Nattie back to her house. Georgie is still up and I get the sense she rarely, if ever, goes to bed without knowing her daughter is home safely.

Thirteen-year-old habits die hard, I suppose.

She thanks Rhys and it feels like this is a common occurrence – but she saves her best for me, continuing the touchy-feely themes of the day by pulling me in for a hug and saying she never had any doubts either. I don't think Nattie told her specifically but it's no surprise that news of the DNA test has gone around the village.

After that, Rhys and myself traipse solemnly back towards the High Street. He says he lives out past the Angry Sheep, so I'm on his route back. The back lanes of Stoneridge feel even quieter than they did on Sunday. There are few lights in the houses and the warmth of the day has been replaced by a crisp chill.

'Are you and Nattie a thing?' I ask as we walk.

He laughs – but kindly. His words are clear and unslurred. 'We spend a lot of time together but not like that. I started going into the coffee shop to get a sandwich each day when I was working on a job by the school. That's how we met and then we got talking when the shop was empty one day. After that, we started drinking some evenings. She'd come over to my flat to get away from her mum and we'd watch TV, or we'd go to the Horse. Before we knew it, we were in a routine.'

Get away from her mum sounds about right.

'Have you got a girlfriend…?' I try to make it sound as innocent as I can but I'm cringing as soon as the words escape my mouth.

Rhys smiles at that and reaches out to take my hand. His skin is rough, those of a workman. 'It's complicated,' he says. There's a long, telling pause and then: 'I'm not sure girls are for me.'

'Oh.'

He squeezes my fingers and then releases them. I hug my arms across my front, hoping for a bit of warmth, but it's not much good given the night breeze. Rhys is only in shorts and a T-shirt but it's not affecting him.

'I'm still figuring that out,' he adds.

'I didn't mean we should… y'know…' I sound weak and pathetic.

Rhys rubs my shoulder. The ultimate insult.

'I know…' he says.

He's not trying to be unkind but there's a hint of a snigger at the end. Probably nervousness or awkwardness, and yet, perhaps he's laughing at me. Being propositioned by girls and turning them down is funny for him.

The cold has hammered away any sense of tipsiness I had before. I'm suddenly aware that I'm babbling and overcome by embarrassment. The houses, street lamps and parked cars feel very close, as if the village is closing in.

'You okay?' Rhys asks – and I realise I've fallen a few paces behind.

We're close to the High Street and I point to the alley that leads along the rear of the Black Horse. 'I need to go via the back door,' I say.

'I can walk you.'

'No!'

He rocks back slightly, stung by the force of my reply. I apologise quickly but the humiliation is too much. I don't know what I meant anyway. Would I have dragged him back to my room over the pub, or gone off to his flat? Is that what I wanted, or have I drunk too much?

I had a friend – *friends* – and now I've gone and ruined it with at least one of them because I couldn't keep my stupid mouth shut. What happens when Rhys tells Nattie about this? Will they both laugh at me together?

I don't think I take rejection very well.

The last week has been about the opposite of that: being accepted and wanted, becoming part of a family. Now I've ruined it all.

We stand awkwardly at the mouth of the alley, Rhys half-turned towards the main High Street. 'I, um… don't really want to leave you,' he says.

'I'm a big girl.'

'I know, it's just…'

I waft a hand towards the alley. 'It's only through there. I'm fine.'

'I didn't mean—'

I force a cheery smile: 'It's fine, everything's fine! We'll catch up soon.'

'If you're not ready for bed, we can watch some movies at mine if you want? I'll walk you home when you're ready, or I'll sleep on the couch and you can have the bed…? Nattie does that sometimes.'

I shake my head. It sounds good and if he'd suggested that before I opened my big, stupid mouth, I'd have immediately agreed. Not now, though.

Faking a yawn is easy enough and I tell Rhys I'm tired. He takes a step away and replies that, if I'm sure, he'll see me soon. I step into the alley and wait until I hear his footsteps echoing away to nothingness before poking my head back around the wall to make sure he's gone.

What an idiot.

It's only when I turn back into the alley that I wish I'd allowed him to walk me to the door of the Black Horse. The shadows shoot down from the backs of the shops, leaving a thick dark coating across the narrow space. There are wheelie bins left intermittently and the lane is so thin that I have to weave in and out to make my way along.

The shops and cafés of the High Street are on one side and there are houses on the other. Each has high walls that stop me from being able to see anything other than the triangular peak of the roofs. It's even colder in the lane than it was on the road and I hug myself tightly as I continue to dodge around the scattering of bins.

The only time I stop is when I realise I'm at the back of Via's. The yard has been turned into a place to sit outside – but I can't imagine anyone would choose to sip their cappuccino next to the dingy alley, rather than sit on the street in the sunshine, or inside the café itself. The gate is locked but I peer through the metal bars, wondering if the name will change now. Via's was a memory of what had gone but Mum doesn't need to be reminded of the ghosts from the past any longer. Perhaps I should suggest it to her?

I continue around the next set of bins. With the back of the Black Horse in sight, I start fumbling for the keys. They're not in my back pocket and the only ones I appear to have on me are the car keys. I pat down my clothes, trying to remember if I have some sort of concealed pocket anywhere but knowing I don't.

Damn.

They're in the car. All this and I'm going to have to go to the car park anyway. I should've told Rhys I wanted to stay with him.

I could try knocking on the back door but Pete will be in bed and it's really not fair to get him up at this time of the—

I spin quickly, convinced there's someone behind me.

'Hello?' My voice drifts along the alley, unanswered, but there were definitely footsteps behind.

Unsure whether to go forward or back, I arch up onto the tips of my toes, trying to see if there's someone there. The bins are so scattered that anyone could be crouching behind.

'Hello?'

No answer.

It's little comfort that, if I heard anything at all, it was probably a rat.

I hurry past the back door of the pub, heading for the exit of the alley at the other end. It's only five minutes to my car if I hurry, then five minutes back. I can be in bed soon enough.

The fear has left me as I risk a quick glance over my shoulder. My mind's playing tricks, still dulled by the alcohol from earlier. There's nothing behind – but that's when I turn and bump into something in front.

Before I can react, there's a hand over my mouth, someone clamping the back of my head into their chest as I'm spun around and held tightly. It takes me a second or two to realise what's happening. Another arm is across my front, pinning my arms down with far more strength than I can battle against.

I try to shout, to scream, but the hand is squeezing my jaw together and it's only when I try to open my mouth that I realise it's more than a hand. There's a cloth, a wet rag, or—

THIRTY-TWO

It's dark.

There's something grumbling in my right ear, some sort of rumble like an approaching earthquake. When I push up to try to get away from it, I wallop my head into something solid. It catches me a little over my left eye, leaving green stars swirling in the black.

I slump back onto my side and try to figure out what's going on. I'm lying somewhere tight and enclosed. There's some sort of thick plastic underneath me, the type that's found inside a box as packing for a new television. It's glossy and smooth and I'm sliding back and forth as the growling continues.

It's definitely a car. I'm in the boot and can smell petrol or oil, something like that. The odour of a garage forecourt.

The plastic sheeting can't bode well. In an age of forensics and DNA, the only reason for plastic sheeting in a car boot along with a captive is if something awful is going to happen.

I can still taste whatever it was my captor used to knock me out. It's bitter and burns, like the cleaning fluid someone would use on paintbrushes – but worse. I can taste alcohol, too – but only faintly. The remnants of a night that's almost forgotten.

When I close my eyes, there are dancing purple and pink shapes on the inside of my eyelids. It's tiredness and shock and whatever I was knocked out by – but the shapes offer a strange clarity, too. I'm in a car boot that's travelling somewhere – the bumps and potholes in the road tell me that. No point in banging the boot, trying to get attention that won't be there. I need to be smarter about things.

Instead of trying to sit up and banging my head again, I roll onto my back and spread out, running my fingers across the sleekness of the sheeting. The top of the boot is only a short distance above my face but the space is wide and I can feel the shape of the wheel hubs on either side.

There's no obvious way out – but perhaps I could kick through what will likely be the back seats of the car. I press against them with my palms but there's no obvious give. Kicking them with all my weight *might* help me get into the main part of the car but there could be a layer of metal between the boot and the seats. Even if there's not, there's no way I'll get through without the thumping being noticed by whoever's driving. If I'm going to escape, there's no point in making so much noise that I'll put myself in greater danger.

If I can't think of an easy way to escape for now, then I suppose I need to think of why I'm here.

There can only be one reason… can't there? Someone wants rid of me. Abducting and dumping someone in a plastic-lined car boot isn't about scaring a person, it's about making them disappear permanently.

Olivia went missing once and now it's time for round two.

The only other question is who – and that seems obvious too. Since the time I arrived, it's only Ashley who's been outright hostile to my existence. Whether he genuinely thinks I'm after money seems irrelevant. He's even got the fleet of taxis at his disposal.

My only consolation – if it can be called that – is that I'm still alive. If Ashley was going to kill me, it would already have happened. That's what I tell myself. It's not like he messed around with Iain. He woke up without the use of his legs but at least I have that. I even wiggle my toes inside my trainers as if to make the point to myself.

The tone of the engine dips with a gear change and it feels like we're slowing. I slip across the plastic towards the front of the car and try to hold on as the car takes a bend. After that, the bumps become more severe. The first one bounces me up, my nose hitting the plastic that's attached to the roof of the boot. As soon as I land, I'm sent skidding towards the rear of the car as the vehicle lurches to one side, in and out of a pothole.

We must've been on road before but everything is juddery now, like the beginning of a rollercoaster when the train is being dragged to the top of a slope. My teeth chatter, my bones rattle and it's so intense that I can't think properly. It takes all my effort to avoid being hurled from one side of the boot to the other as the car darts across what must be a track or some sort of gravel road.

Even after the worst of it is over, it takes me a few seconds to realise. My neck is sore from being bashed around, my vision as blurry as if I hadn't stopped drinking. My whole body tingles, my fingertips itching from the ride.

It's only then that I notice we've stopped.

I hear the clunk of a car door opening and closing and panic as I realise I must think of something. Do I bite and fight? Scratch and kick? I'm not tied in any way but everything's such a fuzzy, bumpy mess.

The boot pops open and a bright orb of light burns into my eyes. There's a hand pulling at me and everything's so mixed up that there's nothing I can do. Before I realise what's happening, I'm on the ground, feeling the dust and dirt beneath my palms.

The white sears into my eyes once more and then zooms away, carving a wide pillar of light off into the darkness. It's only then that I realise it's a torch being held by someone.

'Get up,' a man's voice says – and he pulls at me again, gripping my wrist and yanking me up like a child's doll. I'm leaning on the side of the car and not entirely sure how I got there, trying to blink away the brutish glare of the torch.

Something metallic hits the floor somewhere close to the car, but when I turn towards it, I realise the man, my captor, is directly in front of me.

And it isn't Ashley Pitman at all.

2016: LILY, 19

The door on the street is unmarked but the address definitely matches the note on my phone. It's all very grimy and gritty, something from an old noir movie but with added mould on the walls. I head up a set of stairs onto a landing where there is a door marked 'JAMES JOHNSON, PRI ATE INVE TIGATOR'.

I should probably turn around, but it's not as if I have a lot of choice. The best in the business costs far more money than I presently have, which leaves me with a 'priate invetigator'.

The 'hang on' comes almost immediately after I knock and there's a shuffling from the other side of the door followed by what sounds like a chair falling over. It takes a good thirty seconds until the door swings inwards to reveal a scruffy man in a brown jacket with elbow patches. He looks like a university professor who's hit bad times, with a thin peppering of obviously dyed brown hair that's been combed aggressively forward in an attempt to hide the largest forehead I've ever seen.

'Are you, um, Mr Johnson?' I ask.

'Call me Jimmy,' he says, offering his hand.

His grip is clammy and he wipes his palm on his jacket after ushering me into the office. I'm not sure what I expected from a private investigator's office but it wasn't such emptiness. There's a tall pot plant in the corner of the room, a single desk with a computer and phone on top, plus chairs on either side, then two filing cabinets in the furthest corner. Nothing else. It's like a photo from the cheapest page of the IKEA catalogue. The living room of Dad's house... of *my* house... is bigger than this.

Jimmy sits behind his desk and starts drumming his fingers on the surface. 'How can I help you, Miss...'

'Armitage. Lily Armitage. My dad died a month ago and I found this in his top drawer.'

I slip the envelope across the desk and he removes the contents, scanning both pages before returning them.

'You're adopted,' he says matter-of-factly.

'Right. I didn't know. I only found out after he died.'

'Oh...' The investigator is not good at hiding his surprise.

'I'd like to know who I am. I've been online, but you have to register your details and hope the other person – hope your *parents* – haven't opted out of contact. It took them more than a week to let me know that my mother *has* opted out. She doesn't want to hear from me. I made a couple of phone calls but they say it's impossible.'

'You want me to find your real parents...?'

It's only a word, three letters – 'yes' – and yet it sticks in my throat.

I want to know and yet I don't. Every question answered only leaves another question. Why didn't my dad tell me any of this? I know there was a time where I would have been too young to understand. Perhaps, when my mum died, they were getting ready to say something? Maybe it would've been later, like they had an idea I'd be ready at twelve, or thirteen? But then Mum died and it was only me and Dad.

And the question of 'why?' is what I've been asking myself for the past few weeks. The thing is, deep down, I think I know the answer. With Mum gone, Dad had only me. If he'd said I had another family out there somewhere and I'd gone looking for them, where would that leave him? I understand and yet I don't.

What's worse, I'll never have the opportunity to ask him because he isn't here any longer.

'Yes,' I say.

Jimmy nods slowly, eyeing me closely and focusing on my chest for a moment too long. 'You don't sound so sure.'

'I'm not sure but I want to know anyway.'

'How old are you?'

'Nineteen.' I slide him over my driver's licence – Lily Armitage – and he skims the front before passing it back. 'I saw your rates online,' I add, 'but it was a bit unclear how much everything actually is with all the expenses included. I didn't know if there was some sort of cap, or…?'

'It's eighty pounds per hour, plus expenses.'

'What sort of expenses?'

'It depends, but generally travel. Sometimes I might need to pay someone for information. I'd imagine this might take a little of that…'

Which means he'll likely bribe someone for the information. I've wondered that myself. Is there someone I can find that works with the adoption agency who I would be able to pay off? Even if there was, how would I find that out? And what if they say no and report me to the police? I've not looked into the laws either I or the person inside the agency might end up breaking. Could I go to prison?

'If it's eighty pounds an hour, do you know how long it might take?' I ask.

'How long's a piece of string?' he replies. 'It might take an hour; it might take twenty or more. If you have a ceiling, I can always keep in touch and let you know if I'm close to the limit.'

I suppose a part of me was hoping he'd go easy because I'm a teenager with a sob story. If I learnt anything from Zoe, it's that manipulating men can be easy. *Can* be. It depends on the man.

'I'm selling a house,' I say. 'I'll have money but I don't have a lot right now. Can I pay a certain amount and then the rest of the balance down the line…?'

Jimmy shakes his head. 'Sorry. I do take a deposit but that's only to cover expenses. There are weekly payments due, depending on how long things might take. You'd get regular updates with that. It could be done in under a week, of course, but I'd require the full balance being cleared before handing over information.'

For the moment, I have a little over five hundred quid in the bank – but that's for everything: food, fuel for the car… I could spend all that and more with Jimmy but what then? The house *will* be up for sale, but not yet, mainly because it needs such a lot of work doing. Dad had no savings and what little he had in the bank is going through probate. At some point, when the house is sold, I'll have hundreds of thousands of pounds – but not right now.

The alternative is to wait, come back in however many months once a sale has gone through and ask again. Either that, or go somewhere else, find someone cheaper.

But what do I do until then?

I know I can't let this hang for however many months it might take. My life is on hold, a trawler out in the middle of the ocean for which turning back would take too long.

'I can pay a couple of hundred up front and show you the documents to prove I own a house. I'm hoping it'll sell sooner rather than later.'

Jimmy taps something on his keyboard and stares at the computer monitor for a moment. It's obvious he isn't really doing anything but then he pulls a calculator out from his top drawer and bashes some numbers into that as well.

'Hmm…'

He stands and rounds the table until he's behind me and then it's impossible not to wince as his fingers start massaging my shoulders.

'Nineteen,' he coos and I know what's coming next. 'I suppose the question is how much do you want to find your parents?'

'I need to know who they are.'

'Hmm...' His fingers stop moving but they've tensed my muscles rather than relaxed them. 'I suppose we could come to some sort of arrangement...'

THIRTY-THREE

It might not be *Ashley* Pitman but it's close.

Max has a torch in one hand and an enormous hunting dagger in the other. The blackness of his hair is almost blue in the moonlight but he seems thicker, stronger than I remember. He was probably always like that; it was when compared to his brother that he felt smaller.

Behind him is the gravel of an empty car park. The moon is hidden by the height of the surrounding trees, leaving only a misty sapphire glow.

He nods to the ground. 'That's for you.'

It's a spade, crusty and well used; something that might've been abandoned on a building site at some point.

'What do I do with it?'

He's disconcertingly calm. 'For now, carry it.'

'What about that after that?'

'Dig. I thought you were smarter than everyone, remember?'

I pick up the spade and am surprised by how heavy it is. The handle is thick and meaty, the end solid with square corners.

'Don't even think about it,' Max says.

He's right – he's given me something that *could* be used as a weapon but only because he has both hands full with the torch and knife. There might be a time where I can use it – but it's not now. Not while he's on his guard.

'Where are we going?' I ask.

He uses the knife to point towards an opening between two large trees. 'There's a path through there. Keep walking until I say otherwise.'

'What if I don't?'

I'm testing the waters, trying to stop my voice from wavering.

He shrugs and twirls the knife between his fingers, in complete control. 'Then don't.'

There's a wicked glint in his eye and it's clear he doesn't mind which choice I make. One means a spade versus knife fight right here – and I don't fancy my chances – the other means I might have time to think of something else.

I turn to head towards the path, but the moment I do, there's a rustle of... *something* off towards the other side of the car park. Max spins the torch around, shining the light out towards the noise, but the space is too far for the gloom to be penetrated. There's a moment, only the fleeting glimpse of a thought, where I think this is my chance. I even raise the spade a little – but Max is thinking ahead of me. He's taken enough of a step back so that he's out of range and he turns from me to the noise and back again.

'A deer,' he says. 'There are all sorts of beasts in these woods – now get on.'

He jabs the torch into my back and there is no other sound as I scuff my feet towards the gap in the trees. The light from Max's torch shines out ahead of me, illuminating the way. When I risk a glance backwards, he hisses for me to turn around – and he's a good couple of lengths away. Swinging the spade is not an option. I have to keep going for now.

There's a sign for 'Riversway Country Park' – which I've never heard of, but the setting makes sense for this sort of thing. Aside from family visits on a weekend, country parks are surely there for dogging in the car park and the odd bit of body burying.

The path is largely made of dirt, with intermittent small stones to help with footing when it's wet. I keep an eye out for anything large, even though the chances of scooping it up and somehow hitting Max in one swoop would be lower than using the spade.

The enveloping trees quickly swallow the moonlight and the only light of note is the flickering pillar from Max's torch. I can hear him walking behind, keeping at my pace. He never seems to get any closer but his presence is always there.

It's a few minutes until we reach a fork. There are no signs but Max calls 'right' and I do as I'm told, still scuffing my feet. The spade is starting to feel even heavier in my hands and I wonder if I could turn, throw it at Max and make a run for it. I'm already a few strides ahead and might get a couple of seconds more. The obvious problem is that I have no idea where I am. If I follow the path, he has the advantage; if I don't, then the forest bed is a series of traps. Even in the light of Max's torch, I can see the twigs and branches strewn across either side of the path. There are bushes, too, plus tufty plants and other things to fall over. In daylight, there would be a multitude of leg-breakers hidden from view; at night, I'd be lucky not to end up flat on my face within seconds.

'Why are you doing this?'

I try to sound as vulnerable as I can, nineteen years young; weak and defenceless.

'Shut up.'

'Do you think Mum would want this?'

'Shut up and keep walking.'

'I won't tell anyone if you let me go. We'll pretend it never happened.'

There's a pause and a fraction of a second where I think, perhaps, he's considering it. Then a weary: 'Do I *really* have to do this here or can you just shut up?'

I stop talking but, even though I'm quiet, the forest is a hive of noise. There is endless rustling from both sides of the path; the scurry of night-time critters shuffling around looking for food.

Max mentioned a deer and, who knows, perhaps a miracle will happen and one will appear from nowhere, shocking Max and giving me a chance to run.

Snap!

I freeze, twisting towards the sound which has come from behind. Max heard it as well. He's staring along the path but quickly spins back to me, holding out the knife and then edging a step or two back the way we've come. It sounded like the crack of a twig, or the collapse of a tree branch. Something wooden.

The moment I think about lunging with the spade, Max turns back, sending the arc of light directly into my eyes and dazzling me once more. I squeeze my eyes closed, gasping and staggering before I feel him pushing me along the path with the torch.

'Get going,' he says. 'It's only a deer.'

'I can't see.'

'I don't care. Walk.'

He shoves me once more and I have no option other than to stagger along the path. It's only a few seconds until the stars have cleared but the moment of brightness has left me feeling more disorientated than before.

It's my mind playing tricks, I know it is, but I try to convince myself the snap of wood wasn't a deer. It was help – a saviour who happened to be out in the middle of nowhere and is now following at a distance. The rustling continues intermittently from either side and then there's another crack of wood – this time from far in front of us.

Help. It has to be help.

I clasp the spade tight with one hand and untie my hair with the other, looping the tie around my wrist.

'What are you doing?' Max asks.

'Nothing. I had an itch. I'm walking.'

'Get on with it then.'

We reach a spot with two dog waste bins next to a bench. There's a metal plaque on the back rest of the bench and the light of Max's torch glimmers bright against it.

'Right,' Max says.

I stop but don't turn. 'Right, where?'

'Into the woods.'

He flashes the light in the direction he means but, even with that, it seems eerily dark.

'Get on with it,' he says.

I do, scratching a foot against the verge and continuing. It's only then that it dawns on me we must really be in the middle of nowhere. If Max was worried about being seen, he wouldn't be using the torch. I don't know where Riversway Country Park is to have any idea what the nearest town or village might be, let alone in which direction. The sky is clear enough to be able to see the stars but things like constellations are a mystery to me. I'm far too used to using my phone to navigate.

My phone.

It's hard to hold onto the spade with one hand and I almost drop it – but I do manage to establish it's no longer in my pocket. Max must've poached it when he knocked me out. Not a surprise, I guess. The time to fully panic is getting near.

'Missing something?'

Max sounds like his brother when he gloats.

There's another crack from behind but neither of us turn this time. It's one noise among hundreds of others. Deer, squirrels, rats or those giant leopard-like cats people always see but never get a good photo of.

Max keeps the light a little ahead of me but all it really shows is that tearing off without a torch is madness. Every other step has something to trip over and, even with the spotlight, I still stumble on a number of occasions.

I've lost all track of time, not simply from when I was in the alley but since the car stopped. I could've been walking for five minutes or thirty. Neither would surprise me.

We walk for a while longer but it's slower going over the rough carpet of plants and weeds. Out of nowhere, Max says 'stop' and I do. The light hovers on my back and flickers from side to side. It's hard to know for sure, but it feels like we're in some sort of clearing. The moss is thicker and the whole area is covered with a peppering of clover leaves.

'Don't move.'

The torchlight shines away from me, sweeping through my peripheral vision and then, presumably, off behind me until it reappears on my other side.

'What are you looking for?' I ask.

'Shush.'

The light makes another arcing sweep from side to side and then stops on an outcrop off to my left. The ground dips down into a shallow bowl and the moss is slightly lighter than the rest of the surrounding area.

'There,' Max says.

I risk turning but he's further back than I thought, a good half-dozen strides away. His features are largely hidden by the night, though I can still make out his outline.

'What?' I ask.

'There are bones buried there.'

I turn to focus on the outcrop, wondering if he'll add anything else. *Bones*.

'Is that why you gave me a spade?' I try to sound confident and assured but my voice wavers. I can't help it.

'You really are the smart one, aren't you?' he says.

'Why do you want me to dig up some bones?'

There's a pause and the light flickers slightly as he breathes in. 'I don't, not really. I nearly came out here myself just to check.'

'Check what?'

Another silence. Longer this time. 'I know you're not Olivia Adams.'

I can feel him watching me through the darkness – and then it's obvious. He knew all along. We've been playing this game back and forth, but there are only two people on the planet who know I can't be Olivia.

Me... and the person who killed her.

THIRTY-FOUR

'How'd you do it?'

Max is quieter when he next speaks and it's almost funny what's happened over the past week. He'd have known I was an imposter the whole time but was unable to say anything about it. Then I agreed to the DNA test and he must have thought I'd be exposing myself. It's no wonder he seemed so spaced out when Mum read the letter to say it was a match.

'Do what?' I reply.

Anything I can do to delay the inevitable.

'You know. How did you fake the test?'

'I didn't.'

He laughs but there's menace there. 'Get digging and we'll see you're lying.'

I really don't want to do it. I know I'll be digging my own grave. It won't be one Olivia in there any longer, it'll be two. But digging up those bones will take time and that's one thing I am running short on. I move over to the spot and Max trails behind, holding the light steady.

'There,' he says when I'm standing over the hollow.

'How far down?'

'Get digging and we'll find out. We've got all night.'

It only takes one shunt of spade into ground to tell me this isn't going to work. The ground is hard from weeks without any sort of rain. It takes so much effort to get even one spadeful of dirt out that I know it's going to take hours. We *have* hours, but that's not the point.

'I thought you were your brother,' I say. Talking is my only hope.

'Get on and dig.'

'I *am* digging.'

And I am. Slowly.

'When I was in the car,' I add, 'I woke up and I thought it was Ashley who'd taken me.'

Max scoffs. He's standing a short distance away, keeping the light steady on the curved pit. 'My brother is many things – but the major thing is a big mouth. He does a lot of talking but he doesn't know half of what's going on around him.'

I crunch the spade into the soil again, twisting and wriggling it until another square full of dirt, dust and plant roots come up.

'Does that mean he doesn't know what happened to Olivia?' I ask.

A pause and the light flickers. 'I thought *you* were Olivia…?'

I don't reply to that, instead shovelling out two more mounds of earth. My shoulders and biceps are burning.

'That little cow was a trap,' Max says.

'Olivia?'

It feels odd to be using the name to talk about someone else. I'd spent so long getting used to the name being mine. Olivia Elizabeth Adams. It's my name and yet it isn't.

Max growls his reply: 'Sarah would have stayed with him forever because of that girl. Didn't matter how unhappy she was or how much she wanted to be with me. I wouldn't have had a chance.'

That explains one thing. It's not entirely a surprise, I suppose. Whatever the media might have thought, Stoneridge is far too inward-looking for villagers not to have noticed a strange car or van in the vicinity. If the idea of a stranger staging an abduction is discounted, then Olivia had to have been taken by someone who knew her. Who had more to gain than Max? On the back of what happened, he's had a thirteen-year relationship with his childhood sweetheart. Georgie said he followed Mum around like a puppy and this is why – pure infatuation.

'Mum told me she slept with you while she was married to Dad.'

The light darts up from the ground to my face, temporarily blinding me before flickering down once more.

'She what?'

'She said you were together a few weeks before Olivia went missing.'

The light wavers from side to side.

'What else did she say?'

'That the marriage was in trouble whether or not Olivia disappeared.'

There's silence for a while, followed by a softer: 'Dig.'

I shovel out a couple more piles of dirt but I've barely made an impact on the overall space.

'Did she love him?' Max sounds as if he genuinely doesn't know. That he's spent thirteen years asking himself this but has never been brave enough to ask his wife.

'Yes,' I reply.

'What about me?'

'I think so.'

Three more mounds of dirt come out. It's getting easier now the top level has gone. The earth underneath is mushier and the spade carves through it comfortably. Depending on how deep Olivia's bones are, this might not take so long. All I can do in that case is try to drag things out.

'What did you do to her?' I ask.

'Olivia?'

'Who else?'

There is no reply for a moment and then a crisp, unemotional: 'Her neck was snapped before I pulled her over the back gate. She wouldn't have felt much.'

That's it. He speaks without remorse and could be talking about driving along the motorway or making a salad.

I indicated and moved into the outside lane before switching back.

I chopped up some tomatoes to go with that lettuce. I think there's some French dressing in the cupboard.

Olivia means nothing to him.

I dig out a couple more spadefuls and then stop for a moment, leaning on the nearest tree.

'I didn't tell you to stop.'

'My arms are hurting. I need a minute.'

Max seems to think this over – though it's hard to know because I can't see him, I can only see the light.

'Who are you?' he asks, the question echoing through the dark.

'Does it matter?'

'No one gets one over on me or my family.'

'It's not like that's what I was trying to do.'

The light darts up to my face and down again. It's definitely not an accident this time – if it ever was – it's a deliberate ploy to dazzle me.

'The only reason you're still around is because I've got a dodgy shoulder,' Max says. 'That won't stop me digging the hole myself if I have to. Your choice.'

The torchlight glints to the blade of Max's knife and it looks larger than before. The tip is razor sharp. If there was any question that talking is delaying the inevitable, then he's confirmed it.

'You a gippo?' he asks.

'A what?'

'Gippo. Gypsy. Pikey. Traveller. Didicoi. Whatever you call 'em.'

'No.'

'That was some story you spun Sarah. She believed every word. I figured you must be something to do with the gippos.'

'I made all that up. Took me months.'

I shovel out another heap of dirt and have cleared the surface of a good square metre or so. Everything below will be easier.

'Credit to ya,' he says. 'It sounded good.'

That was the point, I suppose. It had to *sound* good, to be conceivable. People want to believe there are demons on the other side of the garden gate. That's the fear upon which newspapers and horror movies both prey. They're two sides of the same coin.

Travellers roll into town and people are trying to move them on before the handbrake's been lifted. Mine was a story that was easy to believe and hard to disprove. By their very name, they're travellers. They *travel*. They could be anywhere. As soon as I thought of it, I knew it would sound plausible.

Max isn't done. 'Ashley believed it,' he adds.

'I thought he was the one who *didn't* believe me?'

'Oh, aye. You had him hook, line and sinker. His problem was he thought you were after his money. Not that he has much.'

Another pile of soil. It's crumbly now.

'What's your name?' Max asks. 'Your *real* name?'

It feels wrong to say it now, as if it belongs to someone else. In many ways it does, of course. It's not mine to use any longer.

He takes a step towards me and sounds firmer this time: 'Come on. I'm not messing around.'

'It's Lily.'

He stops and the light holds firm on the ground. It's my only way of knowing where he is.

'Lily what?'

'Armitage.'

He repeats the name and it sounds foul in his voice. 'Lily Armitage,' he says again. 'Should I know that name?'

'No.'

'How did you fake the test?'

'I didn't.'

He steps forward again and the light flashes from side to side.

'You're going to tell me, Lily Armitage. Was it the lab? You knew someone there?'

'I didn't.'

'You paid someone, then?'

'I didn't pay anyone and I don't know anyone at the lab. Mum fixed that up, remember. Not me.'

'Don't call her that. She's *not* your mother.'

He spits the final sentence and the controlled anger is now closer to outright fury.

'I'm only going to ask you one more time,' he says. 'You *will* tell me: how did you cheat the test?'

2016: LILY, 19

Call Me Jimmy invites me to sit and I do. He rounds the desk and locks the door to his office. It clicks ominously and then he's fussing at the back of the room.

'Fancy a tea?' he asks.

'Not really.'

He clicks the kettle on anyway and then rests against the table at the back of the room. The tea table is a new addition to the office. Nothing special, of course – that's not Jimmy's style. He's got a cheap side table, a cheaper plastic kettle, a box of teabags and a small carton of long-life milk. God forbid he gets a fridge.

I sit and he slouches against the wall as we wait in silence. What is there to say to each other? He's forty years older than me and we have nothing in common other than that I need something from him and he craves something from me.

When the kettle clicks off, he swills a teabag around a grimy mug with a grimier spoon and then swirls a splash of milk before taking his seat back on the other side of the desk. It's all for show and I've learnt that if I try to make him hurry, he only takes longer. He knows where the power lies because, in the end, I need him more than he wants me.

'How have you been?' he asks.

'Do you care?'

'I'm being nice! Isn't that what you want?'

'Yes…'

He sips his tea and mutters something about it being hot. 'So...
how have you been?'

'Fine.'

'How's the house?'

'Unsold.'

He nods slowly but doesn't add anything, then he starts opening
the pile of mail on his desk. Despite the scumminess of his office,
Jimmy has a fancy letter-opener with an opal handle and a razor-
sharp tip. He slices open the top couple of letters and skims the
contents. I know he's not reading them, not really.

The investigator glances up to me: 'Do you want to clean up?'

'What?'

He nods to the door. 'There's a bucket and some bleach in the
hallway cupboard. I figured you could mop the floor...?'

For Jimmy, it's all about the humiliation. One thing after
another. He wants me to walk away – except I'm not going to do
that. Not now it feels so close.

Instead of complaining, I do precisely as he suggests. He tosses
me a key and I unlock the office door and head into the hall, using
the key to unlock what turns out to be a storage room. There are
two mops, one bucket and an enormous drum of bleach, the type
of thing that can only come from a cash and carry. There's also a
small sink.

I fill the bucket with bleach and water, trying not to feel too
woozy from the fumes. Back in the office, Jimmy continues opening
his mail and fiddling with his computer as I mop the floor around
him. He tells me to open a window, so I do. Then he tells me I've
missed a bit, so I swab away at it before moving on.

When I'm done, the water is black and the room smells like a
hospital ward. I tip the murky liquid down the sink and then return
everything to the cupboard before heading back into the office.

'Lock the door,' he says.

I do and when I turn around, Jimmy has shrugged his jacket off onto the back of his chair. As far as I can figure out, he wears the same clothes every day – the brown suit with the elbow patches, a white shirt and a brown tie.

He undoes his tie and hangs that on top of his jacket and then starts to unbuckle his belt.

'You said you had news…?'

Jimmy stops unfastening his belt and presses both hands on his desk looking down on me. 'What's the rush?' he replies.

'It's just… this is the seventh time I've been here.'

I know I shouldn't have said something. It's never worked before and any time I question him only makes things worse.

The belt comes off and then he drapes that over the chair, too.

'I've got all the information you want,' he says.

He's grinning, brimming with arrogance, but it feels like he's punched me in the face.

'You've… what?'

I can barely get the words out.

'I know who your mother is. I've got your birth certificate – and, let me say this, it's a *very* interesting name indeed.'

I listen for any sense of ambiguity. He's done this before: getting my hopes up, only to say I'd taken something the wrong way.

'What do you mean?' I ask.

'Precisely that. I know your mother's name. Once I had it, I did a quick Google search or two and, what do you know, if you choose to contact her, she's going to have one hell of a story for you.'

I stare at him and he's smiling, relishing the power he holds.

'Can you tell me?'

He remains where he is for a moment and then surprises me by standing up straighter and moving to the filing cabinets at the back of the room. He pats his pockets elaborately, acting as if he doesn't have the key and then taps the top of the cabinet before turning back to me.

'Not yet,' he says.

'When?'

He undoes the button of his trousers. 'We've got business to attend to first.'

'I can't. It's my time of the month.'

His hand hovers over the zip. 'We can do other things.'

'I want to read it first.'

His eyes narrow as he straightens, then he rebuttons his trousers and digs into the front pocket for a key. He unlocks the cabinet and hunts through whatever's inside before pulling out a buff-coloured cardboard wallet. Jimmy takes his time, using agonising seconds to re-lock the cabinet and readjust his crotch. If I ask again, he'll find a way to delay giving me the information. I'm lucky I've got him to comply this much.

Jimmy crosses back to his desk and sits. He flits through the contents of the file, making the odd 'hmm' sound along with a muttered, 'that's interesting'.

I hate him.

'Are you sure you want this?' he asks, waving it towards me mockingly.

'Yes.'

'Are you *really* sure? It's one thing to *think* you want it; another to *actually* want it.'

'I want to read what's inside.'

'Hmm.'

He grips the folder tightly and then passes it across the desk. My hand is shaking as I reach and I fully expect him to snatch it away.

But no.

It's in my hand and my fingers are trembling as I lift the front cover to look at what's underneath. There are eight or nine pages. A birth certificate. Adoption forms. A letter addressed to Mum and Dad. More letters. Another form.

I flick from one page to the next, faster and faster, until I stare up with rage that's now impossible to conceal. 'What is *this*?' I demand.

'That's everything you wanted.'

I toss the file onto his desk. 'All the names and information are blanked out. It's useless to me.'

'I've got the full, unredacted version. Don't worry about that.'

'Where?'

He grins broadly and viciously, showing his teeth. 'You get the full version when I get paid.'

His mouth twitches wider, a kid on a rollercoaster having the time of his life.

'I thought we had an agreement,' I say.

The smile doesn't shift. 'Is there something in writing that I'm unaware of?'

He unlocks the drawer of his desk and reaches in, taking out two pages of paper and placing them on the desk, side by side.

It's an itemised bill, listing hours worked, miles travelled and all sorts of other things. The final item is 'miscellaneous', which, given it's the largest amount of money spent, I can only imagine is some sort of bribe.

The only figure that really matters is the one in the final column of the final page.

£2,357.

'That's plus VAT,' Jimmy says.

'I don't have the money,' I say.

'No money, no information.'

'But I'll have it – you know that. You know the house is for sale.'

'I guess you'll have to wait then…'

I haven't cried in a long time but the lump is in my throat again. 'I thought we had an agreement…?'

It's more of a whimper than a statement – but that's exactly what gets Jimmy off. 'That was the deposit,' he says. 'Enough to cover initial expenses but nothing more. If you wanted to find another way to pay for services rendered, you should've said.' He licks his lips. 'And, let's be honest, you're not *that* good.'

He rolls his chair back a little and unbuttons his trousers once more, spreading his legs wide. 'Now are you getting on your knees, or not? I can knock fifty quid off the bill if you want? My problem is that I'm too damned nice.'

Jimmy sneers at me over his desk as he unzips his flies and then pushes his trousers to the floor. He's wearing flannel checked boxer shorts, as ever. I'd like to think he has a lot of matching pairs but it seems unlikely. The dirty bastard never changes his clothes.

He checks his watch. 'Come on. I haven't got all day.'

I'm on autopilot as I stand and round the desk. The floorboards are still a little damp from where I mopped up and the bleach singes my skin as I fall to my knees. Jimmy grins wider and wiggles his backside, slipping his boxer shorts down until they're around his ankles.

'Let's call it forty quid off the bill,' he says. 'Perhaps if you're *really* good, I'll bump it back up to fifty. Be careful with the teeth.'

He laughs and then it's like I'm watching someone else. It's someone else's hand that reaches onto the desk and picks up the letter-opener. Someone else who thrusts forward and plunges it into the private investigator's stomach. The blade comes out and then thunders into his throat, his chest, his stomach for a second time, then a third.

Jimmy doesn't get a chance to fight. His final word is 'teeth' and then he's on the floor, blood seeping onto the floorboards and pooling around the legs of the table.

I don't know how long passes as I remain sitting on the floor. The investigator's bare arse cheeks are facing up, riddled with stretch marks and pockmarked cellulite.

In the end, Dad was right. Sometimes people need to be put down like dogs. I might be adopted, but I suppose we share something in common. I didn't know I had it in me but here we are.

There'll be DNA in the office – but not only mine. Any other clients he has will have left skin cells and hairs. There's not a lot of point in trying to clean up the scene, I'll simply empty the drum of bleach over the body, floor and chair and leave it at that. Besides, I've watched enough crime shows on television to know I'm not on the DNA database anyway. The only way this can be traced to me is if I'm in his files. The alley on which his office lies is far too dingy for anything like CCTV. I came on foot and can head to one end of the alley, drop over the barrier to the lane below and then be in the park in moments. Nobody will have a clue. The only worry is the blood on my own clothes but I have a jacket that will hopefully cover that until I'm home.

Jimmy's calendar is easy to find on his computer. I click into it and delete my name from today's schedule, before searching for 'Lily' and deleting any other reference. I remove myself from his contacts list and then slip his phone from his jacket pocket and put it into my own. I've never emailed him, so no need to worry about that, which means the only other place I am in his life is within his files.

I set the computer to search for any references to 'Lily' or 'Armitage' and then unlock the filing cabinet.

His put-on search for my file was nothing but a show – 'Armitage' is at the front. I flick through a few more just in case but it seems unlikely I'd show up anywhere other than in my own file.

I know I need to get the bleach – but I've already waited too long for this. My fingers are trembling once more as I flip the front cover of the file and skim the first few pages.

There are two birth certificates – an original and the amended one. The writing is spidery and complicated on the original. No father is listed – but my mother's name is there and so is an address.

It's an anticlimax – someone named Sarah Hanham from a place called Stoneridge.

I've never heard of her or it. Was he teasing when he said it was an interesting name?

A few pages on and there's a marriage certificate between Sarah Hanham and Daniel Adams. That also happened in Stoneridge, which makes it a good place to start looking if that's what I want.

There is more in this file than the false one Jimmy first offered. It'll be lots to take in but there's a petition of divorce, a news story printed from the Internet about a missing child, a second marriage certificate.

Ultimately, as interesting as everything else will be, only one thing matters: I know my mother's name.

THIRTY-FIVE

I can't see Max but I can feel him staring at me through the dark.
'You're adopted?' he says.

He doesn't sound convinced.

'The DNA test confirmed it,' I reply. 'I had the papers before
that but the test proved she's my mum. It was confirmation for
me as much as it was for her.'

'I don't understand. I've known Sarah since we were children.
When were you born?'

The spade clunks into the earth at my feet and I close my eyes for
a second, saying a silent prayer for the sister who's buried beneath
my feet. I can never say sorry enough for stealing her name – but
it was the only way. Before I came, it never occurred to me that
she'd been murdered by someone in the village. I assumed – like
everyone else – that she'd been abducted, never to be seen again.
Nobody ever comes back.

'You must know your birthday…?' Max says.

'I do.'

'How old are you? It's the thing that always confused me. Olivia
would have been eighteen and you *look* eighteen.'

'Olivia would have been eighteen years old and six months.
I'm twenty and four months.'

I still can't see him clearly through the dark but the cogs must
be whirring in Max's mind. I'm almost two years older than Olivia,
which means…

'You're my dad.'

Silence.

The critters and rustling undergrowth has hushed and even the animals have stopped to listen.

'I can't be...'

'You are. I didn't know that before I came here, but you're my father.'

'Stop saying that.' He snaps his words and then the light darts from me as Max marches away from the grave, ending up in a hollow between the trees. The moon seeps through the trees, providing him with a halo. For the first time in a while, I can see his face. His eyes are wide, staring out to the darkness. The torch is aimed at the floor, the knife limp in his other hand.

I drop the spade onto Olivia's resting place and walk slowly across the clearing.

'Stop.'

The light flashes up to my face and then settles on my feet. I freeze where I am.

'Sarah went missing for a year,' Max says. It's the softest I've ever heard him speak. He's genuinely hurt. 'Her mother wouldn't let her leave the house.'

'Georgie told me.'

Max looks up, but I don't know if he can see me properly. Apart from my feet, I'm in the dark. He's still being spotlighted through the trees.

'That bitch always hated me,' he adds.

'Georgie?'

A shake of the head. 'Sarah's mum. She was always poisoning her against me, telling her to find some doctor or lawyer, or something. When she locked her in the house all year, I assumed it was to keep her away from me. I didn't realise she was pregnant.'

'She made her give me up for adoption.'

'How do you know that?'

'Mum sort of told me. Not quite – she was talking about Olivia. She said her mum wanted her to put Olivia up for adoption but she chose not to. She said she was tired of being told what to do. I think that's because her mum had already forced her to give up one child for adoption and she wasn't going to get rid of another.'

Max doesn't argue. It's speculation but the times match. The only real question is how Mum managed to get pregnant twice by the age of eighteen. I suppose she wasn't the first and won't be the last – and the fact Georgie was also pregnant at a similar age means there was something not quite right about the sex education at the local school.

It's not a question I'll be asking if I ever get the chance.

'I can't believe she never said anything…'

I don't reply – and it's not as if I disagree. Mum's carried this secret for twenty years. I wonder if, deep down, she has an inkling that perhaps the DNA test wasn't all that it appears. Ashley will never know how close he was when he pushed my dad and told him that the test didn't prove he was the father.

Because that's how I think of him.

Dan might not be *my* father but he is *Olivia's* father and I'm her. Lily's parents are both dead and so is she. All that's left is the money from the sale of the house – and I'll be switching that into a new account as soon as I have one in Olivia's name. Now I have her birth certificate, I'll be swapping everything else, too. I might even retake my driving test with her details. I've been driving for long enough to know what I'm doing.

Except none of that is going to happen because I'm stuck in the woods with my other father. Dad number three. The one who's going to kill me.

'I never wanted children,' Max says. He's calm and introspective, looking at his feet. 'I would've never wanted you and I didn't want Harry. All I wanted was her.'

It's awful but there's something about his brutal honesty that's almost to be respected. He loves a woman so much, loves *my mum* so much, that he's done all this.

Almost to be respected.

It's terrifying. If Max could snap the neck of an innocent girl and callously bury her in the middle of nowhere, then what's he going to do to his own son? There will be a day where Mum pays Harry too much attention and then that poor little boy will have 'an accident'. Or he'll go missing, too. There is no length to which Max won't go.

He stands straighter and the devil is in his eyes. It's only there for a moment, then he steps out of the moonlight into darkness once more. The torchlight flares into my eyes, sending green and purple shapes spinning once more.

'I'm done,' he says. The knife flashes up in his grasp, the blade catching the light and glinting. 'I've already killed Olivia Adams once and now it's time to do it again.'

THIRTY-SIX

Low branches and hidden tripwires or not, there's no point in hanging around now. I've got a couple of metres' head start and bolt sideways. The light flashes towards me and it's then that luck finally strikes. Max trips on something and I hear him crashing to the ground with a bellow of fury. The light spins away from me and I don't waste a second in looking back to see where it's gone.

The earth is a mix of moss, caked soil and branches at ankle height. I dodge around a large thick clump of bushes, head down, and race towards what looks to be the darkest area of woods. I've not got much chance of outrunning Max, especially not as he has the torch, but I can at least find somewhere to hide.

There's a gruff succession of swearing from somewhere behind and a series of cracking, crunching twigs. I've got enough of a lead that Max will hear me before he sees me, so I slide behind the trunk of a thick tree and hold my breath.

The bark is rough and there are no low hanging branches. I couldn't climb it even if I thought it was a good idea.

Silence.

There was so much rustling on the walk here but the creatures that live in the woods must have pulled up the deckchairs to watch the show.

'Lily…'

The name stings. It's not mine any longer and Max knows it.

'Come out, come out wherever you are…'

The light of the torch sweeps from one side of the tree to the other, not slowing or stopping. The beam is wide and dim, so he's not *that* close.

'C'mon, Olivia. We can talk about this. You're my daughter.'

I remember Call Me Jimmy in his office, pants round his ankles, and it strikes me that this murderer's blood is a part of me. Some people talk about nature and nurture and I had it from both sides. One father says that bad people have to be put down like dogs – and another snaps the neck of little girls.

What chance did I have?

It's an excuse, I know. Easy to blame the parents. I killed that private investigator because I wanted to and I'm not sorry.

A twig cracks and the white flashes past again. It's brighter this time, the light stretching further into the distance. Max is closer.

I risk a quick breath, following the sweep of the torch. He is at least giving me an idea of what's ahead. There's another bush off to the right, a series of trees ahead and a clearing with newer, spindlier trees to the left.

'I'm your father, Olivia. Or Lily. Whatever you want to be called. I'm asking you to come out.'

I can't believe he thinks that will work.

There's a crack of a twig and a rustle of bushes. It feels as if someone's close but there's no way I'm risking a peek around the tree to check. Instead, I hunch low, ready to spring away if need be.

The light swishes past again. It's closer still and I can hear his footsteps sliding across the dry dirt.

I try to crouch lower but realise there's something under my shoe. I carefully lever myself up and remove the stone. It's not too large, perhaps the size of an egg. Not enough to go on the attack with – in a knife versus egg-sized stone fight, there's only one winner – but it could still be useful.

When the light sweeps past from the left to right, I wait for it to pass and then fling the stone hard to the left. Nothing happens for a second or two and then there's a solid *thwick* as it cannons into a tree.

The torchlight flashes across the land towards the noise and I wait, holding my breath.

Wait.

Wait.

Wait.

And go!

As Max heads in one direction after the stone, I bolt in the other, darting what I believe to be towards the clearing and Olivia's body.

It takes him a couple of seconds to realise what's happening and there's a roar of anger as he turns and shouts after me.

I've got a much bigger lead this time. There's no point in worrying about the pitfalls underneath my feet, so I don't. There are a couple of times where I stumble but I keep my footing each time and race on, past the clearing and the spade, barrelling into the next copse of trees and ploughing on.

When I reach the path, it's such a surprise that I almost trip over the ridge connecting the woods to the trail. I know I'm in the right place because of the dog waste bin and I skid on an errant stone as I twist to avoid crashing into the bench.

There's a howl of triumph as Max bursts from the trees but he's not got me yet.

I race along the trail and the light of Max's torch bobs up and down as it follows me. When I get to the car park, I'm going to have to run to the road and hope for the best. Hopefully there'll be someone passing; if not I'll have to find a place to hide.

Any tipsiness from earlier is long gone – but what I can't avoid is that I'm not used to this. I don't exercise and I'm anything but an athlete. Max might not be a runner either but he's bound to have more stamina than me.

I can hear his footsteps and his breaths. He's going to catch me. He—

Wham!

Something slams into my back and then I'm hurtling to the floor. I manage to use my hands to stop myself landing face first but that's about the only thing I achieve. My right knee hammers into the hard path and the earth scrapes deep into my palms. I skid and roll, hoping I'll somehow land free and be able to spring up.

That doesn't happen.

Even if I was clear, my legs aren't working properly. Pain shoots upwards from my knee and I can't do anything other than collapse down onto the path. Max is clinging onto my other leg. He yanks me backwards, spitting and snarling, and all I can think of is poor Iain in his wheelchair. He assumed it was Ashley but I suspect it was Max. After all, in Max's own words, Ashley is all talk.

That doesn't help me now though. I won't be waking up in a hospital. If I can't get free, I won't be waking up at all.

I kick and thrash, connecting with something solid, though it makes little difference. Max rams an elbow into the knee I landed on and then, before I know what's happening, he's straddled across my waist, knife in hand.

THIRTY-SEVEN

BANG!

There's a fleshy thump and Max slumps to the side. It takes me a moment to realise that he's no longer on top of me. I kick his legs away and roll onto my side, oohing and aahing the entire time.

The moon has crested over the top of the trees, lighting the length of path, and there, standing in the bluey glow, is Dad.

It's not a ghost or an illusion, no figment of my imagination, it's *Olivia's* father.

My father.

The moonlight reflects from his shaven head and he turns to me, blinking and disorientated.

He opens his mouth to say something but then Max groans from the floor and tries to roll over. I instinctively roll away from him but Dad launches himself onto Max, straddling across his middle and swinging his fist down hard. There's a pulpy, mushy *thunk* and I realise he's not simply punching with his fist, he's holding the type of stone I was looking for. Fist-sized and unforgiving.

I lose count of the number of times Dad hits him and there's a terrible moment where I know I could stop it. One word and he'd drop the stone.

Except I don't.

It's like I can only choose one father and he's the one I want.

For Dan, for *Dad*, it's the years of frustration after Max stole his wife. The wasted opportunities, the thirteen years. He doesn't even know the other man took his daughter, too.

Blow after blow thunders into Max's skull until it's not a skull any longer.

For as long as I live, I will never forget the spongy sound of stone on flesh.

Perhaps Dad knows I'm not Olivia. Perhaps, perhaps.

I should stop it but I don't because I'm my father's daughter. My *real* father's daughter – and this is what Max would've done.

When he's finished, Dad falls backwards and drops the stone. He rolls onto his knees and covers his face with his drenched hands and sobs. He's out of breath, drowning in another man's blood and it's awful. There's nothing I can say because he knows what he's done and he knows it's not something from which he can walk away.

I take his hand and pull him further along the path, away from the horror, until we're next to a bench and another bin. There's a plaque that says it's in memory of someone named Alice who walked her dogs here every day. It's normal in a world where there is no more normal.

Dad is panting when he sits. His face is smeared with blood, but so is everything else. His clothes are spattered as if he's opened an exploding ketchup bottle.

I wasn't sure if I believed my third dad when he said that some people needed to be put down like dogs. If I wasn't certain before, then I am now. Max would have killed me and probably found a way to get to Harry as well.

It was this or nothing.

Dad is out of breath, wide-eyed and in shock.

'I told you,' he says. 'Didn't I tell you? I told you, didn't I? I said I wouldn't let you down again. I said that.'

I stroke his hand but only really succeed in smearing the sticky slickness into this already tainted skin.

'You saved me, Dad.'

He stares into the woods and he's breathing so quickly that he's spitting through his teeth.

I squeeze his hand. 'Dad.'

'I told you. Didn't I tell you?'

'Can you breathe with me, Dad? Slower.'

I try to count for him but it makes little difference. When I reach around to his wrist and press for a pulse, I can feel it racing.

'How did you find me?' I ask.

'I told you I'd be watching. Told you I wouldn't let you down. Told you.'

I don't think I'm going to get a better answer than that, not yet anyway. There was a moment in which I thought there was someone behind me in that alley along the rear of the Black Horse – but then I turned and someone was in front of me. Perhaps it was Dad skulking around the bins, keeping an eye on me from a distance? Maybe he's been watching all day?

'Why here?'

His two words are breathed rather than spoken.

It's not like I can tell the truth – that the bones of a poor six-year-old girl are buried deep in the woods – because I *am* that six-year-old. The only person who can say otherwise is an unmoving mess around the corner.

'He wanted to kill me,' I say.

'Why?'

'He thought I was here to get his money.'

Dad turns to me and there's such sadness in his face that it leaves me shattered. 'Why *are* you here?'

I take a breath and then say the most honest thing I've said all week: 'I want someone to love me.'

THIRTY-EIGHT

TUESDAY

Nattie is waiting for me on the steps of the police station. Her hair is down and she's wearing sunglasses. When she takes them off, she's bleary-eyed, still hung-over from the night before.

'I thought *I* had a bad night,' she says with a weary smile.

I don't have it in me to laugh but she wraps her arms around me and whispers that the police are at Mum's house. It's not a good time to go there, so we head to hers and I take a long, hot shower before borrowing a dress. Sometimes, there's nothing quite like putting on clean clothes, even if they belong to someone else.

It's a lovely day but my mood is dark and everything feels far too bright and sunny after the events of the previous night.

We don't say a lot as we walk through the village, following the stream out towards Olivia's memorial. The calligraphy letters of her name look so beautiful in the knot of the tree and I'm glad I didn't burn the wreath when Nattie suggested it.

It's not mine to burn.

We sit and rest our backs against the tree, my head on Nattie's shoulder. There are a couple of parents with kids in the play park. It feels like they're watching us but pretending they're not – but then I've been thinking that for days. Nobody dares to come over.

'You're all anyone's talking about,' Nattie says.

'What's new?'

She sniggers but there's no humour there.

'Do you want to talk about it?'

And I do. I *really* do, because it's too much to keep to myself. I tell Nattie about being in the alley at the back of the pub and then waking up in a car boot lined with plastic. I talk about the country park and Max with the knife. Of how we walked into the woods and that he wanted to kill me – and then Dad turned up to save the day.

I don't mention Olivia or her grave. Those are my secrets.

'Ashley's in custody,' I say. 'I don't think he'll be in for long because he didn't actually do anything.'

'I can't believe it.'

There's a lot Nattie can't believe – but that's hardly surprising. I'm not sure I can.

'I think the police are going to want to talk to you and Rhys to match up the times we left the pub and here,' I say.

Nattie's head lolls against mine and I suspect she'd still be asleep in more or less any other circumstances. It feels very appealing.

'I don't remember much after leaving the pub,' she says.

'That's all you'll have to say.'

'What else is going on?'

'Max's car was still at the country park when I left, plastic in the boot and all,' I add. 'They've got the knife, too.'

'What about your dad?'

'I don't know what's going to happen to him.'

It's hard to think about, let alone talk. I didn't know he owned a vehicle but there was a rusty Vauxhall in the car park close to Max's taxi. There were few moments of coherence until the police arrived and all I could get from him was that he was looking out for me. At some point, I'm sure he'll explain... I *hope* he will. I scuffed my shoes whenever I could – and if he'd followed Max's car out to the country park, there's every chance he'd have been able to follow.

Nattie and I sit quietly for a while, watching the kids playing in the park. I count eight children who are all five or six years old and it's hard not to think about little Olivia happily having fun in her own back garden. She'd have been full of innocence, immune to the idea that someone like Max could do something so awful. Much like Iain's story, one moment she was playing by herself, the next... nothing.

The laughs of the children ripple around the park and I close my eyes, listening and thinking of the girl whose life I've stolen. It's then that Nattie asks the same question that everyone's going to have. The one Detective Inspector McMichael was so keen to ask.

'Why?'

But that's the thing: I can never give people the real 'why'. I told the inspector that Max kept shouting about money, saying I wasn't getting any of his and he was going to make sure of it. It's the same thing that Ashley said at Mum's house in front of everyone.

In many ways, it's the perfect, clean story. Everyone in the village will know it's the truth. They'll believe it, because half the village have their own views on the Pitman brothers anyway. Rhys said it was all about family feuds and soap operas round here. Villagers will remember Ashley spreading rumours from his taxi and him storming into the Black Horse, only to be told by Pete that he's barred.

It all makes sense.

But it isn't the truth.

There are bones in the woods. Olivia is no longer here but neither is Lily. My mother was forced to give me away and then had a second daughter stolen from her. She's known loss before and is now a widow. She's suffered too much to lose this all over again. She doesn't even know it and yet a man was so infatuated with her, he was willing to kill twice. If she'd dumped him and left it at that, would any of this have happened? Or would he have latched on to somebody else and ruined their life, too?

And me?

I couldn't risk returning to Stoneridge as Lily to find out I was the unwanted child who was still not wanted. I had to be the one who was kept. The one who was cherished.

'Money,' I say. This is my story forever. 'Max thought I wanted his money.'

Nattie gulps and she believes the lie in the same way everyone will.

We sit in the sun for a while longer, listening to the joy of the children until Nattie's phone starts to ring. She answers and only says a few words before hanging up.

'They're done at your mum's house.'

We walk to the post office and then I drive out to Mum's. I've barely finished parking on her driveway when she's racing out of the house in a flood of tears. She squeezes the breath from me, clasping on so tight that it's as if her own life is on the line.

When she pulls away, her eyes are ringed red. 'I'm so sorry,' she says.

'It wasn't you.'

She shakes her head and glances towards Nattie, who is out of the passenger seat and leaning on the bonnet. She talks to both of us, her voice croaky and rough. 'Deep down, I knew Max had that side to him.'

'You couldn't have known he'd do this.'

Mum gulps back another sob. She's clinging onto my hand and I'm not sure who's comforting whom. 'I only wanted to be loved,' she says. 'When you disappeared, after everything with your father… I wanted to be loved and Max was there.'

I squeeze her fingers and we share the most perfect of instants in the worst of circumstances. It's a momentary locking of eyes, a glimpse of her very soul, and it's in this moment that I realise more than anything that I am my mother's daughter.

THIRTY-NINE

WEDNESDAY

The trail through Riversway Country Park looks completely different in daylight. At night, it was like the woods were far closer, the trees and foliage denser and darker. Everything felt as if it was on top of me, nature rising up to show its ominous, overpowering glory.

During the day, the path is perfect for a pleasant stroll. It's wider than I remember; firmer, too. All the stones and low branches I saw as hazards are barely noticeable, certainly nothing to be worried about.

I take my time following the trail and there are constant flashes of recognition. The shape of a tree that seems familiar; a patch of grass on the side that I remember wondering if I could use it as a space to swing the spade towards Max.

There is police tape sealing off a patch of the path, with signs telling walkers the trail is closed. A day on from everything and there's nobody to enforce it, so I head a few metres into the woods and walk around the track. It's hard not to look back towards the trail and the pool of red that's stained the ground. It will take a good period of rain to get rid of that and then Max's final resting place will be unmarked – as it deserves to be.

I continue back onto the path, taking the fork I remember and then finding the dog waste bin next to the bench.

There's nothing obvious to mark the route into the woods that Max made me take – but there are subtle signs. A couple of plants have been trampled down and there's the scuff mark I left on the ridge by the path. I wasn't sure why I did it at the time but it's a useful marker now.

There is no trail through the trees but it feels as if I know where I'm going. Trees and bushes *seem* familiar and there's never a moment where I'm lost.

It takes a little over ten minutes until I reach the clearing that is seared in my memory. I know it's retrospect because I'm aware of what's there – but the shallow bowl that nature has carved into the ground seems so obvious as a place to bury a body. Even if there wasn't a spade part-covered by the layer of clover and moss, not to mention the mounds of dirt I cleared, the curve of the land is a slightly lighter green then anything else in the clearing. I wonder how many people have walked through this way in the past thirteen years – and it can't be many. This is proper middle-of-nowhere territory and there's no reason for hikers to leave the trails.

Max found himself the perfect spot to get rid of that poor little girl.

Of my sister.

I pick up the spade and shovel the dirt I removed back into place. The plants will grow back over the coming months and it won't take long until it's covered with the same carpet of green as the rest of this clearing.

When I'm done, I walk a little further into the woods and slide the spade underneath the densest bush I can find. The branches are brittle and sharp; the leaves small and thick, and I can't believe it will ever be found.

The closest tree to Olivia's grave has a blanket of vines and leaves clinging to the bottom. It's the thickest in the clearing, stretching so high that I can't see the top among the intermingled branches of all the other trees. I sit among the plants and lean back, the rough bark scratching through my top.

'Olivia Elizabeth Adams.'

I close my eyes and listen. There's a gentle breeze, barely enough to ripple the leaves on the trees but I can feel it tickling my ears.

My voice is the gentlest of whispers, two words: 'I'm sorry.'

And I am.

I'm sorry that Olivia, the *real* Olivia, will never have her story told.

This is not what I expected when I came to Stoneridge and I suppose the question I have to ask myself is whether this was all worth it. Harry will grow up without a father; Dan – my dad – might go to prison. I didn't mean to but I'm the person who caused this.

But I have a mother and she has a daughter. The question of 'why?' that's haunted her for thirteen years has finally been answered, even if it's with a lie.

Sometimes lies are better than truth.

I've got a younger brother and a best friend. I'm going to be loved.

So was it worth it?

I wrap my arms across my front, hugging my knees tight. It takes a while but I sit and listen for an answer until a warmer purr of wind caresses my face.

'Thank you,' I say, opening my eyes slowly.

I take a few moments to stare at the patch of land under which Olivia is buried, knowing I'll never return here. Then I set off back to the trail, ready to live a life that might never be mine.

A LETTER FROM KERRY

There is a big, big spoiler in this letter – so, if you're having a sneaky look before reading the book, you really should not continue on…

If you ask any author which question it is he or she gets asked the most, I can almost guarantee you it will be, 'Where do you get your ideas from?'

It's the standard question that everyone asks, whether family member, friend, blogger, TV, radio or newspaper interviewer, reader, stranger in a pub, and so on. Everyone asks it.

I'm never quite sure how to reply, because there isn't a definitive answer. There's no single place from which ideas come. It's everything and nothing. It's observing people and things but it's also being by yourself and allowing your mind to wander.

I think that, perhaps, the difference between someone who does this sort of creative job and someone who doesn't is simply that we allow ourselves to listen to those mad thoughts that pop into our brains. Instead of dismissing them, we note them down because, one day, it might become useful.

For me, the core of a story usually comes in one of two ways. Either the 'hook' for the beginning, or a twist or reveal for the end. Once I've got that in my head, the rest of the writing is working either forwards or backwards to try to join the dots.

Not everything works. I can spend weeks on something before realising I don't have enough. That's hours of work, thousands of words, that get abandoned to digital dust.

The Girl Who Came Back has a unique origin for me because it was neither a beginning nor an end when it popped into my head. It was simply one line – which is still in the book. It's at the end of chapter 34, broken across two sentences:

... there are only two people on the planet who know I can't be Olivia.

Me... and the person who killed her.

I didn't have a name for Olivia at the time, I simply had an idea of someone trying to pull off the almightiest impersonation job and being caught out by the person who knew with absolute certainty that it couldn't be true. Crucially, that person couldn't say anything, else he'd expose himself as a killer. I liked the dynamic of this cat and mouse game in which neither person could figure the other out.

Everything grew from that one line.

There is also another story behind this. When I originally wrote it, it was called *Thirteen Years*. Somehow, I'd written a succession of books with numbers in the title. There was *Ten Birthdays*, this, and then, a bit later, *Two Sisters*. I'd finished my second draft and sent it off to my agent and then, literally that week, a show appeared on BBC iPlayer called *Thirteen*.

The show's description was, horrifyingly, rather similar to my outline for this – that a girl returns home having been missing for thirteen years. It was one of those moments in which you're not quite sure what to do. The coincidence of the idea being so close, even down to the title, was rather extraordinary. I'd never heard of the show before but watched the first episode with great trepidation, obviously hoping it was nothing like my book.

Luckily, it isn't. It shares a premise and (at the time) a title – but little past that.

I suppose what it does show is that different writers can have the same weird ideas pop into their heads, even down to titles. Oh, and when people say some coincidence can never happen... it probably can.

Anyway, I do hope you enjoyed the book. As ever, if you did, a review would be terrific. Nothing helps to spread the word better than that. You can also contact me via @kerrywk on Twitter, or through my website, kerrywilkinson.com

Cheers for reading,

Kerry